BLUE
CINNAMON

CHRIS BLOUNT

POWERHOUSE
PUBLICATIONS

Powerhouse Publications
Unit 124. 94 London Road
Headington, Oxford
OX3 9FN
www.powerhousepublishing.com

CONTENTS

CHAPTER 1

(Cauliflowers and Confessions)

Father Conor O'Liam was approaching 50 and had been the parish priest of St. Augustine's for ten years. During that time, he recalled, he had never really heard a challenging confession. There must have been plenty of sin committed in the rather down-at-heel North London suburb, for which the ugly, crumbling 1950s church catered to the spiritual needs of its dwindling congregation.

Maybe this Saturday afternoon would be different. For once, he noticed an unfamiliar person, kneeling a few rows back from the "usual suspects." He hoped this man was a serious penitent, someone who might spice up his afternoon. Perhaps he would ask forgiveness for a juicy fraud, or a long-time affair, now over. Preferably no violence or intimidation. Please God, not a murder. Nothing tricky that could put a priest in an uncomfortable position. Nothing where the police should be involved. Something which could be resolved between God and the sinner, with Conor acting as the honest broker between the two.

But Conor would have to wait for that; he would have to hear the regulars first. Just the usual three this week, and these days, and almost every week; Bridie Morrogh, Colleen Hegarty, and Pat Loughlin.

'Nothing very interesting there,' thought Conor, though Pat had the most potential. There was that 'affair' she had two years ago, when she was already in her mid-sixties.

"Could I see Conor 'out of hours'?" she had asked. Didn't want to be taking up more than the statutory two and a half minutes. Tongues would wag — Bridie's particularly. "Times the entries and exits, that one," Colleen had once confided to Conor. Now surely, THAT was a sin.

Pat had come to the presbytery, not wishing to be 'timed,' and Conor had listened patiently.

"You mean that you and Ken, your husband, actually go searching for this young man, Steve, up and down the aisles in Morrisons? And Ken encourages you to find him?" Conor asked, gravely.

"Oh yes, Father, it was his idea. He knows it's my little thrill, and he was there at the time! If he sees him first, he will shout out to me, 'Aisle 14, fresh fish!'" Or sometimes, 'Aisle 8, fruit and veg!'"

"But, Pat, isn't this poor chap, Steve, terribly embarrassed?"

"Oh, no, Father, he is very proud of what I call him. They even call him 'fresh fish' or 'fruit and veg' in the warehouse and now he's going to have a courgette tattooed on his arm and a salmon around his waist, only I haven't seen that yet, of course. Oh, but he has got such beautiful buttocks, although sometimes, his shorts do slip down a bit too far at the back because of the heavy lifting he has to do —"

"Pat, I think that's enough. It's certainly no sin, but I would worry about what you're doing for his job prospects."

"Oh, no, Father, Steve's now got quite the following and lots of the regular shoppers look out for him every Friday, and there's even talk of him getting a promotion and introducing 'Steve's' to other Morrison stores. Of course, it was my idea in the first place, but now I'm not so sure that I should have introduced all this vanity and lust, so I thought I better tell you, Father —"

"There's nothing more I need to know, but perhaps you might let Ken do the shopping, and when he gets home, you could be waiting for him. That might make him feel rather better about your feelings for him."

Conor was more than a little pleased with this rather basic piece of counselling.

"It's not as if I can give you five Hail Marys for something like this, Pat."

"Oh, I know, Father; I should probably say a few extra prayers each week for a whole year, and I expect you'll have to tell the bishop."

"The bishop? Why?"

"Oh, Father, surely you remember; he blessed the store when it opened last year, and, well, that's why I thought I should confess, because when Steve was by the cheese counter, well, that's exactly where the bishop stood when he said the prayer and cut the ribbon...you know, just next to the rabbi and the Muslim gentleman, and —"

"No, Pat. No need for you to recite but if you wouldn't mind doing an extra rota of church cleaning before the wedding next week, that would be more than enough."

Conor stopped reminiscing and waited in the box. Pat came and went. No excitement this time. "I felt jealous of my sister and her new car," and "I had to leave Mass early to put the joint in," was all she could manage.

Bridie Morrogh came next. Perhaps, the English Penitent would wait until the regulars had left.

Bridie spoke in a rush.

"Oh, Father, I bought a condom."

Conor could feel the heat of her embarrassment through the grill. Though strict on matters of tradition, he was inclined to be liberal in the contraceptive department.

'A bit late for that, Bridie,' he thought. 'You should have remembered that forty years ago, before you had Tommy, Paula, Bernadette, Frances, Colin, Derry and —'

"I just had to find out what they looked like. It's the programme, Father; you know, on Wednesdays on BBC2, about the teenagers. You know they keep going on about them. Well me and my Eddie never used them, and he was so good about waiting ('well, not all that good,' thought Conor), and to him, it was, well... as bad as a swearword. I thought he wouldn't mind, but then, Father, I thought you ought to know, as you can recognise the Devil in all his forms, so I brought it in, Father, so I wouldn't be tempted, and I thought you could, well, keep it in your safe with the..."

"No, Bridie, I don't think I'll be needing it, thank you. It's no sin, but you could put the cost of the condom in the poor box."

"Thank you, Father, you're such a good man."

By now it was a quarter to six, and Conor was about to leave the box to take Saturday evening Mass. No sign of the Englishman. No fraud or fornication in the air. Conor scolded himself for such thoughts. "I don't need evil to brighten up my life, Lord," he prayed.

Sometimes, it was very boring in the confessional on a Saturday afternoon. Conor thought he would far rather be at home, watching the racing. At the last annual parish dinner, he had asked the guest of honour, the rather serious newly-appointed bishop who had blessed the new Morrisons store, whether he had the same experience. The bishop replied that, if boredom was Conor's problem, he should come to the cathedral and make his own full confession. That might give him a few new ideas rather than the traditional penance of five Hail Marys, which Conor usually administered.

Finally, the door to the confessional opened. "Bless me, Father, for I have sinned. I couldn't possibly tell you how long it has been since I made my last confession. Over the last five years, I have been involved in…"

For the first time since Conor had been parish priest of Saint Augustine's, the 6pm mass started twenty minutes late.

CHAPTER 2

(Bridget's Student Recollections)

Setting up a specialist institute, able to perpetrate a universal fraud, next door to one of Britain's toughest prisons, without its inmates being the slightest bit aware of its significance, was a perfect irony. My sister, Bridget, had named the institute the UK Association for Genetic Predictions (UKAGP), cleverly disguised on the nameplate as BD Enterprises and concealed on the second floor of an anonymous 1960s office on Pentonville Road and within a stone's throw of the eponymous prison.

Donald was a brilliant scientist. Genetics fascinated him. He read (and sometimes wrote) anything he could find which would increase his knowledge of the subject. He was a shy man, and his partnership with Bridget was a perfect match. My sister was enthralled by the practical implications of the subject and was especially keen to share that knowledge with laboratories around the world. She aspired to be a scientific celebrity, but at the same time, if this discovery brought her untold riches, so much the better.

She admired Donald intensely, and it was not long before that intensity developed into something more carnal. Bridget was not a typical white coat lab assistant. She dressed immaculately; partly to impress Donald and partly to be fully prepared in a white blouse and a short black skirt should an inquisitive journalist request a meeting to discuss genetic data. She would never reveal any information of that type without asking Donald, whose natural caution had inevitably slowed the advance of genetic discovery.

Donald William Sheard had become progressively more taciturn, and had he not been a dedicated scientist, he could well have been mistaken for a history don, under the carapace of a gown, a sports jacket and spectacles. He was happily married to Marion with two young sons, and his relationship with Bridget was similar to an absent-minded professor with a lively young puppy, by whom he was captivated, but whose wild antics he found incredibly frustrating.

***

The most recent series of trials in Ghana, the UK and Sweden had all produced the same results; employing a selection of ages from different ethnic origins, the same gender split in each country, and from a complete socio-economic spread.

There was nothing new about healthy lifestyles and environmental factors contributing to longevity, but a genetic dimension, even if it was only responsible for 25% of an individual's lifespan, was a significant breakthrough. Both of them understood this was common knowledge, but as far as they could ascertain, the impact of what they spoke of between themselves as "The Fourth Dimension" was strictly classified.

"Donald, we can't get more conclusive proof than this." Looking at the figures, Bridget became more and more animated.

"Let's make a qualified announcement."

"But we don't know why," Donald queried, ever the cautious one.

"You know they will want proof…irrefutable proof."

Over the last few weeks, the inevitability of the "final proof" had become clear to Donald, but he seemed curiously reluctant to accept it. He wondered whether he just did not want to confront the implications of such a life-changing discovery, or was he just exhausted by the grinding monotony of research at the UKAGP?

***

Donald and Bridget had been tantalisingly close to the result they had sought for four years, but each sample had left enough area of doubt to prevent a public announcement.

"We know if you follow the lifestyle rules, women can live to an average age of 88, and men to 85, but we don't know the exact date unless we use the fourth dimension. The professors of geriatrics and biostatistics will smile and say it's all been done before, but we know they can't predict dates unless —"

"Let's go home. We can run through the implications of using the fourth dimension tomorrow. There is little more we can do tonight."

Although the world had, as yet, no inkling of the consequences of their research, Donald and Bridget both knew that the reaction of governments the world over, as well as the international scientific community, not to mention religious leaders, ethical bodies, and the world's press, would be every bit as challenging as the four years of research.

New developments in genetics were occurring all the time, globally. Donald did not want to lose out in the international genetic race, but privately, he was terrified of facing the media and of having to explain the background to the institute's findings.

Donald offered Bridget a lift home. For once, Bridget declined, choosing the solitude of the walk home to gather her thoughts.

The university term was barely a few days old, but the students were already partying. She passed a small group, clearly enlivened by the liquid product displayed freely on their T-shirts, and she wondered how the "momentous discovery" (Donald's personal interpretation of the fourth dimension) would "enrich their lives."

Bridget started to think about Claire, her daughter, now in her second term at Edinburgh. She shuddered slightly, thinking about how evasive she had been whenever Claire had expressed an interest in her work. Claire knew that her mother's job was sensitive, but Bridget felt Claire's resentment at not being treated as mature enough to be trusted with at least some of the "lab secrets."

When Claire left home for the first time, Bridget fussed over her, warning her not to drink too much, and to eat "plenty of slow food." Since then, Bridget had been overwhelmed by "the UKAGP project'" and, guiltily, she realised Claire had hardly crossed her mind.

Claire had come home for Christmas, excited about her course, her new friends and the lively social life in Scotland's capital. Since then, she had reassured herself that Claire had settled in happily and had unconsciously switched off her mother gene. An escape from the lab was long overdue. She resolved to take a few days off to visit Claire. Donald wouldn't like it at this critical time, but tough.

She started to reflect on her own student days in Newcastle. She had primarily spent her time with other medical students. In those days, men outnumbered women by three to one in that department. This should have guaranteed a very good time for all the girls. Most of the male medics, however, seemed to have other priorities, dedicating themselves to drinking and rugby rather than dating.

Newly released from the supervision of the headmistress Reverend Mother and her henchwomen, the six ugly sisters, and freed from the watchful piety of her mother and seminarian brother, she was looking forward to meeting the male species first hand.

After a brief flirtation with a fly half, Bridget set off on a one-woman mission to prove that convent girls really do have all the fun.

Students of physics, geography and economics all had the opportunity to enjoy her charms, not to mention a professional footballer, a night club owner and even a policeman (not wholly off-duty). But a one-night stand with a most unlikely candidate, an intense, bespectacled Welshman doing a geology PhD, coupled with an unfortunate lack of understanding of the principles of contraception, proved her undoing.

The university medical school kindly consented to Bridget resuming her studies after the birth, by which time she had become Mrs. John Hughes-Renton.

Twenty years on, and Bridget was devoutly hoping that Claire, the much-loved issue of that night of scientific passion, was taking care not to make the same mistake. Claire was unaware about the circumstances of her conception, and Bridget thought it was time to trust her simultaneously with her personal and professional confidences.

By the time Bridget was reaching for her front door keys, she had already resolved to call Claire tomorrow to fix the weekend in Edinburgh. By the time she had closed the door behind her, the flashing answer-phone was to change those plans dramatically. It must have been a very late call for John not to have answered it. There was no message, but 1471 revealed it was the presbytery at Saint Augustine's, timed at 1.18 am. If Conor was ringing this late, it could only mean that their mother had finally been released from the torment of her mind. Bridget wept a little, more from relief than grief. In her eyes, Mrs Maeve O'Liam had already died…seven years ago.

CHAPTER 3

(Irish Wake)

"Grant them eternal rest, O Lord, and may perpetual light shine upon them."

"…Almighty God, Our Father, we firmly believe that your Son died and rose to life. We pray for our sister, Maeve, who has died in Christ. Raise her on the last day, to share the glory of the risen Christ, who lives and reigns…"

Even if my belief has withered on the vine in the intervening years, I am sure that Conor has contributed to it. His part as the "Good Shepherd" is undermined by a distinct lack of care for his flock and his determination to maintain a professional lifestyle.

We should have buried her seven years ago, instead of letting her slip into that humiliating half-life and the indignity of dementia. Even in the matter of her death, the Very Reverend Conor O'Liam has been playing God.

Mercifully, the present incumbent is not prepared to give up the position just yet.

"…I am the resurrection and the life, says the Lord. Anyone who believes in me shall live and will not die. Alleluia…"

I am the youngest and most secular of the three of us, and it is surely inappropriate of me to have these thoughts at any time, let alone during our mother's funeral. However, the least saintly of the three is confident that it would not have been our mother's wish to have her corpse spirited across England and Wales and the Irish Sea, to be buried on a windy hillside in Howth. Conor, my holy brother, thought our mother would have wanted to be together in death with the da, that rogue whose only legacy was to bugger off with a floozy on the ferry all those years ago. So, Conor sought out the place where the bastard had spent his last penny and drank his last pint, emailed a few Hail Marys to the local parish priest, and here we are, a few rosaries later in the land of the little white bungalows.

Did he ask his little brother and sister what they would have liked? Did he, shit. We don't have many things in common, we three siblings, but it's undeniable that we shared a mother, although from time to time, it has been implied, to me at least, that we didn't all share the same father.

No, funerals are God's business, but during His extended leave of absence, the responsibility for at least some of these events appears to have been delegated to Conor.

What does he look like, wearing a biretta? When did a priest last walk the streets, crowned with an ecclesiastical bowler? I suppose he was trying to out-Monsignor the local guy, whom I'm sure could have done the job just as well.

He did, at least, let Bridget read the lesson, but there was no chance of Conor letting me into the pulpit. He whined on about our mother's suffering not being in vain, and now she is being reflected in the holy light, where she is joined once again with the blessed Declan, our da. Well, if our da ever got into the heavenly kingdom, he must have got Larry the Lock to make a master key for the pearly gates at the same time as the NatWest job.

Conor insisted she was kept alive even in those last few dreadful weeks. The devoted nuns who looked after her pleaded with him to let her go, to no avail.

For Bridget's sake, I promised not to rock the boat, so we sit in silence in the car back to the hotel, where there is to be a "reception." A reception…well there's only Conor, Bridget, her daughter Claire, the local dog collar Father O'Rourke, and me, and, to her eternal credit, and, I hope, salvation, Biddy Tugley, mother's oldest friend, now 85, who has made the journey all the way from Bexhill.

The Clontarf Hotel has done a passable job, and, at least, Conor hasn't stinted on the booze. I chat to Biddy, to Father O'Rourke, and to Claire, who is 19 and is undoubtedly going to have many admirers or probably has already. She is now in her first year at Edinburgh, reading biochemistry, so she has inherited her mother's brains as well as her beauty. Bridget, whom I have not seen for nearly a year, looks painfully thin. She is beginning to grey, and her smart black suit hangs limply from her shoulders.

I want to talk to her, but there seems to be no way of disengaging her from Conor. Finally, even Conor feels the call of nature and has to leave the room for a priestly piss.

Bridget turns to me — I hug her warmly, but she pulls away and smiles weakly. I notice she has broken a tooth. I am surprised she has not had it fixed, as she was always very fastidious about her health and her looks. She is wearing virtually no make-up. The famous green eyes now shine far less brightly, and she looks as though she has spent too many late nights in the lab.

"I know," she says. "We wouldn't have done it like this, but I couldn't deprive Conor now. He'd planned it for so long."

She takes my arm the way she did back when I was seven, and she was all of ten. She was always wise and sensible, and I was always in trouble. Suddenly, Bridget "in loco matre" makes me realise what we have all lost. I try to stop the tears, but I can't.

I feel I must pull myself together before Conor returns from his ablutions. I have no idea what I am going to say to him. However, without my realising it, he has witnessed the entire spectacle and puts a fraternal arm around my shoulders.

Perhaps I have misjudged him. I follow Bridget's wishes and do not raise any objections. He seems subdued, even saintly, joined to me, if only briefly, by our mutual grief. We make dutiful conversation. I haven't spoken to him in five years, and he seems genuinely interested in my life. He then tells me he might be transferred from his middle-class North London parish to a more 'challenging' inner city patch or possibly even to Africa.

I am surprised as I cannot see him ministering to the homeless, or even less, teaching in a missionary school, and I wonder briefly what he had done to deserve this when he seemed on course to become a bishop.

I wish him well and promise to keep in touch. He has put on weight and lost more hair, but it suits him — it makes him more approachable, more of a priest and less of a preacher. We part amicably, and I wonder if it will be another five years before I see him again.

CHAPTER 4

(Turkish Delight)

I am an actuary for an insurance company called Fife Life. I have a comfortable life in South-East London with my wife, Clodagh. She seems relatively content with her lot in life, but her eyes glaze over and her ears close when I mention the word actuary.

There's really not much one can discuss about this profession. I have to admit that my colleagues are as boring as I am, too. It is a pity that it sends Clodagh to sleep because there are problems at Fife Life which will affect all of us before long. I, too, find it easy to fall into an actuarial slumber in front of the TV. Sometimes, she will wake up from the sofa and call out, "Sean, is anything wrong?" as I let out a discordant grunt from a malevolent dream about Fife.

We have two children, a boy called Cork, and a girl called Kellee. Amazingly, they both want to be actuaries. Cork is already showing signs of an actuarial instinct, while Kellee prefers to spend her time sleeping, following her mother's example.

I am flattered by their apparent desire to follow my profession. Outwardly, neither of them shows any signs of a will to study, at least not sufficiently to earn an actuarial qualification. I ask them frequently what is so attractive about my job. Cork tells me that I have lots of long lunches, and Kellee says I finish early nearly every day, leaving lots of time for shopping.

From time to time, I do reflect on my lunch habits. How have I grown to such an inconvenient size and weight? I, who could outrun the ponderous Conor from the age of ten. After all, have I not considered the impact of obesity on longevity for the good of Fife Life, only to casually dismiss that there is no more than a passing correlation between the two?

Little did I know that my comfortable life was about to change. I suppose it was only a coincidence that the paths of the three O'Liam siblings were all going to divert at the same time. Conor's infatuation with horseracing was about to cause him untold grief, and Bridget's profound conviction in determining precise life expectancy would lead her into a genetic battleground. And I was about to liven up my actuarial world with a spot of adultery and forgery.

***

In the days when assured lives ended when predicted, employees became pensioners when they intended to, and there were plenty of government bonds for insurance companies to buy, the life of an actuary was a happy one. There was full employment, and if there were a temporary vacancy, Fife would take on anyone the agency could send us.

To this day, I cannot imagine how she passed their test because she could barely speak English, let alone write in it, but perhaps my reputation as the soft underbelly of the actuary speaking world was already growing. Her name was Hurriyet, which is Turkish for "freedom." She came on a two-week holiday visa.

Margaret, my secretary, was on holiday, and someone in the HR department was clearly too closely involved with the agency to check the need for, or the quality of, any temporary replacement. However, in the quiet summer weeks, she seemed a decorative, if unnecessary, substitute.

Because of my weakness for decorations of this nature, I was in a forgiving mood when she presented herself in my office on that fateful Monday morning, with a very full cleavage and a very empty timesheet.

Though I am easily distracted in these circumstances, I felt it was my duty to explain the principle of composing an email and even drafting a letter. Neither of these forms of communication were strictly necessary, and it was only when I looked more carefully at the previous reference, requested from the agency, that it became clear that it was composed by one of their staff. I was already completely won over, and the Turkish accent that overlaid, "I am liking it very much here, and please can I stay with Fife Life company," was the winning touch.

The weeks passed, and Hurriyet stayed on while I struggled to find clerical things for her to do. Her charms were not lost on the male members of staff, and if it ever looked as though she had nothing to do, there was competition to help her compose correspondence or to assist her in opening filing cabinets. Only Margaret, freshly back from her holiday, was not amused.

The prospect of Hurriyet staying for more than the statutory two-week visa period seemed irresistible. I have had some experience of dealing with the Home Office in the past in my capacity, so I called my old chum, Archie Longworth. Archie was a former 'Fifer', and now an experienced, if somewhat casual, member of a team which specialises in immigration matters.

"Hi Archie, how are you? Long time, no lunch!"

"My thoughts, exactly, Sean, old boy. Is it my turn?

"Actually, could it be down to you? I got a bit of a roasting for a five-hour session with old Lukie at The Little Seamstress. Have you been there? Great place! All sorts of entertainment! Better next time, perhaps."

"Lukie is a bit dangerous. Wanted me to wave through some Gambians for six months. Not sure what he was really planning, but he came out with a real 'sob-sob' request just at the end of the session, when I was pretty rat-arsed. Just came to my senses in time. Suddenly I saw a proper colleague outside The Seamstress, gathered myself, pointed him at Lukie and fled. Lukie is now doing a bit of time at an HMP I sometimes "recommend" but the "immis" don't like me handling guys like Lukie on my own."

"No, Archie, nothing like that, I promise. Just an enquiry."

"We'll behave for once. Let's say The Tug at 1.30pm on Tuesday. That suits me, I have been watching this houseboat on the other side, and it's been there a bit too long."

It ended up being a great lunch at The Tug, and I always learn so much from Archie.

***

"It's just a short-term staff matter. We took on this Turkish woman on a two-week holiday visa while Margaret was on holiday. You remember Margaret?"

"Oh, yes, very strict lady, reported me a few times!"

"Unfortunately, she had a car crash in Spain and this brilliant temp would just cover for the next five weeks while Margaret recovers. The thing is, I believe extending a holiday visa is a real issue and I need to sort it by next week."

"Not a problem, Sean. I'll email you a blank form. Fill in her name, Turkish address and drop it back to me by hand, but you must send me a confirmation that she has left the UK when she goes home, and oh, don't go over the five weeks."

"Thanks, Archie. You're a pal."

"Next time, The Little Seamstress."

"Done!"

I must admit that my infidelity had pushed me into doing something criminal, which I now sincerely regret. Fife has the complete medical history of a substantial number of people, many of whom have now moved into the company's equivalent of eternal life, more commonly known as "permanent filing." A Lancastrian lady, who, having thoughtlessly electrocuted herself at the age of thirty-five, compelled Fife to give a generous life assurance settlement to her husband and three young children, before partly redeeming herself by providing me with the materials for an unplanned resurrection. Hurriyet swiftly became Harriet, born in Accrington rather than Ankara, with an official birthday endorsed by the UK Passport Office, and a stunning photograph, which had more than a passing resemblance to the deceased in her prime.

Thankfully, even Fife Life doesn't pry too deeply into the size of the feet of the insured, as I am convinced that no Lancastrian lass could have matched Hurriy's size elevens. In all other respects, the new Harriet Ribblesdale could not be distinguished from the recently departed version, and I am sure we could have ordered up a husband and three children, at a pinch, to complete the picture.

Soon Hurriy had an employment record and a National Insurance Number. No problem opening a bank account once I had found her a flat in Maida Vale to provide a utility bill or two. I had winced at the cost of offering such accommodation, but she could hardly sleep on the streets, and I needed the cover of respectability. In any event, should she pass her sell-by date, the flat would have been a useful investment.

She slowly walked around her new home and declared, "But Seanie, it's so large! How many here do I sleep with?" Resisting the obvious, 'just me should be enough,' I assured her the flat was just for her, and that she could have as many visitors as she liked, but she must tell me if anyone stayed overnight — according to our curious English laws, anyway!

"You, Seanie, is wonderful. Already, you tell me how many can sleeps here with me!"

This sounded ominously as though I had diversified into pimping, and I was sure that I did not want to hear this unintended recital of illicit love quite so soon. Maybe they were already queuing back to Swiss Cottage, and now I'd have to keep a record of Hurriy's genuine visitors, with the neighbours still thinking I am running a brothel. Happily, for me, Hurriy was thinking along more familial lines for her visitors.

"There is my brother in 'Olland, and my mother, but she has never left Izmir, so she needs my sister to bring her, but my sister never wash so I could not live with her for long. But my mother is very good cleaner! And my brother, he will get very good job when he comes. You find him job, yes?"

Clearly, Archie is going to have a lot of explaining to do. Well, of course, I should have guessed, illegal immigrants never come on their own.

CHAPTER 5

(Publication?)

They held hands across the table in the candlelight at Mama Mia's in Lambs Conduit Street. Bridget recalled the moment as one of enormous release. Their dinner together to celebrate the end of this stage of the project meant a new beginning for her. Donald had finally agreed to go public, but only if they could release the preliminary information about the fourth dimension at the same time. This meant so much to Bridget. No longer would she have to hold back from touching him. Quiet asides would be a thing of the past. She could finally stop making up stories for John. Perhaps she could now persuade Donald they might even spend a night in more up-market accommodation than the Goswell in Southampton Row.

She had worked out what to tell John and Claire, but did Donald really have the balls to tell Marion, his wife. Halfway into the affair, Bridget had wanted to go public about their relationship, but Donald had persuaded her to keep it quiet until the project was complete. Now, surely, was the moment.

She was sure the team knew already. Ruth had already hinted as much, and, if Ruth knew, then Craigie, her alter ego, would also have the full picture.

Bridget had noticed both Ruth and Craigie listening to every word between her and Donald. Over the following two weeks, a series of investigative comments ensued.

After Christmas — "That's a lovely bracelet, Bridget. Christmas present from John, was it? I love that modern jewellery. Such clean, simple shapes. How clever of John to find something like it."

The possibility of John ever going into a designer jeweller's was so remote that Bridget knew Ruth couldn't possibly believe what she was saying. She even wondered if Ruth had seen Donald buying it and bringing it back. Perhaps she saw him put the box in his top drawer. Maybe she had slipped open the box while Donald was away and memorised the bracelet, waiting for it to appear on Bridget's wrist.

No, surely this was paranoia.

She lied. "No, Claire bought it for me in Edinburgh. It was so sweet of her."

Ruth clearly wasn't impressed by this explanation. Perhaps she really had seen the Hatton Garden address on the little bag the gift had come in.

"And I like Donald's new ties. So chic, so tasteful, so clearly Marion's choice, don't you think, Bridget?"

Bridget blushed; she felt so visible.

"Can't say I've noticed," she said, pretending to be absorbed by the Ghanaian test spreadsheet in front of her.

God, that did sound bitchy about Marion; Ruth would certainly pick that up.

"I mean, Marion always looks very smart when I see her, but as far as Donald's ties, well I'm not really an expert, but they seem fine to me."

So now she had admitted that she had noticed; what an obvious cover-up. Shit! Ruth tried another tack.

"Did you know she was going skiing with the children at half term? I think Donald ought to go too. Do him good and he doesn't see enough of the boys. I mean he's here most weekends."

Of course, she bloody knew. They'd planned it for months.

"What a shame half term is in the middle of February, just when we are going public on the project."

Bridget remembered Donald practising it, so Marion must have been persuaded.

I've got to be here that week. You go with the boys, soak up the glaciers and the gluhwein, even if you don't ski. The boys will love it. I know they're really keen."

Marion must have been persuaded because reports on the boys' prowess on the slopes came through on Donald's email throughout that week. And with John on a lecture tour in the States, Bridget was really looking forward to a whole gorgeous week with no excuses.

"Yes, I guess he could do with a holiday," Bridget said.

"I'm sorry, Bridget, that sounds like I don't realise how hard *you* work. I know you spend some of your weekends here too."

'So that's how you get your kicks; imagining us hard at it at the

Bedford,' Bridget thought to herself. 'I bet your old man hasn't shagged you in years. Can't say I blame him. Bit of personal hygiene wouldn't be amiss. No wonder Donald fills his room with the smell of aftershave!'

"I only come in occasionally; as you say, Donald is in nearly every weekend."

Ruth was relentless.

"We are going to that new French restaurant in Montague Place on Friday. Have you been there, Bridget?"

Christ, they'd only been there last week, she recalled. Has this woman planted a hidden camera on one of us? Perhaps she hides in the bushes in Russell Square, waiting for us to come out. Whoops, no, that's what they garden boys do in Russell Square! But then, no self-respecting man, straight or gay, could ever, *ever* want to disturb Ruth…but how the hell?

'This is bizarre,' Bridget thought. 'Why don't I just come out with it? Donald and I went there after work. We got absolutely slaughtered, took a few pills and had sensational sex all night. Actually,' she recalled wistfully, 'we were both so tired, we nearly fell asleep before the truite meuniere.'

"Ruth, I've never been inside, but Donald took a

junior minister there last month. Apparently, the politico was well impressed."

CHAPTER 6

(On the Brink)

Mrs Wilson seemed very surprised to see me at my desk at 7pm. She had been our cleaner for 10 years, but I could only recall seeing her at office parties, and in the pub, after someone was made redundant.

Her duties started well after the 5.15pm had left Charing Cross. She may have been surprised, but I was more than a little shocked.

"So, how are you, Mrs Wilson?"

"Can't complain. Still get memegrains. It's all them com 'puters. They give orf things, you know, like bugsandthat." For someone surrounded daily by viruses and dust, I thought Mrs Wilson looked remarkably fit. However, her presence, on which I had not reckoned, left me with a bit of a problem. Having always been regarded as something of a maverick, even a rebel, I had never been considered "management potential."

But, while it was extremely rare to find me in my own little glass box after hours, it would not be so exceptional as to attract comment. I needed, however, to get access to Phil Jewell's office. Phil was Fife Life's Deputy General Manager and Chief Actuary.

While I had always believed (probably erroneously) that Phil had some professional respect for me, I was quite aware that he looked down on my casual approach to life and my work ethic in particular. Indeed, if he could ever find a pretext for my dismissal, he would use it.

Excluded as I was from the complete Fife Life financial picture, I could only guess from the calculations I was required to make, and from the limited briefings which trickled down from the tight-lipped board above me, that all was not well.

In the early 80s, Fife decided to take an uncharacteristic risk by offering particularly attractive annuity rates to smokers. At the time, the UK press was full of reports of record numbers of deaths attributable to lung cancer and emphysema. At the same time, the connection between tobacco and coronary heart disease had become irrefutable.

Fife's board at the time was an exceptionally Presbyterian group under the austere chairmanship of Sir Malcolm Carrick, who quite simply disapproved of any conceivable activity which could give pleasure to man or woman.

Sir Malcolm's particular distaste was reserved for tobacco, and it was his steadfast belief that the Lord would justly punish the habitual users of this drug with premature and painful death.

Thus, he saw an opportunity to both make money (in his mind, simply the execution of the biblical rules outlined in Matthew 25 (verses 14 -30), and to carry out divine wrath, simultaneously.

He was convinced that no man or woman who had smoked 20 or more cigarettes a day for 25 years would live beyond the satanic age of 66 and 6 months, and he, therefore, offered unmatchable guaranteed annuity rates should they reach their planned retirement. For several years, annuity rates were extremely high, and smokers could get 10% better rates than non-smokers. Fife offered smokers 15% better terms and the company was always the financial advisers' favourite.

While most life companies would make provisions for the higher life expectancy of women, and therefore offer lower female rates, Sir Malcolm thought that women smoking was even more abhorrent and offered identical rates to men and women of the same age. To him, males and females would both perish in their predetermined year. In those days, the board was very weak, and even a polite cough at one of Sir Malcolm's more outrageous proposals could stoke his suspicion and warrant the threat of dismissal.

Sir Malcolm, however, had not taken advances in modern medicine to heart, and had seriously underestimated the increasing social changes that had begun to stigmatise smoking as a habit.

Thus, Fife was left with a large number of coughing annuitants on their books, determined to outwit both their Maker and their insurer, hopefully well into their eighties. Several thousand had already outlived the redemption dates of the British Government Stocks assigned to them. Treasury 9 ½%, 1999, and Treasury 9%, 2000, had expired well before their annuitants, and even the last of the high coupon gilts, Conversion 9%, 2011, had now been repaid.

The practice of life companies buying gilts (the commonly used term for British Government Stocks) is an arcane subject. The principle is that a clever actuary calculates the likely dates of death of the life company's annuitants and then matches those dates by buying stocks, which are redeemed (paid back by HM Treasury) in the years of their expected demise. While the British Government has so far always honoured its commitments and paid on the due date, the same, unfortunately, cannot be said of the annuitants. Too many of them obstinately live on after the life company's appointed hour with the help of better healthcare, a greater regard for their own longevity and an unfortunate habit of reneging on their previous vices of tobacco, alcohol and saturated fat.

The great difficulty for Fife is that when an annuitant passes his or her sell by date (66 years and 6 months in the case of the smokers as prescribed by our late lamented chairman), their life expectancy has to be recalculated. Strangely, having passed their sixties, many of them can be expected to live on into their mid-eighties. Fife Life takes no pleasure in government campaigns such as Smoking Kills and, in a desperate moment, I was sorely tempted to send all the reformed smokers 10 packets of heavy-tar fags, a bottle of whisky and 20 bags of crisps to celebrate their 67th birthdays.

The actuary now has to buy a stock which may not be redeemed for 20 years. When interest rates are low, as they are today, the life company must buy more stock because the yield is high, yet the final redemption value of the stock will be much lower and so the interest with which a life company can pay the annuity is much lower.

Of course, the position is reversed if we have sold a whole life policy. Fife Life hates early deaths. We are the first to write and offer our condolences to a 45-year-old widow. It is a real tragedy for us. There are just too many accidents these days. Already, there was a substantial shortfall, and Fife had to dig deep into its reserves. The problem was compounded by the progressive fall in interest rates in recent years, and the need for Fife to buy much larger amounts of stock to provide the return which was needed to match the annuities.

Fife was, therefore, headed for disaster. This much I knew, but when and how big the collapse would be, I could not tell without a closer look at Phil Jewell's spreadsheets.

Phil had been the bright young secretary to the board, when Sir

Malcolm's sanctimonious decision had been ratified 20 years ago. He was now the only surviving executive still working for Fife. Sir Malcolm himself, no doubt to the great satisfaction of the tobacco barons, had been vanquished by a particularly unpleasant malaise, caused, I am told, by clenching two matching parts of his anatomy together for long periods without release.

Phil was thus reluctant to publish these statistics. He was likely to be considered more culpable than the current board, though he had appointed some trustworthy non-execs to give him credibility.

From the information which I was frequently asked to provide, it was clear that this issue was ongoing and apparently insoluble. Fife, being a mutual assurance company, is not answerable to shareholders. Currently, neither the auditors nor the Financial Conduct Authority, nor even the press, and certainly not the policyholders, had any suspicions, but the truth could not remain suppressed for long.

Once the noise of the Dyson had faded for the night, I crept into Phil's office and sat in front of his PC. I knew Phil to be a very logical man; I also knew his distinctive middle name. I needed his Excel spreadsheets, and I was sure his password would reflect his personal and biblical roots. It just had to be, and it was. Ezekiel opened like a dream. While there was clearly no time to track every individual annuitant, I got what I wanted to know, the total liabilities for each year.

CHAPTER 7

(Tragedy)

Claire reflected what a lovely evening she had had with Tom and his friends in The Highlander. Until now, their dates had been exclusive, so she felt that meeting his circle of friends was a big step. She had worried whether they would accept her, coming from London with her plummy voice and nervous laugh, but, like Tom, his friends were soft, kind and easy-going. Though Claire sometimes had difficulty penetrating his accent, Tom always smiled gently at her efforts and encouraged her with an, "Oh, wee lassie," which made her feel warm all over. That evening, she felt confident that he was 'the one', and she knew then that he was all she wanted.

Tom, an electrician's son from Dunfermline, was a tall, dark, and heavily-bearded chemist. He would not have been Bridget's choice for Claire's first serious relationship, but, as she recalled, he was Claire's choice, not hers, and at least she wasn't replicating her own extra-curricular activities of 20 years ago.

As Claire and Tom left The Highlander, the rain was relentless, and the fallen autumn leaves made crossing Princes Street even more precarious, covering the pavements and blocking the drains, causing gutters to overflow into fast-flowing streams.

As they left, Claire slipped, falling forwards into the street. Tom stretched forward to take her hand, but the cars streamed past creating waves and soaking pedestrians without a thought. A lorry dispatched its wash between them, Claire slipped from Tom's grip, and he fell awkwardly from the side of a bus.

In the inside lane, unseen by Tom and Claire, was Hamish McFallichan on his Kawasaki 900. Tom had seen him in The Highlander earlier in the evening, seemingly a loner working his way through a bottle of malt. There was no sign that he was the owner of that powerful machine, which had been parked discreetly behind the pub, nor was there any evidence that he was even planning to ride home. He did, however, leave the pub unsteadily on foot a few minutes before Tom and Claire.

McFallichan was only thinking about riding as fast as possible down Princes Street and challenging anyone and anything that crossed his path. Against the background noise of the pub, they had not heard the throaty revving of the weapon that was to kill one of them and ruin the life of the other.

Unknowingly, unintentionally, Claire and Tom were about to meet that fate.

CHAPTER 8

(Bridget's Unexpected Request)

The conversation I had with Bridget at our mother's funeral had been brief, and we promised each other we would meet again as soon as we could. Tom and Claire's terrible accident in Edinburgh meant that it was several months before we could actually get together.

I had been reluctant to call Bridget, with Claire still in hospital, Tom's funeral, and all the legal issues concerning the accident. To my surprise, Bridget called me, briefed me on Claire's condition and told me she was going to see Tom's parents at their home in Dunfermline.

"Dunfermline? Isn't that in Fife?" I asked her.

"Quite right."

"Did you know that despite having worked for Fife all these years, I have never been there? I think the name comes from our belated chairman's ancestors, which has rather put me off the place."

Curiously, the blessed Phil wants me to go there and address a small disaffected group of Fife annuitants, who, many years ago, out of misplaced loyalty to their kingdom (yes, it really is a kingdom. Can you imagine having a Kingdom of Essex or a Kingdom of Surrey?) put their trust and money into Fife Life.

So, the following Tuesday, my sister and I were sitting in a smart first-class carriage pulling out of Kings Cross and heading for Edinburgh Waverley. After that, we would change to a less pleasant train to take us the last leg of our journey to Dunfermline. It was all exhilarating, as if we were still ten and six, and I was with my big sister looking after me and taking me to the loo if I needed to go!

After I had asked about Claire, Bridget got straight to the point.

"What do you know about genetics and longevity, Sean?

"Very little, but I wish my predecessors had done a lot more research into those subjects. That might have prevented Fife Life landing in this mess."

"We may able to help. We have conclusive evidence, from mice, that increased longevity is in their genes and increases with each generation. This alone is not enough for us to reach our target, partly because each family of mice come from a different starting point and partly because we need to continue breeding from the same stock until longevity peaks, and then expand the breeding pool until their longevity settles at current levels. Are you interested?"

"From a geneticist's view, that must be fascinating, Bridget, but Fife can't force their wheezing, arthritic old annuitants to mate with each other! Currently, the effect of what we call the genetic signature accounts for 15% of longevity with lifestyle responsible for 85%. Passing on this newly understood rodent behaviour to our annuitants would be equivalent to mass murder!"

"That's not what we are trying to do, Sean but any data you have would help"

"I think it's ridiculous, Bridget, but I am prepared to give you some information. By the way, I'm terrified of mice, and if I find any either at home, or in the office, or in Hurriy's flat, the whole deal is off. Nor is there to be any mention of Fife Life. If you need a foundation, just use the Roe and the Dent families!"

"I promise you, Sean, absolutely no mice anywhere near you, and thank you, this really will help us reach the fourth dimension."

CHAPTER 9

(Conor's New Career)

Conor was standing in plain clothes at the paddock at Kempton. He thought it unseemly to be wearing his dog collar at a race meeting, particularly when large amounts of money were changing hands. He was, however, a familiar figure to the jockeys and trainers. His singular interest on that cold February afternoon was a novice hurdler called Light My Fire.

Conor had decided that this particular horse would be the first stage of his "recovery plan." He had convinced himself that the key to his plan was "sensible investment" not "mad speculation." Measuring his stake at 10% of the total collection money the previous Sunday seemed "sensible." Light My Fire had, after all, only twice left the comfort of an obscure Yorkshire yard (and on neither occasion had earned any reward for his owner) and was priced "on course" at 20-1.

Conor always said a short prayer before the race, feeling the need to get the Almighty's blessing, but concerned that the Lord might not smile too benevolently if the stake was too large.

Light My Fire was running in the last race. He was a chestnut colt ridden by an apprentice, unknown to Conor. The going was soft, and the paddock resembled a mud bath. The horse walked round the ring like a woman wearing Paul Smith boots for the first time. This did not bode well when he was shortly to face five-foot fences. Conor considered hedging his bets but seeing the favourite at 11-8, did not have the stomach for another commitment.

At the off, he looked heavenwards for salvation from his precarious financial position, and then down for more immediate assistance from the soft ground, which, Conor had been assured, would greatly assist Light My Fire. Judging by his delicate avoidance of anything muddy, this seemed unlikely. Four minutes later, this was proven when the horse fell at the fourth and so did Conor's investment.

At his ordination, Conor had sincerely believed his vocation would be strong enough to take him through the perils of temptation. The sins of the flesh never interested him. As he grew older, he increasingly wanted a "comfortable" life. His cellar was well stocked, his presbytery was well furnished, and his belly showed too much prosperity for a man of the cloth. Charity, he thought, is easy, but poverty is much more of a challenge.

In the beginning, he had been convinced that winning minds and saving souls would be enough, but twenty-five years on, it had all become routine. Yes, he still believed, but more out of habit than real faith. He was not a rebel, inspired by some objection to the Church's teaching. No, he would do no harm, but he was increasingly bored with saying Mass, visiting the sick, conducting weddings and presiding over funerals that required him to eulogise the life of the deceased whom he often didn't know.

It was partly out of a misguided sense to help the Church that he embarked on his ambitious Roof Fund scheme. Churches in the 1950s were not built to the standard of their predecessors, and St Augustine's desperately needed a new roof. Tiles were notable for their absence. It was fashionable at the time to install Velux windows above the altar, to create the effect of the guiding light from above. These had, however, been constructed with only a passing acquaintance to sealant and grout. By now, the frames shook noisily during gales and the rain could not be kept out. Mass was often conducted with splashing buckets competing with the sermon.

A series of temporary repairs had not sufficed. The rain had reached the roof timbers, wet rot was diagnosed, and a new roof was the only solution.

Tenders were invited. A rather dubious parishioner in the construction trade won the contract with a suspiciously low price-tag of only £30,000. The diocesan surveyor, delighted by this unexpected generosity, attributed it wrongly to an act of benevolence, and rushed to accept.

In his heart, Conor knew it was not enough. It did, however, give him the opportunity to save money for the Church, and to enjoy himself simultaneously. At this low point in his ministry, he was ready for adventure.

He was in the habit of meeting an expatriate group of Irish parishioners in the Durham Arms on a Monday night. They were keen racegoers, and occasionally Conor joined them at Sandown or Kempton. After his experience with Light My Fire, he was, however, rather less inclined to rely on his own judgment of equine ability.

Bernie Kelleher was the leader and the most prosperous member of this group. It was three weeks since Conor's unfortunate experience with Light My Fire and, with Bernie's encouragement, he was ready for more excitement.

Bernie was trying to buy a novice hurdler called Holy Orders.

"15,000 euros," he said. "Cheap price. Look, I'll put in 5,000, if the rest of you can manage 2,000 each."

Conor thought about the Church Roof Fund, considered his own need for greater home comforts, and committed himself. Work wasn't due to start on the roof for another three months, and the diocesan advance was already in the Church Roof Fund account. If it all went wrong, he could just about find 2,000 euros from his own resources.

"Okay, I'm in. I can't really say no to a horse called Holy Orders, but I think you're having me on. I bet that's not its real name."

"It is now!" said Bernie Kelleher.

"But you can't change a horse's name after it's been registered,"

"Watch me," said Bernie.

Despite the questionable start to his investment, Conor was really excited about owning a leg. Well, not quite a whole leg, he thought. What Conor had forgotten to ask, and what Bernie had "inadvertently" forgotten to tell his new partners, was the issue of the ongoing cost of keeping and training Holy Orders.

The horse was being trained in Ireland. Over the next few weeks, "Holy" ran three minor races on relatively obscure Irish courses and secured two firsts and a second. The prize money was just enough to cover his keep, his travel and his training.

As most of the races were held midweek in the middle of Ireland, and all the partners lived in London, none of the syndicate had had an opportunity to enjoy their success in person. After the second victory, Bernie invited the syndicate members to his house for a celebration. Bernie had DVDs of all three successful races, and these were shown several times accompanied by many bottles of the cheapest champagne Bernie could find. While he did not rate the taste buds of his fellow investors too highly, he had not bet on Conor being rather more knowledgeable on the subject.

Conor arrived late. Clearly his partners were enjoying their increasing acquaintance with the sparkling liquid. The videos were shown to increasing applause. Several risqué jokes were made, based on the suggestion that Holy Order's success was attributable to his gelding status.

At this point, Conor came into the bar.

"Would you like to see the videos of the three races?"

Conor was delighted and this clearly called for the syndicate to have their glasses refilled. The cheering escalated with each successive showing of the victorious colt. By now, every part owner was convinced that 'Holy' could win the Gold Cup!

"Now, I've got a plan to make us all very rich men, not just this 500-euro nonsense. Father, I'm not sure if you should be a party to this, because you could call it greed, and I know you are, like, sworn to poverty."

"I'm not a monk, Bernie. I am allowed some creature comforts. And as for greed, well…"

"Well then, listen up. I'm saying we should take our profits on "Holy." He's done us proud, but he is only going to go so far, and I, that is, we, the syndicate, have been offered a very good price for him."

"But sell him? The Holy one? No, that's not right." Joe the glazier said.

"Wait, Joe. With the proceeds of 'Holy', we could buy 50% of a really serious jumper, called Revealed. Your stake will be diluted, but this is a proper animal, trained by Jodric O'Mahon, and good enough to win the Champion Hurdle. And," he paused for effect, "he'll be racing in England, so you can all go and watch him, even if Diana House (Bernie's new development of not-so-luxury flats) has to go without windows for a few more days!"

"Trained by Jodric himself," Joe said. "Well I'm in."

The others were in no mood to disagree.

Larry, Mick and his son, John, all worked in some capacity for Bernie. They may not have fully understood what "your stake will be diluted" meant, but they had never had such fun, and they wanted more.

"And you, Father… it all depends on you. You have every right to refuse and you can sell your stake back to the other members of the syndicate, but the terms of the agreement state that the buyer can insist on the seller's original cost price, no matter what "Holy's" value is now."

"You don't need to twist my arm, Bernie. Let's celebrate."

A few more bottles of the fizzy stuff went down. Bernie produced the paperwork and all the members signed it. Conor sincerely hoped that his taste in cheap fizz was surpassed by his expertise in buying horses.

"Now all will be revealed!" Bernie proclaimed.

Conor later questioned him on the cost of Revealed being trained at the renowned O'Mahon stable.

"Sure. What's the difference? One horse eats as much as the next. Anyway, Jodric is an old friend of mine. My brother built some of his yard."

It did not answer the question, but Conor was not thinking clearly, and, now he had signed, there was no going back.

Revealed was only seven years old, still young for a top jumper, so Bernie reckoned he could go on winning for at least five seasons. Indeed, in the two races prior to Cheltenham, Revealed had enjoyed two wins. Bernie had backed him for the Champion Hurdle before the first win at a generous 20-1. He reminded the syndicate to follow his example at 100-8 before the second victory, and on the day of the big race, he had been backed down to 8-1.

It was the day before the Cheltenham Festival that Bernie received his first bill from O'Mahon for the cost of keeping and training Revealed. The bill was three times the cost of looking after Holy Orders, but he decided to keep that information to himself, and, predictably, he also failed to inform his partners that he had opted out of the horse's permanent injury policy, with which the other co-owners had protected their investment in Revealed.

The day of the Champion Hurdle was the first dry day for weeks. The Cheltenham going was officially "soft" but several trainers had withdrawn their runners because of the very soggy conditions. Jodric, though concerned, knew that "soft" going suited Revealed. Bernie was convinced that only an Irish horse, accustomed to the sodden ground, could win this race; he put £5,000 of his own money on Revealed.

Bernie had taken a box and had treated the syndicate to a trip on the early race train from Paddington, complete with champagne breakfast. By Reading, Larry, Mick and John were already discussing how many lengths Revealed was going to win, by Swindon they had calculated their profits, and by the time they reached Cheltenham, they had decided where they were going for their exotic holidays.

Bernie had extended the offer to Conor, and he agonised whether to go. Finally, he decided that the risk of being seen at such a public and extensively televised event by his bishop or his by parishioners (even, or indeed especially, if he was in secular disguise) was just too great.

Bernie was so convinced of success that he remained completely sober during the day so that he would appear in the Winner's Enclosure without embarrassing himself.

The conditions determined a relatively slow start, but even with riders taking exceptional care, six of Revealed's twenty-one rivals had fallen by the time they came up the hill past the grandstand for the first time. The field spread out, with Revealed at the back of the leading group of five. Bernie was ecstatic. The commentary accelerated as they entered the second and final circuit. Revealed had eased into third place behind the co-favourites, but at the 17th, he slipped while landing and fell awkwardly on his neck. His jockey was thrown, but the rest of the field managed to avoid him, and he escaped injury. The horse was not so lucky. To Bernie's horror, Revealed did not get up. The vets were called, the screens went up, and Bernie cried for the first time since his mam's funeral.

Conor, watching from the comfort of the presbytery, was distraught. The TV cameras did not show the whole picture. Viewers were spared the gruesome details. The next of kin were consulted, but in this case, no decision was necessary. It was not only the end of a lovely animal, but also the last day of Conor's career as an owner. The Bank of Church Roofs was going to have to cough up its share of the trainer's bills and there would be no point in calling the insurance company.

CHAPTER 10

(Royal Infirmary)

The wave of disinfectant at the Royal Infirmary took Bridget back to her student days, which only accentuated her fears for Claire. The feeling in the pit of Bridget's stomach was telling her there was little hope for her daughter. Tom had already been pronounced dead and Claire's life was hanging by a thread.

She was shown into Claire's room. There were tubes everywhere, charts at the foot of the bed, medics checking her pulse and heartbeat at alarming frequency. Walls pale blue, nurses green and white, fruit, apples and bananas, red and yellow, presumably a legacy from the last occupant. Surely, they shouldn't be here? Hadn't they heard of MRSA? Why was her mind wandering like this, distracting her, when she should be thinking about Claire? Trauma playing its old tricks. No, of course it wasn't fruit, just the colours of a first aid box.

The "Acute Room" they called it now. It used to be "Emergency" when she was training. Acute sounded worse, closer to finality. Had the last occupant died or recovered? She scolded herself for focusing on these diversions. Knowing the human brain as she did, she realised this was the release mechanism for not confronting the real issue — Claire.

***

Claire lay very still — was it because of sedation or a coma? Please God, not brain damage. The bike had thrown her and Tom a long way, Tom into the path of a bus, it was instant. Poor bus driver, nothing he could do. Train drivers who experience suicides never recover. Never drive again. Slower, much slower with a bus; he must have seen it all happening. Stop drifting. At least, think about Tom's parents. At least she had their phone number and address. She couldn't face contacting them today. Wait till John arrives from London tomorrow and go together. Must ask about his funeral. Wreath or flowers? And tell Claire? She broke down at this point. Maybe there will be no Claire to tell.

"Mrs Hughes-Renton…" The doctor must have been there for a minute before he thought it right to disturb her grief. Professional and he looked it. Probably only 30, soft Morningside accent, and black, very, very black.

"It's Doctor Hughes-Renton, actually." Bridget recovered her composure. She reckoned there would be no bullshit if he knew she was one of them.

"Yes, of course. I'm so sorry about Claire, but the outlook is not too bad. The initial scan has revealed no brain damage. Sight and hearing are OK. She is semi-conscious, with light sedation, so she will only wake gently. There could be some spinal correction, but it is not broken. Neck badly bruised, two broken vertebrae, three cracked ribs…"

"But will she make a full recovery?"

"The concussion could lead to amnesia. We will only know when she is fully conscious. Once she has gently woken, we will carry out the recognition tests and can make a complete assessment."

"You mean she might not know me?"

"It's possible, at first, yes, but that is unlikely in my opinion, from our initial examination of the scars and the bruising. I'm sure you will remember… (Bridget found this patronising, especially as she hated trauma and had opted for research as soon as possible rather than life in a hospital or general practice).

The doctor paused respectfully, slightly restoring Bridget's confidence in him.

"And I'm so sorry to hear about her friend, Tom. DOA I'm afraid. I have seen his parents."

"Yes, poor Tom, just terrible. I shall call them tomorrow and arrange to see them as soon as possible."

"And the guy riding the bike?"

"He tried to leave the scene of the accident, but he was too badly hurt. He was taken to City Hospital, where the police have spoken to him, possibly to arrest him, when he is well enough to leave. He may lose a leg."

"Just a leg? When he has killed one person and seriously maimed another? Hardly seems like justice."

"I really mustn't say any more, as I might be called to give evidence regarding Claire's injuries. Naturally the pathologist —"

"Of course."

"We will call you as soon as Claire is conscious, probably in a couple of days. Would you like me to tell her about Tom? If her memory is okay, she will ask immediately, and it will be difficult to wait until you can get back here. Are you going back to London?"

"No, my husband and I will both be here tomorrow. We need to be here as soon as she's conscious, it's really our duty to break the news to Claire and be with her at that moment."

CHAPTER 11

(End of Life for Fife?)

Philip Ezekiel Jewell sat in his office overlooking Euston Road and felt utterly depressed. Fife simply couldn't afford to pay its annuitants. Reserves had been squeezed, costs had been cut, but the company only had funds for four months, six at the most, if they lost a few more annuitants than usual this winter. Phil wondered if he should pray for three months of ice and snow or a flu pandemic, but thought better of it.

What more could Fife do?

It was strictly against the rules to "borrow investments" from another fund within the group. The FCA would close them down. Fife would go into administration. Phil and even the non-execs would go to prison. 'Ford Open Prison, probably,' thought Phil. Quite convenient for family visits. Five years, he estimated, three with remission. He'd be 46. Emily and Beth would be at university. Oh my God, no. Something must come up. It was this desperation which pushed Phil into calling to discuss the figures.

I already knew the figures, of course, and I was actually keen to help Phil — okay, mainly out of self-interest (my job would die long before the bloody annuitants), but also out of professional pride. Fife had been good to me. The company had ignored my frequent afternoon absences and had paid me well. I wanted Fife to survive, but Phil undid all that goodwill in the first few minutes with his patronising approach to my professional knowledge.

"You may not be aware, Sean, what a serious position Fife is in."

Of course, I was aware. Did he think the figures I had been giving him for the last two years meant nothing to me? After all, I am a fucking actuary!

"I can see we will have several years of underfunded "puffers," but, of course, I do not know the whole picture."

Where did I learn to be such an expert liar?

Fifers always referred to smokers as "puffers," partly because Sir Malcolm could never bring himself to use the word "smoker" and partly in the hope that our continued use of the word would encourage them to "puff their last." Phil then showed me the figures, which naturally matched the ones I had extracted from "Ezekiel."

"Bloody hell, Phil," I said, putting on the most horrified expression I could muster. "The manure is well and truly hitting the fan very soon."

Phil winced at my vulgarity but said nothing. I felt I had the upper hand. Phil was a capable manager, and, except for insuring the puffers, which was not directly his decision, he was an expert at assessing an insurance risk. He was, however, extremely uninformed about markets, particularly the bond market. For as long as I could, I pretended I had not seen the figures before, and studied them assiduously, and then with that spark of genius, to which only qualified actuaries could possibly aspire, replied gravely,

"Phil, I think there may be a way out of this."

After mumbling something above his head about the gilt market, I said, "it will take me a few weeks."

"Sean, we really haven't got much time before —"

"I know, I know, the audit is due at the beginning of March and the FCA return shortly after that."

"I should have called you before, but the board thought we had to keep it to ourselves."

'Too bloody right, you should have called me,' I thought. Not that I had any idea how to rectify the situation.

"Okay we'll meet on 2nd of February. That gives me three weeks."

I have no idea why I gave myself such an impossible timescale, except that I just loved the idea of telling him when we were going to meet!

As he left, I said, "...and Phil, how many people know about our position?"

"Just the three execs, Doug, Rob and myself, and now you, of course. I need hardly say that no-one, and I mean no-one, must hear —"

"Sure, sure…"

I waved him away. I had never felt more like a chief executive. Oh, what fun to see him on his knees. Silly prick.

"You have my word; absolutely no-one."

Interesting though, just the old triumvirate keeping it to themselves. Not a thought about consulting the non-execs. Did they think they could bluff the auditors and the FCA? Of the three directors, I was sure that Phil and Doug would keep absolutely mum, but Rob? I had heard it on the actuarial grapevine that he had been entertaining a lady from the Pru — or was it a Scottish Widow? Either way, I don't think I've got long to save Fife.

On paper it seemed a hopeless task, with gross redemption yields on gilts at 2% and the annuitants needing 11%. Did I need a challenge like this?

Ezekiel opened for me again the following Tuesday. Although interest rates had started to rise once more, there was nothing I could do about the shortage of quality bonds or the low yields, which they offered. Neither the yields, nor the amount of stock on offer, were going to match the increasing number of annuitants Fife had to pay. I had to know the scale of this liability and if I had any chance of saving the company and keeping my job.

I checked my own estimates with Phil's figures. Fife had undertaken to provide annuities for 32,000 smokers with annuities from age 66 years and 6 months believing that none would have defied the Grim Reaper beyond that age. Fortunately, since Sir Malcolm's time, the board had become more realistic and half the annuities since then had been based on more realistic assessments of life expectancy. 5,000 of the 32,000 had indeed left us for a smoke-free world. 10,000 would reach 66 years and 6 months within the next three years, some within only a few months. 4,000 of those were covered by government stocks which matched their predicted lifespan, but 6,000 had no matching gilts beyond 66.6 years.

9,000 of the remaining 17,000, who had already passed that age, also had no government stocks to be their guardian angels. Fife therefore had to fund annuities for 14,000 wheezing puffers out of its reserves. It was too big a download to cover the whole alphabet, so I selected surnames J to L (coded John Player Special to Lambert & Butler), saved them to my memory stick, exited Genesis, and discreetly withdrew from the House of Ezekiel.

By this time on a Tuesday night, I would normally be taking Turkish classes, but, for once, Hurriyet was not my main priority. She, of course, had not stayed that long after Margaret's return from her holiday. I could not justify her retention as a temp. Even now, Margaret cannot resist, on encountering those rare letters dictated and typed during her annual leave that year, that the error must have occurred during the "Ottoman Empire."

Besides which, Hurriy's disconnected sentences are barely enough to bear on Tuesday and Thursday, let alone reading them on office copy.

My family had long accepted that on Tuesdays I was teaching the Institute of Actuaries Professional Exam Part 1, and Thursday evenings were dedicated to the future of the actuarial profession in Birmingham and Manchester, which inevitably required my absence from the marital bed.

Even so, I was chancing my luck, and sooner or later, Hurriy would have to go. But go where? Sure, I could evict her with a plausible excuse, but could I just leave her homeless? I am a rogue, but I like to think I am not that heartless. Yes, she has a proper identity and another job, with the doner kebab king of Cricklewood, but she could turn nasty, very nasty. This will require careful planning.

CHAPTER 12

(Brotherly Love)

Pizza Please on Euston Road would not have been my first choice. It's usually crowded. There is no privacy, and the food is so predictable. However, Bridget said she needed to be near the lab and couldn't take more than an hour. For someone who is used to rocket salad for her midday meal, a Napolitano was quite a step up. For me it was lunch in the wrong direction.

She had called to tell me about Claire, and I suggested lunch. Bridget had just returned from Edinburgh, as, contrary to medical predictions, Claire had not regained full consciousness. She was, she told me, ready to drop everything and rush to Stansted for the next flight as soon as Claire was awake. John was also on red alert.

Despite the terrible news, Bridget looked much better than when I had last seen her, at our mother's funeral. I had often wondered what Bridget wore to work. I had only seen her once in "lab mufti." Did she really wear the long white coat?

So, I was surprised to see she was elegantly and, as far as I could tell, fashionably dressed. I can't tell one designer from another, but it all looked good to me.

We talked about Claire, and I was relieved to hear that the doctors were confident of a complete recovery. Bridget, clearly that much more closely involved, and much more knowledgeable, was less confident.

"The trauma will be huge; the concussion could have all kinds of side effects... and she doesn't know about Tom yet. Still, at least she's alive, unlike poor Tom. His parents are devastated. He was an only child. I'm flying up for the funeral on Friday and will call into the hospital on the way back, I hope Claire will be well enough to be told."

"I don't envy you that; it puts all our other problems in perspective."

"Anyway, how are you?" she asked — trying to put Edinburgh to the back of her mind? "I can't imagine it's very easy at the moment. How do insurance companies manage with interest rates as low as this?"

"With great difficulty, Bridget…Fife, especially."

I trusted Bridget implicitly, and despite giving my word to Phil, I told her the whole Fife story. I reckoned he must talk to his wife, though I doubted she would be as quick to pick it up as my sister. Bridget immediately recognised the issues, particularly the returns which the annuitants required and the poor yields on short-dated gilts.

"But Sean, that's a disaster for you, and for the annuitants, not that I have much sympathy for lifelong smokers, though, as you say, most of them have given up now."

"Well, for me that's just tough if Fife goes down. But thank God I'm not a director. I can't be held liable. I only provide information to the board. It's down to them if they don't act on it. The annuitants may well be okay. Their annuities are guaranteed, so if Fife goes to the wall, they may well be bailed out. There would doubtless be an enquiry, which would drag on for years. Meanwhile, everything would be frozen. It doesn't bear thinking about."

What is worrying me is that I am now in possession of all this information, following my meeting with Phil (I couldn't bring myself to admit the little matter of "Ezekiel"). Technically, I should now go to the authorities, or at least inform the auditors, who, incidentally, are coming to Fife next month.

I had told Phil that I had an idea which might help us get out of this mess. I was bluffing, though there's a chance that some of our annuitants may actually be sicker than we think. We never know until we see the death certificate.

"And this is what I wanted to ask you. I guess anyone can get cancer at any time, but, in theory, their chances of lung cancer are many times greater than the average non-smoker. It's the same with heart disease. I know it partly depends on how 'well behaved' they have been since they gave up. Are they still drinking heavily and eating badly (like "yours truly")? Although smoking was never my thing, they usually go together. We know many have given up, because we get these pathetic letters asking if we can increase their payments as they have given up. What kind of guys are these? Are they really that simple? Don't they realise we actually want them to carry on smoking, and snuff it as soon as possible? A miserable pay-out before 66½ is a small price for Fife to pay to avoid subsidising a grossly inflated annuity for the next fifteen, even twenty, years.

No, cancer is not the issue. We can make a pretty good actuarial estimate on that one, though, of course it would be helpful, if we knew exactly how many had given up smoking. Bizarrely, we are not even allowed to ask them. No, cancer's not the problem. It's emphysema. There have been several articles recently in The Lancet, and other medical publications. It may surprise you to know that life companies employ consultants to interpret these. The people we use then send their reports to me. You will know all this, I guess, but apparently, in your sixties, the natural age-related deterioration of the lungs' function accelerates pro-rata if there has been early life damage due to smoking. The problem for us is "pro-rata with what?" and "what constitutes early life?" Anyway, maybe these guys won't last into their seventies after all!

Research in the US now confidentially predicts that familial longevity runs through family trees by as much as three decades. So, genetics is catching up with lifestyle choice as a contributor, but eventually, it will level out. The question is when?"

Bridget had no idea that life companies did all this medical research, but she could see the logic of it. She could also see that this would be the perfect test for the Death Date Gene (UKAGP). This could be the perfect opportunity to produce irrefutable proof here in the UK, with the evidence right on her doorstep. This would be so much more persuasive than Ghana, where the Institute had been carrying out tests, and a claim for its success could be made available almost immediately if it were done here. She also appreciated how much it would help with Fife's problems. Perfect!

"Sean, I have to go now, but I have an idea which could help both of us."

Only Donald and Bridget knew the results of the Ghanaian DDG research, plus Gloria who was currently en route to London. She was certain that no-one else had any knowledge of what she called the "the fourth dimension."

Last year, a freelance journalist had written a speculative "what if?" article for *The Daily Mail*, but it did not provide any evidence, only conjecture. At the time, Donald and Bridget were quite shocked, but there was no follow-up, and surprisingly few reader comments. God bless *The Daily Mail* readers, so obsessed with their own little lives. She guessed it would have been different if the *Mail* had run a campaign. "Death Date Gene." "Could it be true? We demand to know!"

I had no idea what she was thinking, but my lasagne was well cold by now.

Finally, Bridget said, "Sean," (a good sign – last used when I was in very short trousers), "that's amazing. We are currently doing some work on this. We could really use the data and help you at the same time. But I will need to speak to Donald, before I can take it further. In the meantime, I will not tell a soul about Fife and promise me you will not say a word about our research."

"Done," I said, looking at her across the table, "but I have only got a couple of weeks."

"Yes, I know. You said so earlier. Why are you looking at me like that?"

A smile crept across my face.

"Some things never change."

Our agreement was sealed by the exchange of my empty plate for her untouched but tepid Napolitano.

CHAPTER 13

(Saying Goodbye)

They reached the chapel where Tom's father was waiting for them. Tom's funeral had been family only, as his parents could not have coped with all his university friends at his graveside. Now, the same chapel where the funeral had taken place a few weeks before was packed with undergrads as well as Tom's local friends.

Hugo McLaren warmly welcomed John and Bridget.

"We really appreciate your coming all this way. We had so hoped that Claire would be well enough to come. My wife called the hospital to find out how she was, but they wouldn't tell her. Something to do with patient confidentiality, I gather. You would have thought, given the circumstances, which she explained to them, they could make an exception, would you not? Helen, my wife, was very distressed."

John and Bridget were visibly moved by Hugo McLaren's kindness.

"We would have really liked her to be here, but maybe she would have found it all too much. We would really like to see her, although we only met her just the once, when they were courting. We would like to include her in our prayers today, if that's alright with you. If she is out of danger, we can thank the Lord for her recovery."

John, almost in tears himself, thanked him and readily agreed to this request.

"They have told us she can go home, and we are picking her up from the Royal Infirmary this afternoon."

He hesitated before talking any further about her condition, in case her survival might in some way seem more distressing to Hugo, the father who had lost his only son.

They followed him into the chapel, where the only seats still unoccupied had been reserved for them, just behind Tom's family.

Both of them felt the full force of Claire's grief over the next 60 minutes.

***

Bridget had already talked to the Admissions Tutor, and the university had agreed to hold her place for the next academic year, assuming she made a full recovery.

By the time John arrived at the Royal Infirmary, Bridget was in reception, standing beside Claire who, though fully dressed for a Scottish February afternoon, was still on a stretcher. Bridget had arranged a private ambulance to the airport. The porters lifted Claire into the vehicle; Bridget sat next to the semi-comatose Claire, and John took his place beside the driver. He was greatly concerned there was no nurse, and he was not all that convinced that Claire was fit for the journey. He guessed that Bridget had bullied the hospital with her outdated medical qualification and that the Royal Infirmary, always desperate for beds, had agreed.

The journey took nearly an hour through the Edinburgh evening rush hour, and Claire still seemed delirious. She kept murmuring "He's dead, isn't he?" without really demanding an answer.

John had, as usual, underestimated Bridget's organisational skills. A nurse and a porter were waiting at the airport to take them straight to the departure lounge. Twenty minutes later, they were crossing the Cheviots and heading for London.

CHAPTER 14

(Data from Ghana)

From: gloria.okane@bigpond.gh

To: b@271h.co.uk

I have finished the analysis of births and deaths for three generations in my home village in the North. My uncle has complete records. I also have details of any inter-marriage between first or second cousins. This is a sensitive issue in my tribe. My uncle may not have told me the whole story. The figures are on a spreadsheet. Do you want me to send it as an attachment? Last time you were worried about security. The total number of living cases is 16. I have 42 cases of deceased but only 28 with three generations. Many of the cases are very young as you requested.

Kind regards,
Gloria Kumasi, Ghana

***

From: b@271h.co.uk

To: Gloria.okane@bigpond.gh

Hi Gloria, that's great news. Well done. We have experience of journalists trying to hack into our system, so do not email your spreadsheet. Also, please save it to another site and print a copy. I would like you to come to London to discuss your data. Do not reply to this email. This address will be deleted shortly. Call me on my mobile regarding flights etc.

CHAPTER 15

(Mary's Birthday and an Unusual Alliance)

Mary Pollaine had been Conor's housekeeper at St Augustine's for 10 years, and today Conor and his assistant priest, Father Robert Ngeni, were celebrating her 75th birthday. Mary knew that her continued arthritis would eventually restrict her housekeeping duties.

"I think you'll be looking for another housekeeper soon, Father. Those stairs become more difficult every year. It's the knees that do the complaining, you know, Father."

"Oh Mary, you'll still be fit as a fiddle when you reach 90, though I will let you off a few duties every year. We'll get Father Robert to do a bit more cleaning, and then maybe the washing up, and then —"

"Oh, but surely they'll have made him a bishop by then, back in his own country! Will that be soon, do you think, Father?"

Before he got into a long conversation about Robert Ngeni's prospects, the front door of the presbytery opened, and the young Nigerian priest called out to Mary that he had met a young lady in the garden who was looking for a certain Mary Pollaine.

"Well, that will be my Rowena for sure, Father, and I'm really looking forward to you meeting her."

"And I'm looking forward to meeting her, Mary."

"But I should warn you that she doesn't 'hold with' priests or Catholics at all, Father, if you know what I mean. I really don't know why. She was brought up in the proper Irish way."

"Mary, I've met many Catholics, ex-Catholics and people of all religions who have no time for priests. I just have to live with it and try and be as polite as possible. It's just part of the job."

But Rowena proved to be much more amenable than Mary had predicted. She talked about her job applications and even asked if Conor would give her a reference.

"I know it's rather cheeky of me, but I don't know many respectable people in London, Father, and although I have rather lapsed in recent years, I always cross myself when I pass a Catholic church. Do you think that will ever help me get a new job?"

"Well, it won't do you any harm, and I will do my very best to help any relation of your blessed aunt Mary.

I would be happy to give you a reference, so it looks as though it is working already."

"Let's light the cake," Conor said, trying to make Mary the centre of attention again.

There followed the time-honoured candle blowing (75 candles, five attempts) and present opening (three "delighted"), before the two priests left Mary to her niece, with Mary being thrilled that Conor and Rowena were getting on so well.

"Rowena was greatly encouraged by this new relationship, and almost forgot to give Mary her present. And I brought this for you. She extracted an unwrapped pack of Dove cosmetics from her bag.

"Sorry it's not very smart."

"Oh, never mind; it's just what I wanted," Mary said. "And it's just lovely to see you."

They went on chatting about Rowena's early family life until Conor brought matters to a halt. "You'll miss 'The Archers', Mary."

"Oh, good heavens, so I will, and I haven't even started supper."

"No cooking for you tonight, Mary. Father Jeremy and I are taking you out to dinner, just as soon as you are up to date with Ambridge."

CHAPTER 16

(Hurriy Settles In)

I wasn't looking forward to this. Turkish women can be fierce, I had been told. To be fair to Hurriy, I would be pretty pissed off myself if I were in the position she was about to find herself in. It was true I could no longer afford the mortgage on the flat, but not quite true that it was going to be repossessed. I was struggling to make the payments, but I was determined to continue until it was sold, so at least I could recover what I had lost by letting it to Hurriy on the very modest "cleavage rental" which she paid. I really didn't want to throw her out on the street; I was too much of a softie for that. I knew that I would still have to subsidise her lifestyle, only it would probably be a pretty grotty flat in a much less desirable area than Maida Vale. It would cost me more than what I had to make up on the flat and I would have a very unhappy Hurriy on my hands.

I pressed the answer phone and she let me in without speaking. I should have made it quite clear who was pressing the buzzer. I had failed to identify myself on a previous occasion, so I could hardly blame her for not questioning the identity of the caller. Maybe she just assumed it was me at this time of the evening. The flat was on the top floor of one of those attractive Victorian terraces. These houses were built for the newly prosperous middle classes in the 1890s, and they ensured the fitness of their servants by placing the staff on the top floor and the kitchen in the basement. After 110 years, there was still no lift and every week I found it more of a challenge.

Eventually, due to the poor state of my fitness and my taking longer than usual, her curiosity won the day.

"Is that you Seanie?"

I looked up the stairwell and I could see her looking even more stunning than usual. She was wearing bell bottom silk trousers and a revealing white blouse. Leaning over the banister, her assets were fully justifying her reduced rent.

I flopped down on the sofa, looking as stern as I could between puffs of air.

"You don't look happy, Seanie," she said. "It's the flat? I know it's not clean, no? It's the flavour of kebab, yes, from Mehmet? It's all over the flat, and but it's everywhere, it's in my hair, my clothes, in the bed. Seanie, I hate it by the van. I can do other things now. I think I go and learn secretary again. My English gooder now. If I get better job, I pay you more rent, so then I can stay longer."

"You should say "my English is better" just like you said, "if I get better job," except it should be "*a* better job.""

"So, when I use "gooder?""

"Never, Hurriy, never."

"So, when Mehmet says to me, "I am a good lover; I am gooder than your boyfriend," I should say, "No, you are better than my boyfriend." I think he trick me, because I say "gooder," then he say, "okay, let's go home.""

"Yes, if he is playing games like that, I agree it really is time you stopped working for Mehmet. I'm afraid your English is not yet good enough —"

"No, it's "better enough," you just said, why is it not same?"

"Not *the* same, Hurriy my darling."

"Okay, okay, but you would need to go on a proper English course. But, Hurriy, I can't afford that at the moment. I have a problem at work. I may lose my job. I'm sorry Hurriy, but I will have to sell the flat. Of course, I will find you somewhere else, and maybe if I get a good price and the cost of renting is less than the cost of the mortgage, there will be enough for an English course."

This all came out in a terrible rush as I was so nervous; Hurriy might get confused with her elephants, but she quickly spotted the main point.

"Sell this flat? No, Seanie, no!"

"Well, at least you wouldn't have the smell of kebab around any more."

"I like this flat very much, and when I leave Mehmet tomorrow, the flavour will go."

I was getting nowhere and beginning to feel rather sick. Strangely, I hadn't really noticed kebabs until she had mentioned it. Now, I could smell them everywhere.

"Did you say 'leave tomorrow'?"

"Yes, you say it's time I leave Mehmet, so I go tomorrow," she said, nuzzling up to me and undoing my shirt, button by button.

"No Hurriy, not now, not tonight. We have other problems, and I need you to stay a little longer with Mehmet, please."

"What problem?"

"Have you seen any policemen coming up to the van and talking to Mehmet?"

"Yes, a few times, they come. I think one of them likes me."

"I'm sure he does, Hurriy, but what did he ask Mehmet?"

"One time, Mehmet not there. He has seven vans and I think he at Tottenham Court Road, so I send them there. The other time they talk to him about his 'illegal women'. Seanie, does that mean he keep house of women for sex?"

"No, I think it means he has lots of illegal immigrants working for him, selling doner kebabs, not sex, from his vans. When they came to the van when you were on your own, did they ask you your name?"

"Yes."

"What did you say?"

"Harriet, of course. Harriet Ribblesdale. I no longer Hurriyet Anktash. You said I never to use Hurriyet Anktash again, but, Seanie, can I change Ribblesdale. It is not easy for me to say, and I feel silly not saying my own name right."

"And the policeman, what did he say then?"

"He seem surprised. He said, 'I think you are Turkish.' I said, 'Yes, I am Turkish, but my husband is English.' I think I should say husband, not boyfriend, as it is legal then, yes?"

"And what name did you give them as your husband?"

"Sean Ribblesdale and he could see I couldn't say it right."

I put my head in my hands. I would have to change my carefully prepared plan, which revolved round Mehmet running a racket employing illegal immigrants. It would be safer for Hurriy to go home on her English passport for a few weeks, as they might arrest anyone who worked for him and put them in a detention centre. So, now they will check the Department of Immigration records for certain, because it could be a marriage of convenience. Oh, God help me! They won't find any marriage and it won't be long before they figure out that it is a false passport. Oh my

God, this is curtains, and all because of a pair of beautiful...

Well, they weren't the only reason. But as I sat there, they were the largest thing I could see, and certainly the easiest to blame.

I wondered whether I should tell her everything. I tried to pull myself together.

"Hurriy, when did this happen?"

"Yesterday. Why?"

So, I told her the whole story (well most of it, as I didn't think she would appreciate having a real dead woman's identity) and how, obviously, it would all get sorted when we were married (yes, I was so besotted that I even hinted at it one passionate night).

Hurriy was very quiet for a moment after I had finished. Then she stood up and walked across to the sofa and calmly tidied a cushion. I was terrified. Suddenly, she snatched the cushion and started beating me about the head with it.

"Seanie, you promised it was all okay; it was all legal. Could get job. I live always in England. Now, I not want to marry you ever. Ever, ever, ever, you little shit and…"

There followed a torrent of obscenities, which she could only have learnt from Mehmet and his customers. This was one area where she could easily pass an EFL exam. Most were in Turkish, but I still got the gist. In an attempt to evade her blows, I moved towards the front door of the flat. In one skilful move, she pinned me against the wall of the tiny hall and pulled open the door with a strength I could only marvel at. Despite my far greater bulk, the momentum of her anger ensured that a final push sent me to the top of the eight narrow flights of stairs. Just my luck to have found a smart enough house to have a stairwell, which was clearly going to be the place of my doom. If I am spared, dear God, I promise I will go to Mass and the gym every Sunday.

Thankfully, Hurriy had decided enough was enough, or that my weight was too much of a deterrent. She pushed past into the bedroom and slammed the door. She grabbed the phone and started gabbling in Turkish, but I could not understand. Maybe she was phoning her brother right now, to come over and finish the job. She opened the door again briefly, maybe to check if I was still there. I was terrified and convinced she really was strong enough to push me. Somehow by deft use of backside and the stairs, sheer terror propelled me to the bottom.

CHAPTER 17

(A Brush with the Law)

I was sitting in my office at Fife the next day, when a call came through from my loyal secretary, Margaret, who, bless her, was still with me despite all I had put her through over the years.

"Detective Inspector Colthorpe and Detective Sergeant Coyle would like to have a few words with you, Sean."

"Is there anyone in the Board Room, Margaret?"

Margaret informed me that Phil Jewell was out all day, and nobody had booked the room.

"Please show them in and offer them a cup of coffee."

I was shaking all over, but I was relieved that by going straight to the Board Room, nobody except the Croatian temp on reception, who probably thought this was quite normal, would have seen the two policemen.

They introduced themselves as DI Brian Colthorpe and DS Gwyn Coyle from the Immigration Division of the Metropolitan Police. Perhaps they were from the Fraud Squad, finally catching up with Fife, and they were already holding Phil as he was the senior officer of the company. So, I reckoned they would want to see him first.

Then I thought that they must have arrested Mehmet and examined his records. I had woken intermittently during the night, wondering how I could answer questions about Harriet's immigration papers.

"Do you know a Miss Harriet Ribblesdale, who is also known to us as Hurriyet Anktash?"

"I can explain everything," I gabbled.

"We'll decide what information we need, Mr. O'Liam," said Colthorpe.

I didn't like the look of him; he was thin, about six foot two, but possessed that sort of wiry strength, which seemed to be typical of a television copper. He had fair thinning hair and a small, mean mouth, and I judged him to be in his early forties.

Well there was no point in denying it. I remembered reading in a detective novel, that if you turned your eyes to the left, they knew you were telling the truth, and that you were lying if you looked to the right — or was it the other way round? My eyes were opening and shutting like fruit machines and I must have looked as guilty as hell.

"Yes, I do but…" I said firmly, trying to appear amazed that the police would have heard of her and that her name came as a complete surprise. It was as if I was going to say, "…but I can't believe you know her too."

I was cut short by the younger officer, Coyle, who had, up to this point, shown no apparent interest in the proceedings and had been studying two mating pigeons on the roof of the next office block. Coyle, despite his spiky hair and a rather flash leather jacket, which was too big for him, looked smaller and kinder and, I thought, even tried to smile. I noticed that, despite the plain clothes, they still wore standard issue police footwear and that Coyle's shoelaces were undone. I looked down at his feet because I, too, am useless with laces. My loafers looked positively stylish by comparison.

"Miss Anktash is in police custody at Paddington Green Police Station. We are holding her under counter-terrorism measures, and we would like you to answer a few questions. We think it would be preferable if this discussion continued at the station."

I nodded in agreement.

I collected my coat and told Margaret that I would be back by lunchtime, but I was privately thinking I would not set foot in Fife House for several years. In the police car, I began to realise what had happened. Harriet, still furious, must have gone to the local police station very early in the morning to "report" me for having "cheated" her. She must have told them, or, more likely, they extracted from her, all the details, and matched them with the file they were building on Mehmet's activities. What she hadn't realised was that she was now an illegal immigrant with no passport, masquerading under a very dubious British alias.

The police must have transferred her immediately to Paddington Green, the London centre for terrorist suspects. I decided that I would tell them the whole story. At least, I owed that to Harriet, even though I would seriously incriminate myself. I had never been to Paddington Green before; I knew it was a high security centre, but I did not know it was also a conventional police station where members of the general public came to report muggings, lost dogs and "domestics," such as the argument Harriet and I had had last night. I was awed by its sheer size, designed like a skyscraper with 16 floors. I learned later that it also had 12 cells underground, and what is charmingly called the "custody suite."

I think the "custody suite" would have freaked me out, but luckily for me, it was occupied. In the suite, filled with all sorts of gadgetry and recording devices, sat a detainee, under armed guard; he looked an extremely unwelcome character and I wondered if Harriet had been interrogated earlier in the same room. I really hoped not. It would have been truly scary for her.

I was taken by the two detectives to a small room leading off the suite.

"Do you need to use the toilet?"

I certainly did, thinking that this was going to be a lengthy interrogation. They left me there for a few minutes with only a very large and heavily armed officer for company. He was joined by a rather pretty woman police constable, who was a pleasant distraction. I smiled at her when she came in, but this was not reciprocated.

Colthorpe and Coyle returned; I was offered a glass of water and a cigarette. I accepted the water, and though I hadn't smoked for years, was very tempted to accept the fag.

They asked me to confirm my personal details, when I had met Harriet, what our relationship was (I skipped the fruitier details), whether I had any connections in Turkey, how I had obtained Harriet's false identity, and so on. It struck me as strange that they didn't follow up on my replies, but merely seemed to be running through a predetermined list. I was surprised that Coyle, the young DS, was much more aggressive than his senior officer.

When Coyle asked me who paid the mortgage on the flat, I twigged that they were corroborating my story with Harriet's.

The whole interview was timed, and those present all named, including WPC Laura Curtis (pretty name, I thought). Her number, 608, was the registration number of my first car, which must have been a good omen. I was wrong. My bladder was putting pressure on me to ask for the loo again. I prayed that they wouldn't bring some sort of pot, because I knew I couldn't perform with the lovely Laura in the room. She didn't speak, but with a nod of the head, the giant plod got the message and he led me to the little boys' room. I had never pissed with an AK47 inches from my backside before, and it is not an experience I want to repeat. I was desperate, but it still took seven minutes.

When I returned, I was relieved to see the familiar face of DI Trevor Crisp. Trevor, who lives further down my road in Dulwich, did not show the slightest sign of recognition.

He addressed me formally.

"Mr. O'Liam, we are satisfied that neither you nor Miss Anktash have been involved in terrorist activities. However, the falsification of official documents, the harbouring of an illegal immigrant, the theft of an identity of a deceased person, the…"

The list of charges seemed endless. He finished with the formal charge and standard warning about "anything I should say…"

"You will be detained here until the custody officer has received the report on your case. You will surrender all your belongings, including what you are wearing, and you will be given police issue clothing, suitable for temporary custody. If you wish, you may seek legal representation. If you give the name of your solicitors to one of my officers, he will make the call for you. The conversation will be limited to the details of the charges against you, and arrangements for your legal representative to attend this station. When your representative arrives, you will be entitled to hold a private conversation with him or her."

"What about Harriet? What will happen to her?"

"I am not at liberty to discuss the charges against Miss Anktash."

As he left the room, Trevor turned and said, "in the circumstances, as you have fully co-operated with this enquiry, I can tell you that Miss Anktash will be taken to an immigration centre, pending deportation. If the Turkish authorities act quickly, and issue her with a new passport, her stay should not be longer than a few weeks. Currently, two support officers are with her at her flat, helping her to pack, and explaining the procedures. I understand she is very anxious to speak to you."

***

I asked the custody officer if he could call James Latham-Percy, my solicitor. To my surprise, he handed me the phone and let me dial. As I had surrendered my possessions, I then had to ask him to find the office number for Trumpers & Binks. Eventually, I got through to James and explained the charges.

"I can get to Paddington Green by six tonight, and I'll bring my colleague Letitia Roberts, who is an expert in the field. Can you wait that long?"

"Very funny, James. They don't have early closing here, you know."

"Sean, what about your girlfriend, will she need representation? If possible, it would be good to have the same brief. She may, of course, have asked for legal aid. Neither Letitia nor I come cheap, but if we want to prevent her being treated as a failed asylum seeker, facing deportation, we've got to act fast."

"I haven't been allowed to speak to her yet, but I am told she has been escorted back to the flat and is collecting her possessions."

"Okay, put me on to the custody officer; I'll let you know what is happening when I see you tonight."

***

James and Letitia arrived promptly at 6pm. James wore an even wider pinstripe than normal. Letitia looked six feet tall and rather severe. I was very impressed and could hardly take my eyes off her. Out of the corner of my eye, I could see James laughing at my fawning admiration, while Letitia carefully and firmly took me through the steps we had to take.

"We have to convince the Home Office that the "arrangements" you made for Miss Anktash were not intended to be permanent, but simply an act of altruism for a friend, so she could learn English and study British culture. You will have to be prepared to pay for an RDO, so that she can return to Turkey as quickly as possible. She must consent to this arrangement."

"What's an RDO?"

"A Rapid Deportation Order; your case, while unusual, is not unique. Some quite well-known names in the entertainment world, not wishing to wait for the long-winded immigration process, and also being unwilling to commit to matrimony, have used similar means to bring "friends" into the

UK. However, as far as we know, nobody has had the means to recreate a whole personality with a lady from Lancashire, whose life ended tragically early."

"Will I go to prison? And, if so, for how long?"

"We hope you will get away with a PCR, Perceived Criminal Record. If not, then you can expect a two-year sentence, which would reduce to 16 months with good behaviour."

The interview room was grossly over-heated, but I suddenly felt very cold. James took over from Letitia and explained.

"A PCR is used when no-one has actually suffered criminally. Mercifully, no fraud, as such, has been committed, and the only person out of pocket is you. It is very fortunate the flat was in your name, otherwise "permanent intention to reside" could not be denied. The authorities won't worry about Harriet working for Mehmet, although she might be called to give evidence, as he has been running a large and very illegal immigration racket. She has readily agreed to do this, as you would imagine."

"Oh, you've seen her," I said, wistfully.

"No, but I have spoken to her, partly to corroborate your story, and partly to see if she would co-operate. It was too late to stop her going to Campsfield, but I would hope to get her out within a few days."

"And will she co-operate?"

"I'm not sure. She is alternatively very angry with you and then she realises that if she hadn't gone to the police, you would both have got away with it."

"Can I see her when she gets out of Campsfield?"

"Let's concentrate on getting our story right for the Home Office. The problem is the identity theft. That's more serious than the falsification of the passport. If you had gone to a dealer and just had a counterfeit made, you would have got away with it. But stealing an identity; that's a different matter."

"But the woman's dead, for God's sake; long dead."

"Yes, but her husband and children aren't dead."

"And it's only three years since her accident," said Letitia, following on. "James and I will discuss this issue overnight. We could just choose to leave it out of your statement, but we are putting ourselves at risk, and if Harriet

Ribblesdale comes to light again, you are in serious trouble."

"Harriet doesn't know that hers is a dead woman's identity; I thought she might think that rather sick."

"That's good. I haven't seen her statement, but the police will have asked her, and it is now genuinely on tape that she doesn't know how or why you gave her that name. It could have been an 'off-the-shelf' name."

"What? Just like an 'off-the-shelf' company?"

"Exactly, Sean, but *they* are perfectly legal," they said in harmony.

"And the PCR is like a suspended sentence?"

"In a way, but unlike a suspended sentence, it does not appear on your records; but if you offend again, they will cane you, I should think."

***

Hurriyet agreed to co-operate. I paid Trumpers and Binks £25,000 to pass 'under-the-counter' to the Home Office, £12,000 for their fees, and I gave Harriet £10,000 and the cost of her flight to Izmir. I felt full of remorse, and promised to marry her. She didn't believe me, but at that moment I really meant it and would have given my life to go and live in Izmir. Then I realised she had three more brothers in Izmir, who would happily have taken my life. Miss Hurriyet Anktash was going to be avenged one way or another.

CHAPTER 18

(Claire Comes Home)

Claire took longer to recover than expected; the trauma had been huge, and the hospital had warned Bridget that the embolism, which resulted from the accident, could cause a fatal stroke at any time. Despite this ever-present threat, her doctors thought she would recover more quickly at home, though she would need regular checks at a London hospital.

Bridget had chosen the day of Tom's memorial service to collect Claire, though she would be in no condition to attend. John had been back in the UK for a few days, but he was able to get back to Scotland in time.

***

This time, Bridget really only had time for a coffee. She chose a tiny coffee shop in Fitzroy Square, which certainly had the edge on the nearest Starbucks in terms of privacy, as there were no other customers.

I had never seen her so animated. She told me all about DDG, the results of the tests they had taken in Sweden and Ghana, her lingering doubts, and her reluctance to publish the data. With Fife's information, all Bridget's doubts would be swept away. Donald had been extremely keen to publish as soon as possible, but for some reason which he refused to reveal to Bridget, he had changed his mind. The staff meeting at which they had intended to brief their own team had been suspended indefinitely.

Bridget had explained the case of the Fife Life smokers to him, and, initially, he had embraced it enthusiastically. Although, this test really would give them final proof from a source in the UK, Donald had reservations about me becoming a party to the application of DDG. She explained how the application would help Fife and how I was risking my career by passing Fife's data to them. He was a scientist who had little time for the world of finance; Fife's problems were of no interest to him

Bridget pleaded with him, and even threatened to end their relationship; he wanted to stay in the security of his scientific shell, as if the knowledge would be tainted if released. Eventually, he agreed to my testing a token sample of 1% of the annuitants. This was never going to save Fife Life, or so I thought, but at least it was a start.

CHAPTER 19

(Telling Tales to the Bishop)

The last time Conor had been to the Archbishop's House, the baroque Victorian building which sits alongside Westminster Cathedral, was for a party for the London priests to celebrate the 10th anniversary of their ordinations. This visit, however, was going to be a much more solemn occasion.

Bishop Jordan came down the grand staircase to greet Conor in the hall. He was the same bishop who had blessed the opening of the supermarket.

"Good morning, Father O'Liam."

Not being addressed as Conor or even Father Conor was definitely a sign of some future discipline to follow.

Conor shook hands with Bishop Jordan and was ushered into a small study. He was shown to an armchair, so at least he didn't have to face him across the oak table in the corner of the room.

The study was lined with books; an entire wall was devoted to religious publications of every faith, including, somewhat surprisingly, some written by the 'opposition' such as Richard Dawkins's *The God Delusion* and Christopher Hitchens's *God is Not Great*. Conor reminded himself to buy a copy of each as he found he was increasingly being challenged on matters of faith these days, and books such as these were frequently quoted at him. Frivolously, he wondered if he could claim the cost on expenses. More surprisingly, there were whole sections devoted to cricket, golf and rugby. Then he remembered the archbishop had been an international —

"They are a fine collection of books," said the bishop, interrupting Conor's thoughts, "and I expect there is a small section in the archbishop's sporting memorabilia, which you might be interested in, and this is the area I want to discuss. I will come straight to the point. It has been brought to my attention that you have been seen at various race meetings over the last six months."

Conor shuddered, but said nothing.

Bishop Jordan continued. "Furthermore, our informant advises us that on two of those occasions, you were not wearing your clerical collar. She has also assured us that you were betting heavily. I have no objection to you spending the occasional day with parishioners at a race meeting. The Church is not totally opposed to gambling, provided it is in moderation; a small flutter, I believe it is called, a pound or two, would be acceptable. You are meant to observe restraint, and I would remind you of the vow of poverty you made at your ordination."

Conor waited for more, but after a long pontifical pause, the bishop only said, "do you have anything to say?"

Conor was in turmoil. On the one hand, he had to stop himself from saying, "is that all?" He was hugely relieved that there had been no suggestion of impropriety with the church roof money. However, he was fuming at the allegations. If he had brought the Church into disrepute by being on a racecourse, surely it would have been much worse if he had been wearing his 'dog'. And who was the informant?

"Bishop Jordan." Conor smiled to himself. He had only just picked up the biblical connection; he would have been delighted to baptise him in the river, but with one critical difference involving the final position of his head. "I don't deny that I am fond of horse-racing and that I have been to the races on a few occasions. My betting is modest (and so it had to be, he reflected, since his unfortunate experience with Light My Fire). I can't believe your informant could possibly know how much money I was placing, unless she was literally standing behind me. Is your informant one of my parishioners and, if so, surely I am allowed to know her name?"

"I am not in a position to disclose the identity of the informant," replied Jordan pompously, "but I can confirm she is one of your parishioners, and she observed the exchange of money, first hand, on the course."

Conor was speechless. This was completely unjust. The bishop has not asked his accuser for any evidence; he had just taken her word against his. No formal enquiry has been convened, so he could not call any witnesses himself. True, he didn't know all his parishioners by name, and certainly not all the RECs (Remembrance, Easter and Christmas). Surely, even the woman to whom he had rather flippantly said after Midnight Mass, "Happy

Christmas, see you at Easter," would not have taken this much offence.

"Do you feel you have a problem? Perhaps, there is a lady who has a grudge against you for some unknown reason," said the bishop.

He knew what the bishop was trying to imply. 'You can throw the good book at me for many things, but not for that,' he thought.

"I cannot think of any parishioner, man or woman, who holds a grudge against me, or has any reason to do so," he said defiantly.

Excluding the RECs, he had about 250 regulars, of whom about 80 went to the 6pm on Saturday, another 60 at the 8.30 am on Sunday (not being an early riser, Conor left this one to Jeremy Ngeni) and 110 at the 11am Sung Mass on Sunday. Then there were the football swappers; their attendance depended on whether there was a 5.15 match at The Emirates Stadium or White Hart Lane on the telly, or whether it was on Match of the Day 2 on Sunday morning. Surely, he hadn't upset any of them? He might have teased the Spurs supporters in the past, but their performance this season was nothing short of divine! Surely a few jibes in seasons past wouldn't justify revenge on this scale. Surely, the snooper didn't fall into any of these categories.

"Would you like some coffee?" said the bishop, unexpectedly.

"Thank you," said Conor, hoping for some more thinking time while Bishop Jordan went in search of his housekeeper.

Conor could make no sense of it. He looked out of the window. On the street below, he saw two policemen. Scotland Yard was just around the corner, he recalled. Perhaps all this was a trick to get him to admit the church roof fund 'loan'. He felt he was being stalked. He racked his brains for a possible suspect. Perhaps she was a syndicate member's wife. That was unlikely, and, anyway, he didn't actually know if any of the syndicate were married.

Bishop Jordan returned, but without the coffee.

"Unfortunately, I cannot find the archbishop. Until I call you again, you will continue with your parish responsibilities, but you will not discuss this situation with anyone. Please let yourself out."

CHAPTER 20

(Claire's Recovery)

Back in her parents' home in London, Claire was still weak. She knew she would slowly recover her physical strength, though the surgery had been intrusive. Every time she considered returning to her studies in Edinburgh, the thought alone exhausted her.

Bridget had taken compassionate leave when Claire first came home. She attended to her basic needs, but Claire only really wanted to sleep. In the second week she got up and pottered around the house. She looked at herself in the mirror and she barely recognised the pale, tired person who stared back. But it was her mental state that worried her the most. She just couldn't see herself ever reclaiming her energy to study.

Bridget had told Claire about her work on the DDG a few days after she had come home. It was a curious moment to choose as Claire was really in too weak a state to absorb it, and she was still in shock about Tom.

On Claire's second day out of bed, Bridget sneaked a few hours in the lab. "I won't be long, darling," she called, as she adjusted her helmet for the bike ride to the lab. But to Claire, alone for the first time, five hours seemed daunting. The home she had grown up in suddenly seemed menacing: every door seemed to creak, revealing some hidden danger; every cupboard had a secret; its very silence seemed uncanny. Claire turned on as many radios as she could find, and the television too, to hide the silence that still called Tom from every corner. The atmosphere was just too clean, too cold and too sterile. Just as her mother's lab was abandoned every night and left to its functional self, so this house seemed equally unloved. She found solace with Wag, the family Jack Russell, and a few of the treatises among the pile of untidy papers in her father's study. As if she were still a child, she longed for him to come home from his American lecture tour.

Claire thought more and more about how her mother had changed. Bridget was not a tactile woman, but while Claire's internal injuries precluded a big maternal hug, something more than a peck on the cheek would have been welcome. She seemed to be more a lab assistant than a loving mother, and she wondered if was she still a devoted wife?

Every time her father came home from America, warmth returned to their house in Finchley. These were the same days that Bridget became more withdrawn. Was this only how it seemed to Claire? Having no siblings, Claire could not share her thoughts. Claire had wondered, as children often do, why she was an only child. As Bridget conceived her while she was still at university, age had not been the problem. Could she remember her parents being close to each other when she was younger? True, they still shared a bed, and as a young girl she remembered they were always playing games with her. Now it seemed they were never at home at the same time and, if they were, they hardly exchanged a word.

The second day Bridget went back to work, Claire started thinking more about the accident. 'Would it have been possible to have predicted that Tom would die, and I would survive the accident? Will I recover? They said there will always be the risk of an embolism, as a result of the blood clot. If that's fatal, the DDG should be able to predict the date.'

The effort of concentrating and the pain of accepting her survival against the loss of Tom made her feel weak again. The numbness stage of her grief was translating rapidly into anger, an anger she was not strong enough to carry. She struggled back to her room and collapsed on her bed.

Some hours later, Bridget returned from the lab. Claire was lying partly dressed on the bed, and her room was freezing. Bridget felt her pulse and knew that hypothermia was setting in. She wrapped her up and called the surgery, which referred her to the Whittington Hospital.

"I can't drive and keep her warm," Bridget screamed down the phone. "The car is freezing."

Disturbed by Bridget's anger, Claire began to wake up. She was delirious and kept asking for Tom and mumbling, "I'm not going to die."

After what seemed like an age, the ambulance arrived, and Bridget accompanied her to hospital. The doctors at the Whittington took the precaution of keeping her in overnight and agreed to release her the next day, provided she was not left alone.

Bridget felt suitably chastised, but was unprepared for more babysitting. She had meetings the next day, which Donald had forced on her, mainly because he hated talking to the 'men from the Ministry'. They appeared from time to time to check on what was going on at the Institute. Talking to the press was an even greater nightmare for Donald than explaining things to prying civil servants, so Bridget was under pressure to be there.

Bridget was sitting at home and wondering how to resolve this dilemma. Claire was still too weak to be left alone, yet Bridget had to go ahead with the meeting. Donald had postponed it once because Bridget was in Edinburgh. It was clear the Ministry could not be put off again. She thought about asking her cleaner, Elena, to come on Tuesday rather than Thursday. It was always a major problem changing the woman's arrangements as she spoke almost no English and Bridget was somewhat lacking in Ukrainian and Russian. Communication was usually face to face, or occasionally in German, which Bridget spoke competently, and which is widely understood in the Ukraine.

None of this would help Claire if there were a crisis, so she dismissed the idea. The phone interrupted her thoughts. John had never mastered international travel, so this was unusual. However, following a recent incident, he had resolved to become more organised. He had been due to speak in Paris one week and Vienna the next. Arriving at Gatwick, he had forgotten the sequence of events, and finding only the Parisian tickets, assumed he had lost the Austrian booking and was relieved to find there were still seats on the BA flight to Vienna. He made a last-minute booking at the airport and was surprised to find no-one was waiting to meet him. Arriving at the lecture theatre the next day, he was even more amazed to find his old friend Wilhelm Katz, who was due to introduce him before his lecture, looking unexpectedly casual, and enjoying a coffee in the rest room.

"John, it is great to see you, but you should have said you were coming for a few days' holiday. You could stay with Marika and I, and we would show you the delights of our lovely city."

"Wilhelm," he replied, as the truth dawned on him, "I need to make a very urgent call to Paris, and the sight-seeing will have to wait till next week."

The problem of nursing Claire was unexpectedly resolved by the Norwegian weather. He had to come home from Oslo as he could not travel to the University of Tromso in the Arctic Circle. The conditions were too severe even for the Norwegians.

Claire recovered under the watchful and more caring eye of her father, who had been particularly shocked by the setback in Claire's condition. Bridget now fully appreciated that the reaction had been partly caused by not discussing the full implications of the DDG with Claire. Over the next few days, she prepared her explanation more carefully.

A few days later, John had to give a lecture at UCL, and Bridget resumed her nursing duties at home. It was quite mild for mid-February. Snowdrops now had to compete with crocuses, and even green daffodil shoots were vying for attention. Claire came down to breakfast, having been awake half the night preparing her interrogation. She was calm and rational. She didn't bother with a perfunctory kiss for her mother.

"So, what exactly is going on between you and dad, or rather what exactly is not going on? You don't seem to live on the same planet, let alone in the same house."

"Has he said anything to you?"

"He doesn't need to. I can see there's a problem, and I don't think it's him. He's the same, kind dad, but you, you've completely lost it. Is it just the gene thingy? Now, you never think of anything or anyone else."

Bridget sipped her coffee. Claire stirred her muesli into a mushy pulp. "Well, aren't you going to say anything?"

"Claire, I was going to tell you when you were better. You've had so much to cope with, what with losing Tom and the operation."

"Mum, look, just give me all the shit now. Right?"

"Well, it's very difficult. You must know that your dad and I haven't been getting on for months, well, actually over a year now, since you were on your gap year."

"What do you mean: 'I must know'? Of course I don't bloody know unless someone tells me. I am 400 miles away for Christ's sake, and now you're saying it's all my fault for going to Oz last year. You couldn't be trusted to get on together while I was away. Sorrreee! I suppose I was the cement that kept you together. Well, just get it. I won't be staying here for long in this atmosphere, so get some new cement."

Bridget swallowed this, waiting for a further verbal assault. Nothing followed. She broke the silence herself.

"Claire, I'm seeing someone else." It was almost inaudible.

"You what? You're joking! Seeing who? Does dad know?"

Bridget poured herself another cup from the Caffe Torino.

"Yes, he has known all along; he has been very good about it."

"Very good about it! Just accepting your bit of hunk on the side. He deserves a medal. Who is this guy? Why? When did it start? Are you going to split up?"

The stream of questions became a torrent. Bridget sat motionless, wishing she was somewhere else. This was not how she had planned it. When the discussion deviated from her plan, she didn't know how to cope.

"What about me? Will I still have a home? I don't suppose you thought of that. For Christ's sake, tell me who it is. Mum, TELL ME."

The torrent of words became a flood of tears, but Bridget was speechless. The right words just wouldn't come out.

"Do you want to know more about the project?" That was all she could manage.

Claire went ballistic. She brought her face as close to Bridget's as she could and screamed at her. "Yes, I do. I want to know why Tom died and why I didn't and why you couldn't tell me. I want to know all that and more because I think your fucking project is fake, but first of all I want to know WHO."

"Oh, Claire"

Claire pushed her away.

"Don't get all mummy with me."

"It's Donald."

She really only mouthed the words, but it was enough.

"Donald! That little creep! You're shagging Donald. That is so-o-o-o gross. That's disgusting. Is this some kind of experiment to produce a super scientist? Or are you post-menopausal now? Most mothers share that sort of information with their daughters so maybe not yet. So, I can expect some kind of baby Bunsen brother anytime soon? That's just…oh God! I can't believe it!"

She needed to do something physical. She grabbed a piece of her mother's favourite Dresden and threw it at the wall.

CHAPTER 21

(It Helps to Speak Turkish)

Jon Heely was travelling to Izmir in Turkey to investigate claims of a cure for blindness caused by macular degeneration. Having trained in respectable provincial newspapers like *The Wolverhampton Express* and *Star* and *The Birmingham Post*, he had decided to go freelance a few years ago, and chase 'sensationals', some of which were published in the wilder national tabloids such as *The Daily Sport*.

'Woman Gives Birth to Monkey and Human Twins' was his most famous. Stories such as these required little research. They often emanated from third world countries, where the payment of a few dollars would make an enormous difference to the lives of the affected individuals. Jon would spend hours on the phone to an intermediary (usually a brother or father). He would always ask for photographs; when they arrived, he would take them to a colleague for reconstruction to identify fakes or time inconsistencies.

The Turkish blindness healer intrigued him because the cured patients had apparently been examined by eye surgeons in Istanbul and found to be genuine. All the healers had the same reluctance to allow journalists to actually meet the patients, and an even greater disinclination to produce the original medical records.

Jon had decided that the Izmir 'healer' was going to be his last sensational, simply because the stories were ruining his reputation to write anything serious.

As he boarded the Turkish Airlines Airbus A320 for his final cheap headline trip, he caught sight of an attractive woman in her mid-twenties being escorted separately to the rear steps of the plane by two officials, whom Jon recognised as being employees of the Immigration Office. The woman between them must, therefore, be a deportee.

She was dressed remarkably smartly for a deportee, and this intrigued Jon. With considerable journalistic experience of asylum seeker deportation stories, he knew she would be the last one to board and that the cabin staff would be under instruction to watch her throughout the flight. He also observed that the deportee seemed remarkably calm. Usually the final escorting procedure onto the plane would be accompanied by tears in a last vain attempt to be allowed to stay. Alternatively, if resigned to their fate, the air would be filled with anti-British abuse.

The customary procedure (except for convicted killers and terrorists, who would be escorted all the way) would be for the receiving country to provide officials at the other end. They would board the aircraft first and escort the deportee from the plane before the other passengers. This was partly to satisfy the UK authorities, and partly because there was almost invariably a minor crime which the deportees had committed 'at home' before he (and occasionally she) had left the country of origin.

Jon did not know how strictly the British authorities had instructed the Turkish cabin crew to be with the deportee, but he noticed that the 'prisoner' was not being 'observed' by the staff and was allowed to queue by the brightly shining toilet sign unaccompanied and to buy from the duty free. He felt there was a story behind this woman, and like a terrier chasing a rat, he had to see it through.

However, the woman was sitting in the traditional 'deportee' position at the very rear of the plane (so that Turkish Immigration could escort her at Izmir with minimum publicity and inconvenience). She had been given the window seat, and the middle and aisle seats were left deliberately unoccupied.

Her location allowed Jon to make three comfort stops (one genuine, two fabricated) to get a better view of the drama. It was only when he passed close by that he realised that she was stunningly beautiful and as full bodied as the A320 she was sitting in! On really boring trips, he would test his memory by reciting the aircraft's specifications and the safety instructions. This was much more interesting, but what was his justification for talking to her, and would the cabin staff try to stop him?

On the second comfort stop, he caught her eye, and she smiled. Wow! 'Why the hell is the UK deporting you?' he thought. He also noticed she was reading *The Daily Mail*. He had to be careful. He must give no indication to her that he suspected that she was being deported. She would not trust him.

Jon did not speak a word of Turkish, and the language problem was worrying him. Communication with the Izmir healer on the phone had been painful, and there was no middle man. Suddenly, an opportunity presented itself to talk to the glamorous deportee and find out at the same time,

On the third visit, he returned the smile with interest. He allowed himself to pass her row on the way back, and then turned around to face her, as if on impulse. By now she was engrossed in Grazia, but she looked straight at him when he said, "excuse me, this is a real cheek, but I wonder if you can help me?"

And Hurriyet Anktash was only too willing to help him.

CHAPTER 22

(Genetic Factors in a Rodent World)

This time, Bridget and Donald held a formal meeting at the Institute's offices. Bridget wanted to include Craigie and Ruthie, even though she despised the odious pair. But Donald overruled her, fresh in the knowledge that he attributed to the fourth dimension. The essential difference between Donald and Bridget was that, while my sister believed passionately that lifestyle was the principal determinant of longevity, Donald attributed extended old age partially to genetics and only partly to lifestyle.

Recently, however, the pendulum had begun to swing towards a more genetic solution. I recalled my conversation with Bridget at the little coffee shop in Euston. Although I didn't realise it at the time, Donald's growing enthusiasm for a genetic outcome had hugely enthused Bridget to apply a solution which could more reliably predict a death date combined with lifestyle.

Obviously, more research had to be done by both parties, but the templates which the world's most eminent scientists at recent conferences in Boston and Rome were applying were a long way ahead of Donald and Bridget.

CHAPTER 23

(Press Reaction)

Stories about the death date gene were beginning to leak from the two conferences and then appear in small articles in *Science Daily* and *Scientific American*. *The Daily Express* was the first national daily to feature it; just a half column on page four, a filler piece with no attribution: "Now we know when we'll die. UK scientists discover death gene."

It is a strange fact in British journalism that, unless individuals are actually named, the more outrageous the story, the less the use of the conditional inverted commas. So it was with the death gene story. It seemed so improbable that *The Express* did not bother to qualify it.

'Death gene' itself was qualified the first and second time, but the discovery was not. After *The Express* ran it for a second time a few weeks later along the bottom of the front page, *The Daily Mail* quickly followed. Then came the broadsheets. After that, the death gene was considered to be in common usage, and no qualification was necessary.

Rumours of a documentary began to circulate, but no journalist had named any scientist or any laboratories. Their legal teams had seen to that.

The Department of Home Affairs began to worry, but so did the Department of Science and Technology, the Department of Health and even the Department of Work and Pensions. After much arguing about whether the government should make a statement, and if so, which department should make it, Home Affairs made the following announcement:

"In light of recent stories in the national press, the Department of Home Affairs confirms that, as part of the programme to decode the human genome, evaluation of life expectancy rates has been carried out in a number of countries outside the UK, by the special projects of the UK Advancement of Knowledge of the Human Genome (UKAGP). It is not expected that any definitive interpretation of this evaluation will be known for several years."

If the government expected this statement to dampen speculation, they were completely mistaken.

The following headlines appeared the next day;

- *Government Admits Life Expectancy Testing (**The Times**).*
- *Government Refuses To Release Death Date Gene Information (**The Guardian**).*
- *Death Date Gene Is Threat To Planet (**Independent**).*
- *Government Challenged On Death Date Gene (**Daily Telegraph**).*
- *Mail Campaigns For Death Gene Information (**Daily Mail**).*
- *Swedes Know Our Death Dates (**Daily Express**).*
- *Give Us Our Dates (**The Sun** – with skull and crossbones).*
- *I Know When You're A Goner; Swede Boffin Tells All In Lab Sex Romp (**Daily Sport**).*

In fact, *The Daily Sport* was closest to the truth. The Swedish connection had happened because the UK project was, and still is, working with the Institute of Genetics at the University of Gothenburg as part of their ethnic diversity exercise. The Institute thought they ought to issue a parallel statement to the British Government.

In the absence of any confirmed location in the UK, the British press besieged the Swedish university. Various protest groups arrived in Gothenburg, carrying very strong messages. These included the Lutheran Church of Sweden (How dare you play God?).

Internet 'date swap' groups were set up (I'll tell you my date if you'll tell me yours) with, of course, completely fabricated dates of death. Death plea blogs (DPBs) became common (this is my date; I have only three weeks to live and I must have sex with four virgins before I go. Proof of virginity not essential).

All sorts of weird sects set up camp around the university. Eventually, the Swedish army was called in. They set up barricades around the Institute with several hundred big blonde soldiers. Apart from the big blonde soldiers, who were very popular with the female undergrads, the army proved to be an effective deterrent, and both the press and the protest groups drifted away.

In the UK, speculation about the precise location of the project was rife. Almost every scientific establishment was identified as a genetic scapegoat, but nothing was proven. In fact, the project operated under a none-too-clever pseudonym, Predicta Ltd., in an anonymous building in Tavistock Square. Donald swiftly came up with the idea of adding "Manufacturers of Pregnancy Testing Equipment" under the nameplate, and no journalist ever put two and two together.

The government really did know nothing at this stage, because the results of the project had not been reported to any ministry and were only due to be reported as an addendum to the whole human genome research project. Only when the wheels of government started to move faster did questions begin to be asked.

In the city, the shares of life assurance companies doubled, as investing institutions realised there would be no risk as actuaries could calculate their liabilities precisely, only to fall back again the next day, and then halve again, when they realised the shoe was on the other foot. Under Data Protection laws, only the life-assured would know his or her predicted death-date and he or she alone would be able to arrange their life policy accordingly.

Telephone cold calls, usually from Canada or the US, inviting investors to participate in 'guaranteed investment schemes' between now and the investor's death date, proliferated. These schemes, known as 'boiler room scams', manifested into offers such as '50 things to do in your last three weeks' and 'How to handle your creditors after you've gone'. Most people thought that DDG was a joke, but the UK and Swedish governments were not the only institutions who took it very seriously indeed.

CHAPTER 24

(Letter to the Faithful)

His Grace the Cardinal Archbishop of Westminster has instructed the following letter to be read in Catholic churches throughout England and Wales on Sunday 21st February.

"The recent speculation in the British press regarding the so-called 'death date gene' has given rise to a great deal of concern among the bishops and clergy of England and Wales and to large numbers of lay Catholics throughout the country. Following the recent statement by the government, we are assured that there is no evidence that it will ever be possible, from the reconstruction of the genome, to determine the date of death of any living human being.

The length of our time on Earth lies solely in the power of Almighty God, and the destination of our souls in the next life is in our own hands and at the mercy of Our Lord Jesus Christ. We shall therefore pray that we are not distracted by temptation to believe such idolatry and that we continue to serve God, and our neighbour for his sake, as we have been directed."

Given at Westminster on the 20th February in the year of Our Lord.

A parallel archiepiscopal letter was issued by the archbishops of Scotland and Ireland.

The Catholic Church is still one of the richest institutions in the world. 1.2 billion people, around one in eight, claim to be Catholic, even if not practising.

It has to be wealthy. It has over 400,000 priests to pay, a similar number of churches to maintain, tens of thousands of schools to support, radio and TV stations to administer, not to mention the Swiss Guard.

Over the years, the Church has made sensible investment decisions in property and securities; every Sunday, Catholics the world over continue to fill the plate with millions of euros, dollars and even pounds.

Imagine if you were a bit of a naughty Catholic, but you knew exactly when you were going to leave this world. Confession is still central to the Church's teaching. It is almost unique to the Catholic Church, though some Anglo-Catholic churches and quite a few Orthodox also apply the sacrament of reconciliation.

Okay, so what's the point of leading a blameless life? I can screw who I want, I can rob whom I choose, and I can even kill a person at random, provided I can get to confession a few days before my death date.

The Church isn't going to like that. At least Mother Church can keep you slightly on the straight and narrow if you don't know when. You could be caught off guard and plop straight into the eternal flames, or at least spend a very long spell in the Purgatory Penitentiary unless you can get to the local parish priest and receive your last rites. I, Sean O'Liam, still believe this, even though I have strayed; so do millions of Catholics throughout the world.

Large numbers of men and women could simply stop coming to Mass and start behaving badly, because they have a free pass. It might be human nature, but would the Church stand by and let it happen? I don't think so.

The government also had concerns, not so spiritual, more legal and temporal. Would I care a fig about my creditors if I were not here next week, and, in fact, never coming back? I'll borrow anything I can from anyone who'll lend.

I want to get my own back on that shit down the road who smashed my car while it was parked outside my house. He never admitted it, and I could never prove it. There would be time for retaliation this week, confession next week and absolution to coincide with my cremation the week after. I'd be gone long before my trial.

Murders, robberies, rapes, all could be committed without penalty. Anything but suicide bombings, but they were never popular with Catholics anyway!

Schools started planning to ask pupils to reveal their death dates and were excluded if they weren't going to reach 18. Financial planners were extremely busy with Inheritance Tax schemes.

The Careers Services of the Armed Forces had a very busy time. Anyone could be a hero without risk if they wanted to be, forgetting that the DDG said nothing about life-changing injuries.

There were a whole lot of institutions out there who didn't want DDG research to go any further.

CHAPTER 25

(Donald Changes His Mind)

There was a connecting door between Donald's and Bridget's offices at the lab. It was rarely closed, usually only when there was a visit from the ministry, and then only for the comfort of the visitor, rather than because Donald or Bridget wished to withhold anything from each other.

Ever since the discussion about releasing the DDG information to enable Fife to carry out the life expectancy trial on a 1% sample of Fife Life's annuitants, to which Donald had reluctantly agreed, the door had been closed more often than it was open.

Bridget had not really considered this as unusual, knowing that Donald was under particular stress, and allowed him the time to prepare for the public stage of the project. I had been in possession of the genetic data for about a week and had made encouraging progress. For the first time in months, the future looked brighter. Hurriyet had returned to Turkey and there just might be a way out of the crisis at Fife.

The phone rang, but my sister, on the other end, sounded distraught.

"Donald's changed his mind. He has refused permission to use the data. If you try to apply it, he will take out an injunction. He has more or less shut himself in his office for the last few days, refusing to talk to anyone, even me. He stormed into my office this morning screaming about how I was crazy to persuade him to agree to release the information to you 'of all people'."

"But I thought you and he were... close?"

I could almost hear her blush.

"I don't know what gave you that idea."

"Okay, okay, but what has got into him? I mean, what has changed his mind? It's too late anyway. I selected 1% of our annuitants (320 in total, including 50 who have died) and took a random sample by age, gender and address, including some who are technically covered by a gilt redemption and some where we have no cover at all. I've already sent out the 270 questionnaires, which is what we agreed."

"Well, Donald says the whole world will know. He thinks the annuitants are going to suspect something, and that they will ask their financial advisers why Fife wants this information. He says they will assume that Fife is going to reduce the annuity. He believes that, because Fife has written to its annuitants, the city will suspect it is in trouble."

"Fortunately, because we are a mutual, it doesn't matter a toss what the city thinks. We don't have a share price to defend."

This was a bit of bravado on my part, because, obviously, I did not want financial journalists sniffing around at the present time.

"From your point of view, Bridget, I can see that a 100% result from the 320 would be perfect even though the 250 will take a few years to die, but I need to know the death dates of all 27,000 so I can buy the right stocks to coincide with their departures. Bridget, I've put my life in your hands on this one. Please ignore Donald and let me do the rest."

And then it occurred to me. Sometimes, the dull hand of compliance and the tedium of an audit could work in our favour. I would call Phil Jewell in the morning.

CHAPTER 26

(Sharing the Grief)

Claire was on the train to Edinburgh to meet Tom's parents. It had taken a lot of courage on her part to do this. She had only met them once and it was not going to be easy. She knew they were very religious and that they had accepted the accident as God's will, something which she could not agree with. For Tom's sake, though, she wanted to share her grief with them.

As the train left York, she noticed a young guy a couple of seats away. His hair was short and neat, and Claire was unaccountably pleased he had not chosen what men's hairdressers called a No.1, as she hated the extreme hairlessness of this currently popular style. Whenever Claire teased Tom about his long, unkempt locks, he would threaten to go and get a No.1 cut, though she doubted if he really understood this would leave him completely bald, at least for a few weeks.

She reckoned her travelling companion had chosen a No. 2 and that his hair had been recently and expensively cut. She had got bored with reading the beauty tips in *Red* and could not get to grips with her book. She speculated about the other passenger. Across the aisle sat a middle-aged woman she was convinced was treating her elderly mother to a few days in Edinburgh. From her appearance, she was clearly not looking forward to the prospect, though the old lady was obviously enjoying herself as though she was on release from her care home. Rather like a four-year-old nagging her mother, she kept tapping her daughter and saying "sheep" or "church" as though these sights were completely new to her.

Claire's eyes kept straying back to the man with the No.2 cut, but she could not place him. His jeans fit but had seen better days. They were worn and, while not outwardly dirty, had that sort of bar-stool look, with beer stains and a faint smell of salt and vinegar. His shoes were scuffed but stylish. He was writing notes in longhand; funny that a trendy, professional guy did not use a laptop

Then she caught his eye and found herself visually flirting with him; he smiled and looked away. That must be the first since the accident, she thought; she wondered if he had noticed the scar. Her hair had nearly grown back, but if he looked closely, he *could* see — but men rarely looked that closely the first time, did they? My legs are a mess; those scars will be there for years. Plastic surgery before miniskirts; fortunately, her jeans covered all that. There was no doubt that she found him attractive; she reckoned he was about 28 and he had a kind, but determined, face. Then she rebuked herself for thinking such a thing on the way to meet the parents of her dead boyfriend, whom she missed so much.

She wondered whether that mattered, what Tom would have thought, and whether it was healthy. It had not occurred to her until then, but she would be looking at men again — one day.

She wondered why it bothered her so much that this unknown, untidy man admired her, when he was probably getting off at Newcastle and she would never see him again. But it did.

Tom's parents were waiting for her at Dunfermline Station. She remembered how kind they had been when they had met her before. Tom had obviously been so proud of her. He had never introduced a girlfriend to his mom and dad before, let alone a "Sassenach." Claire had felt very touched by this, but was concerned how much she could share with them.

Could she mention the wonderful weekend they had in Berwick, where they had first had sex in that freezing but wonderful room looking out over the North Sea? Would they disapprove, or would they assume the weekend had been totally innocent and platonic? They seemed very naive. They rarely came to Edinburgh and had never been to the university. What would they think about the trip to Musselburgh Races? The whole department had agreed to charter a coach to the watch the racing. Claire had noticed Tom before, but this was the first time she caught him looking at her, and that little butterfly she used to feel in her teens fluttered again.

At the races, they all got horribly pissed. The coach had to stop five times for various friends to throw up. She felt she would be strong enough to tell them that that was when she fell in love with him, but was worried they might disapprove of drinking and gambling.

'This time it would be easier,' she thought. They would bring out photographs of Tom as a baby, of Tom's first day at school, of him in the church choir, and they would cry together with their arms around her.

On the freezing platform at Dunfermline's Queen Margaret station, Hugo and Morag greeted her more like a prodigal daughter than their son's fleeting girlfriend.

Back home in the warmth of their granite terraced house, in front of a warm coal fire and a large Victoria sponge, the questions poured out.

"And what will you do now?" asked Hugo "Will you go back in September to finish your studies?"

"You can always stay here if you can't find any digs," promised Morag.

While they all knew that would never work, Claire thanked them graciously. She really didn't know how to ask them how they were feeling, sensing they would be too proud to voice their grief. She saw Morag shedding a tear when she showed her a photograph of herself walking along the beach holding hands with Tom as a child. She realised that was thoughtless. Perhaps they had built up hopes that she and Tom would marry, that they would have grandchildren to play with. One day Claire would find someone else, but for them, there was no future generation. Feeling that every memory must be just as painful, but unsure how to leave without appearing to cut short the visit, Claire tried to change the subject by suggesting that they might like to come to London.

"I'm sure my mother would like you to come and stay for a few days and see the sights."

There was a long pause, and Claire thought she had offended them.

"Well that's very kind," Morag said finally, "but we couldn't presume. And, you see, we've only got our pensions and Hugo has a wee annuity which doesn't go far at all, so I don't think we could manage a trip like that."

Hugo nodded, but was clearly embarrassed by his wife's revelation of their penury.

Claire decided not to suggest that it was possible to take a return coach trip from Edinburgh to London for only £18. Clearly, the pain of seeing her again would be too great. She had done her duty, and guiltily, she felt quite relieved.

"I think we'll manage to get you on the 4.33pm if we leave now," said Hugo. "Then you'll be in Edinburgh just after five. That'll give you plenty of time to meet your friends and catch the London train."

***

At home, the last few weeks had been calmer. Claire had made a kind of truce with Bridget, but she was still angry. She couldn't control her emotions, which ranged from grief for Tom to anger with the killer driver. Then she felt a wave of sympathy for Tom's parents. Then the anger with her mother returned, followed by, "Why me?" Self-pity was followed by overwhelming grief. Claire was exhausted.

Although Edinburgh University had agreed that she could start her second year again on medical and compassionate grounds, she realised that she would have been quite unable to focus, had she been told to re-start in the summer term.

The days her fellow undergraduates spent at Claire's home were a much-needed medicine. Days of window shopping on Kings Road and nights in trendy clubs ended all too soon when the girls had to return to Scotland.

As the days grew longer, Claire had more and more time to fill, but the prospect of waitressing or bar work did not appeal. Instead, she concentrated her time on preparing a challenge to her mother.

She was not convinced by Bridget's defence of the Death Date Gene and believed the figures had been rigged. She wanted her mother to apply the test using Tom's DNA from an old shirt of his; she had kept the garment as the nearest thing she could get to a living memento. Bridget refused, claiming they must maintain the integrity of the evaluation by confining the testing to the Ghanaians and Swedes.

"But this could have saved him!" screamed Claire.

"No, the date was pre-determined in his genes."

"That's crap, and you know it. A genetic disorder or a family predisposition to cancer, maybe, but a road accident, that's impossible. That's pathetic. It's just out of order."

"Wait till you read the figures. The DDG can forecast any death date, from illness, accident, even suicide, to within a few hours of the event — on man or woman, black or white, old or young, murdered or diseased. That's how I knew you were going to get through."

"So, you did have *me* tested. Why not Tom as well?"

"Tom had already died. I would not have been allowed anywhere near his body. I'm not a pathologist. Even if I could have done it, it would have been most unethical. I shouldn't have done it for you, but I had to know. You must see that. I had the opportunity. I had your DNA everywhere, on your clothes, on your toothbrush, in the house. It was so easy. You would have done the same in my position."

Claire squeezed Bridget's hand.

"Yeah, okay, I can see why you had to do it. So, when is my death date? Surely the damage I suffered in the accident and the embolism must change that."

"It's years away, but it would be completely wrong of me to tell you. It could change your whole life."

Claire caught her looking away, trying to hide a single tear.

CHAPTER 27

(Tea, Cake and Inquisition?)

Bridget couldn't remember ever being in this part of North London before. The last time she had visited Conor, he was offering pastoral care to a more affluent flock. In those days, he was only too happy to entertain in his prosperous presbytery, hinting to his adoring mother and his less obsequious siblings that he was only one step away from a mitre. He even told our mother once that Our Lord had assured him that she would live long enough to see him in a red hat. Sadly, Conor never made it past parish priest. Fortunately, his faith was not diminished by this setback, though his ambition may have been.

As she navigated the heavy traffic, she wondered why she had received this unexpected summons from Conor to 'The Vatican', the facetious description of St. Augustine's. This dull concrete citadel, built in 1964 and dedicated to the founder of English Christianity, may have served God well as a place of spiritual restoration, but in aesthetic terms, it had absolutely no redeeming features.

Bridget approached the presbytery door with some trepidation. Conor had not offered any pretext for the invitation, but since relations between them had been re-established at our mother's funeral, she thought it would seem churlish to decline. Certainly, Conor had become less recriminatory over the years, but he was still 'Father Smug' to her.

He opened the door and embraced his sister warmly.

"It's lovely to see you. How was the traffic?"

"How do you cope with that dreadful North Circular? Is any of your parish on the other side?"

"Technically, yes, but only a few of ours live there. It's mainly mosque and synagogue country. Anyway, I go everywhere on my bike. Good for me, good for my carbon footprint. You should try it."

"Conor, you may recall I have been biking to the lab every day for the last five years. You late converts to fitness and the environment behave as though no-one had ever heard of travel on two wheels before. Still, never mind, I'm pleased. It was time you got some exercise. You look well and relaxed. Is this a demanding parish? And how is your housekeeper? Is it still Maeve, or have you retired her yet?"

"Actually, it's Mary, and she is still very much with me. She's seventy-eight and still going strong. I don't think she'll ever retire. This is her home, and the Church will look after her when she gets too infirm to work."

"And if you get posted to deepest, darkest Africa? I can't see Mary doing your washing in the river!"

"Tea or coffee? You'll have to put up with me making it, as it's a Wednesday; Mary's day off."

"Tea, please, with milk but no sugar."

As Conor disappeared into the kitchen, Bridget absorbed the elegant surroundings. Past presbyteries had been bare, with a few books and functional furniture, with prints of The Sacred Heart on one wall and Our Lady appearing to the children on the other. This room had a very comfortable sofa with matching and well-padded armchairs, Matisse and Fauve prints and crystal model trees, some pretty occasional tables and a tallboy. She wondered what the relatively impoverished parishioners thought of these comfortable surroundings.

True, some of the furnishings seemed to be missing, and tempted though Bridget was to raise the subject, Conor had no intention of suggesting any link with his losses on the racecourse.

Then she spotted a charming whisky decanter in a mahogany cabinet. Was this the image Conor really wanted to project? She did recognise the decanter, which had belonged to their mother, but had not been offered to his siblings — who were not tied to a vow of poverty. Still, to be fair to Conor, he seems to have stuck to chastity and obedience, so why not have a few creature comforts?

"How's life at the lab?" Conor asked, returning with a silver teapot and slices of malt bread and a walnut cake.

"My God, Conor, either the Queen called in when she opened that swimming pool up the road, or the Archbishop's about to pay his annual visit!"

"Well you don't come and see me very often."

"No, but you don't ask me very often!"

"Actually, I'm exhausted so it's lovely to get away for an afternoon. I'm still working on the same project, but we've got a long way to go yet."

"Decoding the human genome?"

"No, that work is done elsewhere; this is looking at the applications," she said cautiously. "I am guessing you want information. Perhaps Mother Church suspects something. I can tell you, Conor, it is all terribly routine. It's a bit like police work, constantly checking loads of boring data."

"But just occasionally, you get a clue, a revelation of what could be applied?"

"I think revelations are more your area, dear brother. As of yet, nothing sensational, but I can see you're fishing for something."

"Bridget, how could you say such a thing?"

"Look, now that mother's gone, I've known you longer than anyone on this planet, and I know, believe me, I know, when you want something. I can remember when you wanted to borrow my new bike for your dear little school friend, but I knew you had a perfectly good bike of your own, which you were not prepared to lend to that boy. What *was* his name now… Spotty something?"

"Gavin Gray."

"Well, he'll always be Spotty to me. He twisted the frame the first time he rode it, and you didn't tell me he'd never been on a bike before… I was livid. I went running to mother, but she let you off, as usual."

"Well, I am curious, actually. You know all these stories about the Death Date Gene —"

"Well, *you* should know. It was your church which set the rumours running by making an announcement in every parish in the country one Sunday a few weeks back, and, of course, everyone thought it must be true if the Catholic Church is talking about it, and then the government comes up with that stupid statement."

"Okay, I don't write the Archbishop's episcopal letter, and I certainly have no input into what the government says, but it was your lot, wasn't it? You're the team who are working on it, aren't you?"

"And if we were? Are you going to get your Opus Dei friends to firebomb the place in the name of The Lord or in case that's too incriminating, get some bible freak associates of theirs to post inflammable prayer books through the letterbox? And then you thought, I can't let my poor sister die in an arson attack. I better make sure she's not there that day. Very considerate, Conor. You've asked me here to tea so you can murder my colleagues with a clear conscience."

"Bridget, please! I assure you I do not have the slightest desire to torch your lab, nor do I know any religious freaks who might want to. I don't even know where your lab is!"

"The Church already knows the principle behind the UKAKHG but not, of course, the evaluation, nor when the results will be announced. The government and the church have simply made holding statements, but that's all. I know no more than that. There must be those who have been involved in the project, who, if they have no doubts about the authenticity of the results, must have come to realise the huge legal, social, financial and, yes, even religious implications. Especially, as I understand it, the evaluation of the data may soon be made public."

"Well, I'm not one of them —"

"Not one of them who has been involved enough in the project to make a judgment, or not one of them who has any doubts?"

"Oh, piss, Conor, you're just trying to trick me into some sort of confession. I'm not playing your games. Can I make my confession here or do I still have to go into that funny Tardis thing in the church and whisper through the grill? If I remember rightly, if I confess to you, you can't release what you learn, because you would be bound by the secrets of the confessional. And you can't refuse to hear my confession. You can't deny me the sacrament of penance, not to a really serious sinner like me."

"'Sacrament of Reconciliation' we call it now." Conor fell straight into the trap.

"Penance! Reconciliation! Whatever! It's nonsense."

"May God have mercy on you. Anyway, your confession would be pointless, because you are clearly unrepentant and have no intention of amending your ways. Also, I can't hear confessions from my own family —"

"Oh, really, I've never heard that one before. So, I couldn't say to you "Please forgive me, Lord, but I have been harbouring thoughts about wanting something awful to happen to my brother."

"Bridget, please. If I knew just a little bit more, I could help you, protect you even. The government and many ethical bodies, not just the Christian churches, are seriously worried. The information is in the hands of a few people, and there are journalists swarming all over the UK looking for you and your team. It's only a matter of time before they find you. They'll follow you to the lab; they'll be camped outside your house. And what about John and Claire? What's it going to be like for them? It's hardly going to do Claire any good in her present state. Once they know where to find you, the extremists will be gunning for you. You'll need police protection 24/7. It'll be impossible to work, and you might have to rush through a statement before you are ready."

"So, who could hear my confession?" she said very quietly.

Conor wasn't sure if she was teasing him.

"Well, my assistant, Father Ngeni usually has supper with the nuns but, I am sure, after that, he would be only too happy to hear your —"

"Father Ngeni…from Nigeria, perhaps. Well you have changed, Conor. I always thought your views were as close to racist as the church could tolerate. How do you get on with him?"

"Jeremy Ngeni is a charming, intelligent and very holy young man, who is universally liked and admired throughout this parish."

'Unlike his boss,' thought Bridget, but she refrained from saying it.

He sounded rather attractive; a sort of clerical Denzel Washington. Mischievously, she wondered if it would be possible to chat him up inside the little box, even stroke him through the grill. Just think of the headline in *The Sun.*

"Cosmofessional! Randy scientist (48) does her penance with virgin black priest!"

Conor poured her another cup of tea and even Bridget couldn't resist Mary's cake.

She thought about the implications, which Donald always refused to discuss. "We're scientists not sociologists," he would say.

"I'll pass on the confession and I'm sorry if I was a bit over the top. At this stage in the project, there is a huge amount of stress; I guess when it is time for the announcement, a little support from the church wouldn't do us any harm, but persuading Donald will be almost impossible. What sort of information are you looking for?"

CHAPTER 28

(Keeping the Annuitants Happy)

Phil Jewell was overjoyed to hear my proposal to circulate a random 270 Fife Life annuitants as part of the preparation for the interim audit.

"Sean, that's brilliant; anything to distract them from identifying the potential deficit. If they can see we are verifying our liabilities as part of our standard procedures, I may be able to defer their report until our own evaluation is complete."

"Phil, I wouldn't bank on that, but it gives us a chance."

"I leave it entirely to you, Sean, **and** our compliance department, of course. Just email me a copy of the final letter to the annuitants for my records."

Ken Mogg, our compliance officer, was a little surprised by my proposal, but when I explained that the circular was in anticipation of the audit, he raised no objection. I had promised Phil I would email him a copy, but I planned to do that well after the letters had been dispatched. He wasn't that assiduous in checking his emails (he had been brought up in the strictly paper era of Sir Malcolm), but I didn't want to draw his attention to the details. His eagle-eyed and ambitious deputy, Ms Mercy Greenfield, my avowed corporate enemy within Fife Life, would have loved to have had sight of the letter, and would have wasted no time in scoring yet more points at my expense. At present, my stock was riding high, and I intended to keep it that way.

I therefore dictated the following:

To: Fife Life B2 Annuitant
Policy No. 648261A

Dear Sir/Madam
It is a regulatory requirement for Fife Life to verify its liabilities. As part of this exercise, we are writing to a 1% random selection of our annuitants and giving them an opportunity to undergo a completely free health check. Part of this check will involve the medical practitioner taking a swab of your DNA. As

this information will be provided to, and will be retained by, Fife Life, the Data Protection Act requires your approval for this to occur. Fife Life promises not to impart this information to any third party.

If you are prepared to have the health check, you will need to sign the attached form and take it to the appointed medical centre. We are sorry it has not been possible to make these arrangements with your own local practitioner, but we have made every effort to ensure that there is a medical centre convenient to you. You should, however, advise your own medical practice once the test has taken place, as they will require the results for their records.

The checks are free and may help to detect any symptoms of disease in their early stage. As the selected medical centres will have no previous record of you, please call our helpline on 0800 003 4200 to make an appointment. Our staff will assist you in locating your most convenient centre. When you make the appointment, you must advise us of any medication you are currently taking.

If you do not wish to take this test, please sign and return the 'I do not wish to participate' form in the envelope provided. You are not obliged to take the test. You will not be penalised in any way if you do not take part.

You must contact our helpline by 8th February. The final appointments must take place by 8th March.

As a token of our appreciation, all participants will receive an additional £100 in their annuity payment for May. For those who receive their payments quarterly, the July distribution will be increased by £300.

Yours faithfully,
Sean O'Liam
Chief Actuary Fife Life Mutual Assurance Co. Ltd

The random test was not quite as random as I had told Bridget, as I had chosen annuitants who lived within 25 miles of one of the selected medical centres. I was particularly keen not to involve their GPs as, in my experience, they harbour considerable resistance to helping life assurance companies and resent third party medical checks. By the time they received the information from the tests, we would have all the information we needed.

Sexual desire may diminish with age (so they tell me), but greed (measured by the prospect of a pensioner getting a bargain) certainly does not. The helpline was overrun by annuitants wanting to take up the offer. A free health check within a few weeks and an extra £100 in May was just too good to refuse. 91% opted for the test, 2% were dying or were too ill to attend (oh, bliss!) and 2% were returned "gone away" but apparently not "gone upstairs" as I checked their payments were still clearing their bank accounts.

5% had already died, but the rellies had never informed us. I was concerned our systems had not picked up that the payments hadn't been returned to us when Mr. Annuitant became Mr. Annuitant deceased, but that was a problem for another time. I was just overjoyed our liabilities had unexpectedly reduced by 5%, at least by number!

The original text of my letter, which had been approved by old Mogg in Compliance, had been a little *amended*. Had he bothered to check, he probably would not have condoned the final edition. Like the good old school compliance man that he is, he actually trusted me. It is such a shame he is retiring next year, as I am sure we will have a nasty officious jobsworth replacement appointed by Ms Merciless Greengage.

The cost of the exercise was £75,000 (mainly due to the greedy doctors at the medical centres), a small price to pay for such vital information.

CHAPTER 29

(From Clever Schoolboy to Brilliant Scientist)

Donald Sheard was born and raised in Rotherham, the only child of a steel worker and a pharmacist's assistant. He was a quiet, studious boy, who did not get along with others easily. Had it not been for his remarkable ability to remember every conceivable statistic relating to Rotherham United FC (popularly known as the Millers), coupled with some modest footballing ability, he would have been teased mercilessly as a four-eyed brain box. As it was, he achieved god-like computer status.

It became a regular feature of the breaks between classes for boys to test each other on Rotherham knowledge; all the correct answers were supplied by the Don machine.

"Who scored for the Millers in the 3-0 away win against Barnsley on 4th December 1955?"

Occasionally, a boy would know the answer to a question like this, but though they were testing each other, what they really wanted to hear was Don's confirmation as to who was right.

"And why was the fourth goal disallowed?" asked Ronnie Mearsby, a cheeky 12-year-old with great dribbling ability, and whom everyone thought was destined to play for Rotherham when he was old enough. In fact, he did have a trial for the Millers when he was 15. To his horror, they did not take him, and he was poached by Barnsley, for whom he played for several seasons.

"'Cos a pigeon crapped on the ball!" shouted Johnny Glaby, a fat no-hoper, who was nevertheless very popular because he took all the jokes about his size and weight very well.

"Noor, it was 'cos Glaby's stomach was offside."

"Half a point to Johnny," said Donald, providing the official answer.

"It's true that a pigeon crapped on the ball, but only after the goal had been disallowed, because the ball hit the pigeon on the way in and was deflected. The pigeon was disgusted by the decision and flew over the ball and crapped on it."

"He was a right Millers' man, that bird," Johnny said.

While the pigeon story was part of Rotherham's folklore, they never tired of hearing it, and Don's reputation grew and grew the more he embellished it. The Don was living up to his name in other ways. Unlike his friends, who were all destined to spend their working lives in the steelworks, Donald was determined to get into grammar school.

It was in his last year of primary school that tragedy struck the Sheard family. An explosion at the No.2 furnace at the Don Valley steelworks claimed the lives of three workers including John Mycroft Sheard, Donald's father. Pat, Don's mother, never got over losing her husband, and died, inconsolable, at 51. Don never forgot his mother's grief.

"If only Dad had known," Don used to say to his mother.

"'Twould' a made no difference, son. He worked that shift every day and he'd never miss a day, even if he was poorly."

"But there must be a way of knowing. It can't just be chance."

"God's will, son," but Don was not convinced.

His father had taught him to build models with meticulous detail and never to leave a piece of work unfinished. Sometimes Don would help him with the simple maintenance work he did as an extra earner at weekends, repairing slates and tiles, replacing gutters, but best of all, mending cowls, which would be strong enough to withstand the Yorkshire gales.

Don got a place at Sheffield University, where he read metallurgy, but while he was there, his mother became more infirm. He spent many hours trying to comfort her and learned more and more about the failure of conventional medicine to cure disease.

He studied homeopathy and he worked at an acupuncture clinic during his holiday, and when the steelworkers' widows finally won their disputed compensation, not a pound of which did his mother spend before she died, he decided he would take another degree in pharmacology (in her honour) at Birmingham University.

Don had a strong anti-establishment streak. He thought everyone in London was a crook, he mistrusted all politicians, he wasn't too enthusiastic about doctors, and despised all religious institutions, which, in his eyes, had failed to offer his mother the comfort she needed in her widowhood.

It was during his first year at Birmingham that he met Marion, a nurse at the city's Queen Elizabeth Children's Hospital. Donald was not conventionally good looking, but he was tall, dark and slightly mysterious, and his thick glasses gave him an air of maturity. Although only 24, he could have passed for 10 years older.

Marion was a doctor's daughter from prosperous Richmond Hill Road, just around the corner in leafy Edgbaston. She was bright, bubbly, plump and pretty. She had no shortage of admirers. In truth, she was everything Donald was not. She was also a great practical joker.

At the time, there was a consultant at the QE who was almost universally loathed by the nurses because of his arrogance. Every October, the nurses held an event which involved floats parading along the local streets. Tins were jangled by pretty short-skirted nurses and considerable amounts of money were raised both for new equipment at the QE and for children's treatment in the third world.

This particular year, the theme was 'surgery through the ages'. The first float showed a surgeon ready to amputate a gangrenous leg, a casualty of a fifteenth century war. He was armed with a saw and a machete, and the patient lay screaming for mercy, as he was fastened to a board with ropes. His screams sounded real enough. In fact, they were recordings from a particularly bellicose collection of films and continued unbroken throughout the parade. Meanwhile, nurses stood on the float with buckets, ready to collect the blood as it flowed from the operating table.

The second float showed nurses incredulous at the arrival of primitive anaesthetic in the nineteenth century, and examples of the unfortunate addictive tendencies of laudanum.

The final float was made as much as possible to resemble a modern hospital ward, including drips and other apparatus. Marion was the living image of the offending consultant with a grey wig, goatee beard, surgical mask and glasses. She was an uncanny parody, especially as he was a man of only 5'4", Marion's exact height. Marion was strapped to the bed, with tape across her mouth, carrying a placard saying "Doctor, help, you can't trust nurses." A nurse, doubling as a surgeon, carried a pair of scissors, pointed at the patient's genitals.

The message may have been lost on the general public, but not on the hospital authorities. Marion and her friend, Louise, were told to appear in front of the disciplinary committee, after the real surgeon had objected in the strongest terms. They arrived and waited outside the committee room. Eventually, a secretary appeared with an envelope for each of them. They were told to go away and follow the instructions. They ripped open the envelopes, but there were no words beneath the hospital's headed notepaper. It was lucky the authorities shared the nurses' sense of humour.

Word of this prank had reached Donald, but though he knew her by sight, he considered her to be way out of his league. Marion, on the other hand, had noticed Donald a few times as he earnestly shadowed a consultant around the hospital. 'He is my challenge,' she thought. Louise bet her that she couldn't date him within a month.

She was pretty sure he wouldn't be impressed by her flirting directly with him, but she had noticed he always lunched alone, so she simply walked up to his table, without a button undone anywhere, and said demurely, "Do you mind if I join you?"

After that, it was easy. He was flattered to receive such attention. She listened attentively to why he was so dedicated to pharmacology, made assenting noises in the right place, and just smiled as he spoke.

Marion won the bet by about three weeks but could not explain to Louise why she found Donald so attractive.

"Okay, so you won the bet, but you can't seriously fancy him? I mean, he is *such* a nerd. What is he interested in, apart from work? You won't have much fun in the lab with him!"

She may have got a date with Donald within a week but getting him into bed took a lot longer. For Marion, sexual chemistry was immediate and had to be satisfied forthwith, as soon as a suitable venue could be found. All her previous partners understood this from the start, and Marion could be as suggestive as she liked.

She was genuinely concerned that Donald would react adversely to this direct approach. Provocative dress seemed to leave him cold, certainly while he was sober. As far as she could see, he rarely touched alcohol, so this, again, was a problem.

Louise's words, "Why bother?" rang in her ears, but she had a counter bet that she could bed Donald within two weeks of the first date, and she was not going to give up easily on that particular challenge.

"He doesn't even know where it is, let alone what to do with it," her friend teased.

"Then I'll be the first to show him. I'll bet you £10… by a week on Sunday."

"Done; but I want evidence."

"Apart from you being in the room or me getting pregnant, how can I possibly give you evidence? Neither of those options is worth a tenner."

"Then I have to hear you!"

They were giggling so much as they hurried onto the Dunlop ward that they collided with the diminutive consultant whom they had lampooned so accurately on the float.

All he could say was, "Not you two again," and they ran off, convulsed in laughter.

Marion's plan was to seduce Donald after administering him with liberal doses of alcohol. She knew an opportunity would arise at the Colmore Circle party, which all postgrads were expected to attend. The party had originally been a ball but was beginning to degenerate into a typical student bash with no formal dress code. There was one tradition which had survived, which was that The Colmore had to be preceded by lots of smaller parties, usually at student digs. By the time the guests reached the Colmore, they were well and truly smashed.

Marion broke with tradition and decided she would host a black-tie event in her parents' garden. Dutifully, they had agreed to go away for the weekend. Her lethal fruit punch, laced with brandy, vodka and Australian plonk did, however, conform with the tradition.

Donald was intrigued to receive Marion's invitation as he thought he must have bored her irreparably as he droned on about his work on their single date. He had no intention of repeating that embarrassing episode. However, his Yorkshire pride told him that he could mix with the smart set and so compelled him to accept.

Donald had never worn black-tie dress and felt distinctly self-conscious. Marion, though rather overdressed in a stunning navy ballgown, introduced him as though they had been an item for years. The under-dressed male student doctors and the LBD-attired nurses were impressed at his achievement in pairing with the ravishing Marion. Louise, determined to win her bet at all costs, did her very best to distract him by arriving late, wearing a VLBD (Very Little Black Dress) and kissing him animatedly before even greeting her hostess.

"Bitch," murmured Marion, "but I'm still going to win."

Donald, ignoring all the LBDs, including Louise, soon found plenty of new colleagues who were prepared to talk about medicine. He was so engrossed that Marion had countless opportunities to top up his glass with the addictive punch without any objection, and noticed to her immense satisfaction (and she so hoped that Louise was watching) that he even squeezed her hand when she put her arms round his waist, by far her most daring action to date.

The minibus duly arrived, and Donald was really enjoying himself. Indeed, though slightly surprised, he couldn't help but be flattered by Marion's request that he must help her tidy up the house before her parents came home later that evening. This was completely fabricated, but Donald relished the responsibility and was happy to accept her story that they would take a taxi to the Colmore an hour or so later.

Before the other guests left, he felt bold enough to say publicly, "Marion, you are simply a wonderful hostess."

"It's all down to you, darling," she said, and he glowed with pride.

While she asked him to clear the room, she rushed upstairs and changed into her own VVLBD. They never made it to the Colmore. The £10 was in the bag and so was Donald.

CHAPTER 30

(Unreliable Informants)

Jon Heely listened to his recording machine for the third time; he tried hard to focus on the content, but Hurriyet's broken English was so erotic that his thoughts were constantly distracted. She was one hell of a woman, he thought, but dangerous, vengeful and a little short on accuracy.

Still, he had a deadline to meet. *The Sunday Times* were keen, and there were only a few slots available for freelancers like him. Next Sunday was publication day and there was just not enough time to corroborate the story with his actuarial and geneticist contacts.

To date, the press had held back from naming any scientists, aware of the possible consequences. Thanks to Hurriyet, Jon had the names and the link between me and Bridget. He had not yet worked out how Conor fit into the picture, but he had Googled his way into discovering he was our older brother and a Catholic priest.

There must be some connection, but he couldn't find it. Was the church paying to prevent publication? Was it in league with the Department of Science? Why was the government waiting?

One part of Hurriyet's story kept coming back to him. It wasn't on the tape, and clearly, she didn't think it was important. Jon was sure she had said that someone in the family had died recently in an accident, but she couldn't recall who it was. If this was true, had the DDG been tested on the deceased?

He called her number in Izmir. Thrilled though she was to hear from him, she was keener to switch the subject to the fortnight in Spain, which he dimly recalled promising her during the Turkish healer fraud.

"Scottiland, I think. Yes, Scottiland, for sure. I remember Sean saying he very much liked his, how you say, his nicey and —"

"Niece."

"No, not Nice; I know Nice; is very pretty place in South of France; you want to take me there and not Spain. I like it very much."

"No, Hurriyet, niece means the daughter of his sister or brother."

"Yes, daughter of sister, I think, the doctor."

"Right, the daughter of his sister; and where in Scotland?"

"Eddie Burr, I think, and boy was hit by bike; girl also. He died, no, she died, he hurt. Jon, I have new passport now. We can go to Spain…or Nice. You said you take me as reward."

Jon recalled his promise to take her on holiday after Hurriyet had exposed the healer as a fraud. She had quickly spotted that the documents issued by the Turkish Ministry of Health confirmed that the peasants whom he had met were blind, and the forms were counterfeits. In truth, they were genuinely blind, and the statements from the eye surgeons were authentic but did not confirm the original ownership. Without Hurriyet's translation skills, Jon might well have been convinced.

"Hurriyet, this is important. Try and remember which. This is for my story so I need to get it right for the newspaper; then I can make some money and we can go to Spain."

"No, you think I like Spain better than Nice."

"Definitely."

"Okay, Spain."

"I remember now; they were hit by a bike and I thought how could a bike kill someone, like a strong young man. So yes, he died, she hurt."

"A motorbike going at 60 miles an hour would kill you."

"Yes, it was a motorbike, for sure; it was day before my birthday and I thought, maybe Sean will forget to buy my present and take me out."

"What day is your birthday?"

"It is 24 January, so don't forget when next year comes!"

Jon was beginning to appreciate Hurriyet's shortcomings. Neither Nice nor Spain looked quite such exciting propositions as he had first thought.

"Also, he had name like mine; I think he also Turkish."

"Turkish?"

Hurriyet had begun to realise she could make things up, and so long as Jon got some information, she might get some time on the beach, though the Costa Brava at this time of year could be rather chilly.

"Yes, his name, I think, was Hurriy Hamish."

"Never mind about the name," said Jon, doubtfully, "You've been brilliant; I promise I won't forget your birthday and I might even take you to Edinburgh instead of Nice!"

"No, no, not Eddie Burr, I want Nice or Spain or —" but Jon was far too busy Googling road traffic accidents in the Scottish capital in the last week of January.

All he needed were the names and *The Edinburgh Evening News* from 23rd January said it all.

'PRINCES STREET TRAGEDY: STUDENT KILLED BY SPEEDING BIKER'

'Edinburgh University student, Tom McLaren (21), was tragically killed last night by a speeding motorbike while crossing Princes Street. A young woman, Claire Hughes-Renton (19), who was with him and who is also a student at the university, is on life support at the Royal Infirmary. The rider of the bike, who was also critically injured, has not yet been named.'

Jon went on Googling. A shorter article in the same paper three weeks later informed him that Claire had left hospital; there was still one problem. Because of the secrecy surrounding the UKAGP and its employees, he could not identify the Hughes-Rentons' address, nor telephone numbers, nor emails. In the end, he resigned himself to two weeks in Spain with Hurriyet. He stayed on the internet and booked two weeks in Benidorm for himself and a very happy young Turkish woman.

CHAPTER 31

(Dressed for the Job)

It was a quiet afternoon and South London, for once, seemed remarkably healthy. Nothing needed dispensing before the early evening addict hour and the usual demand from prescription-less junkies claiming their rights for their nightly fix was absent.

Having qualified in pharmacology and then experienced years of tedium dispensing prescriptions at high street chemists, Rowena's opportunity to improve her lot in life occurred quite by chance. A copy of *BioPharm International* rested unread under an unopened box of Metformin. A free copy was delivered monthly, and rather than staring out at the gloomy outline of Eltham High Street, Rowena occasionally browsed through the careers section hoping for a lab assistant's job in San Francisco or San Diego. In fact, any old San would do so long as she could escape from Sowf London.

Much to her surprise, there was an advertisement from a London-based laboratory seeking a technician. No details were provided but her qualifications were adequate, so she updated her CV, and emailed it to the agents.

A few days later, she received a call from the agent, Melanie Grace, asking her to come to an interview. To Rowena's amazement, the agent was not authorised to provide any information about her prospective employer, other than that it was a most respected research unit. Nor could she tell Rowena anything about the job itself, other than the salary, which was a healthy increase on her existing position, and the approximate location, Central London, which would be a definite improvement on Eltham.

Melanie discussed Rowena's qualifications and experience, asked for references, and assured her that she was sure that her profile fit the role perfectly. Rowena, who liked conspiracies, was intrigued, but was convinced that she was only a bit player in this mystery. She left feeling that she had been cheated and did not expect to hear anything more.

Three weeks later, she received a text message from a woman called

Doctor Grendon, inviting her to call the sender who would like to follow up the interview. Rowena couldn't resist the text message (so much more cryptic than a phone call), although she was innately cautious. So, she phoned the agency to find the number was only able to make outgoing calls. Searching the internet for the agency, Pharmappoints Ltd, revealed nothing. Googling Melanie Grace, recruitment consultant, also drew a blank.

She still had the copy of *BioPharm International* where the advertisement had been placed. The number she had called was quite clear, but she realised there was no address. She recalled that the agent had given it to her. Would she remember the street? She did remember that she had taken a bus to Euston Road and had walked a few blocks.

Rowena decided to re-trace her steps, taking the same bus and alighting at the same stop. She found the building again, easily enough. It was one of those serviced office blocks, where you can rent a proper office for a few hours or a few months. The same bored receptionist was there, still polishing her elongated vermillion nail extensions. Rowena asked red nails if she could give her any other information, but her reply was brutal.

"Nah, can't do that love," said red nails. "It's against Data Protection, innit? They all do it now, them agencies 'n case anyone's got a grudge, see. Can't be too careful what with terrorists and that, canya?"

"Yeah, but they do want to see me. They've texted me, except they didn't say where."

"Oh, yeah. Didn't say when either, I suppose. Look, I've seen it all here. They've all tried it; blokes who were *promised* a job if they came back here next week for a second interview; women who thought they'd get a job 'cos they they'd fucked the boss, but turned out he was only the security man; dossers who'd put on a tie and been asked to wait – they just wanted a kip in a warm office and a chance to nick a Red Bull from the drinks machine."

"Come on," said Rowena. "Do I look like a job tart, or a terrorist or a sodding rough sleeper?"

Red nails was not used to this type of response.

"I dunno who you are," she said, leaning towards the emergency button under her console, "but I'm pressing this red button and that nice man downstairs will be up 'ere quicker than his bruvver, Usain Bolt."

Rowena left the building rather more quickly than she had come in, and headed for the nearest Starbucks. She considered her options. What had she got to lose? Maybe there was a perfectly simple explanation. Perhaps, red nails was right and agencies had to be careful of vengeful, disappointed applicants? After a long swig of her latte, she texted Doctor Grendon, who replied quickly, asking Rowena to meet her at the Novotel on Euston Road on Friday at 6.30. She texted that she would be sitting to the right of the swing doors, with her back to the street, reading a copy of *Biopharm*.

Before she caught the bus home, she passed the Novotel and reassured herself that it was full of innocent-looking American tourists and anonymous respectable businessmen — and that there was more than one exit to the street.

She was intrinsically drawn to this job, though she understood it was the intrigue which attracted her most. Wild speculation surrounding MI5 and MI6 filled both her waking and sleeping hours, though she couldn't reconcile why such organisations would use *Biopharm* to recruit agents.

***

"First time is it, love?" Alphonse asked in Toni and Guy.

"Sorry?"

"I mean, first time with us. I didn't mean first time *ever,* dear, although you should see some of them who come in. Well, I mean, you'd think they'd asked their mothers to cut it on the kitchen table. No, not you love, you've got fine locks, but they just a need a bit of…shall we say…refinement. Now what sort of cut would we like? I think a short brunette crop would suit."

Alphonse showed her a video of a pretty brunette flicking a new cut in front of her boss ('the master spy,' she thought) and Rowena took little convincing.

"Lovely colour, isn't it? It'll really suit you, and so easy to Maintain. And the roots; we can't just leave them, can we? I mean, is it for a special event? I mean, it's all over so quickly isn't it? And it's got to be just right for the photographs, hasn't it?"

Rowena realised that she hadn't actually said a word and in normal circumstances, she would have been out of the salon within seconds rather than endure this monologue, but as she was dreamily considering her new career in the secret service, she let it all simply wash over her.

Two hours later and £150 poorer, she was slightly less convinced, but it didn't deter her from buying a rather sleek Betty Barclay navy suit from Debenhams.

CHAPTER 32

(Sharing Info with Bridget)

I had to be certain that the 50 dead annuitants in our 1% sample had actually perished on the dates prescribed by the DDG. Fife Life retains all data for 15 years after death to establish trends, to measure the effect (if any) of giving up the addiction at an earlier date, to meet any Department of Health request for statistics, and to compare our investment performance with the benchmark.

I restricted myself to batches of five a day and saved the results to my home PC, partly because I had to be absolutely certain that there was no risk of any other Fifer accessing it at this early stage, and partly because I could not believe what I was seeing; I wanted to read them again in the peace of my own home. The first five came in, all exactly on the predetermined date. 'Okay,' I thought, 'just luck, they had all died within a three-year period.' I was still sceptical. I extended the range to cover the entire period, a whole fourteen years. Right on the spot again. Still I didn't believe it; maybe they were all Scots; I checked all their addresses and places of birth. By the end of the week, I had seven Scots, three Welsh, six Englishmen North of Nottingham, three South of Nottingham, five from London, and a Latvian (not sure how he got there!). 25 out of 25!

Maybe the gender balance was wrong. Fife did insure more men than women, but I had chosen 14 men and 11 women, and they all dropped off on the appointed day. At the end of the week, I couldn't resist ringing Bridget.

"If all these results are true —"

"Of course, they're bloody true. God, what further evidence do you need after 25 out of 25?"

The reference to the Almighty by my non-believer sister, in support of the evidence, amused me, but I declined to comment as I really needed her on my side.

"Yes, but it's almost *too* good to be true. I can't wait for the DNA to come back and to try it out on the 270 living. If I had known the exit date of the 50 dead'uns, I could have bought exactly the right gilts, so I wouldn't have had to refinance the annuity when the life-assured outlived the biblical date by only a few months and could have cashed in a much shorter stock for those who failed to make 66 ½ by several years."

"So?"

"What do you mean, 'So?'? It means, dear sister, that if this is reflected in the life expectancy of all the living annuitants, then there could even be a surplus, which I could invest in the equity market which is just starting to get better. Any profits can go towards a bonus payment for the surviving annuitants. Before our little exercise, I didn't even have enough to pay out on all the life policies, let alone a bonus for the goody-goodies! Sister, you are a beauty. I love you."

"I'm delighted the smokers are paying a bonus to those who have abstained, even though they won't know about it. But Sean, how have you convinced the Fife board this is going to work? You promised you wouldn't use any DDG projections as evidence."

"No, I promise you, B, I haven't. I suggested to Phil Jewell that we hadn't done a revised liability check on our annuitants for a few years, and that in the light of medical advances and increased longevity, and allowing for deaths we've missed, wouldn't it look really diligent to do this before the auditors come next month, rather than wait for their recommendation?

So, I dispatched a letter for the auditors which will stay unread in Phil's inbox forever, and which, even if he or Mercy reads it, will not bear much resemblance to the one incentivising our dear annuitants to claim a free health check. If they agree, I have requested that they sign and return the original, confirming their agreement, to me. Sure, some bright spark could photocopy it, but I doubt it.

The result of these checks will act as a pretext for me to reshuffle the portfolio, but, in reality, I will change it to reflect the death dates which you can now give me from all this lovely DNA we will have harvested."

"Christ, Sean, they could put you in Ford for misrepresentation, breaking data protection rules, falsifying a document and God knows what else."

"Ford?"

"Yes, Ford for fraud. Surely you know that one. A lot of quite famous fraudsters have been there. You'll pick up some good contacts! It's near Chichester, not too far for me to come and visit!"

"Bridget, how do you know all this? I thought you were a scientist, not a criminologist."

It finally occurred to me that Bridget was teasing me. I smiled tentatively.

Then she freely admitted it.

"Actually, we *are* sharing the same data. You seemed surprised and delighted that your stats have been 100% justified, but I would have been horrified if they had showed anything less."

"You mean?"

"Yes, we have run all this data before. This is what we call the fourth dimension, but letting Fife apply the data gives you the credibility!

CHAPTER 33

(The Scottish Challenge)

Jon Heely was expecting to meet his fifth Fife Life annuitant of the day. He was quite pleased with himself for tracking so many already. He knew it was possible to buy shareholder lists, although this had become increasingly unprofitable as so many private clients were registered in their brokers' nominees. Only the very small shareholders who had held shares since privatisation still had certificates in their own names.

But it was while he was trawling through the register of a large Scottish utility company that he saw that Fife Life itself had a holding in the company. Eventually, he found three holdings with different designations. Then he saw he had strayed into a different part of the share register. Fife had a holding in each of the company's three corporate bonds. The bonds were due to be redeemed in four, seven and eleven years respectively, so they must relate to the assured's life expectancy.

***

So that's what they pay Sean for; to work out actuarial risk of each life assured and buy a bond with a redemption date which he hopes will coincide with their demise. 'That's quite a risk,' he thought. It is unlikely, but the company might have gone bust by then. After all, no-one had expected some of the banks and ex-building societies to have failed.

It was a small advertisement at the end of the list of bondholders which caught his eye. 'We can provide any shareholder or policyholder registers and movements thereon for the last 10 years. Contact *Shareseekers*, PO Box 9080, Worthing, West Sussex, BN12 7ZZ.' Jon was intrigued; the Worthing address gave it credibility as the UK's largest registrars were located outside the town. But policyholders? He thought that information was covered by the Data Protection Act. Clearly, *Shareseekers* had their own ways of finding it. Still, it's worth a try.

Armed with a fairly unreliable list, which omitted recording the policyholder's death and caused him a lot of embarrassment with grieving widows and angry sons and daughters, Jon tracked back and forth across Scotland and was now introducing himself to Hugo McLaren in a hotel bar.

Jon wasn't clear if Hugo had taken out an annuity with Fife as a result of the tenuous connection with the company via Tom and Claire. It seemed unlikely, but he had responded with eagerness to Jon's request for a meeting. After an Irn Bru or two (Hugo) and a pint of Tennants (Jon), it became clear that it was the letter to the sample annuitants that had caused his angry reaction, and that he had no knowledge of the family relationship.

Hugo had taken umbrage at the letter to the annuitants; what was wrong with his own doctor? And why did Fife feel it had to bribe its annuitants to attend a special medical centre? Jon really liked the sound of the word "bribe," which is nectar to freelance journalists.

"May I see this letter?"

"Aye; I have a copy wimme."

"Did you know that Sean O'Liam, the actuary who wrote this letter, is actually Claire's uncle?"

"No, I'd no idea."

"Do you mind if it gets published? I will try to keep your name out of it, but I can't guarantee that once the national press start snooping around. They are almost bound to call you. They'll track you through the same sources I have."

"I don't mind what you do with it as long as it doesn't upset Claire. I've never met her uncle, though her parents came up from London for the funeral. Claire, of course, was still in hospital."

"Her mother, Doctor Bridget, may also be involved. I am still trying to find out if there's any truth in that."

"Well, I wouldn't like to learn that she's implicated. She's a charming lady."

Jon could have sworn Hugo blushed slightly as he spoke.

"Don't worry. I would let you know first."

"That'll be alright, then," said Hugo.

Jon thanked Hugo and headed home. The annuitants' information was just what he needed.

CHAPTER 34

(Interrogation)

Had she ever had a criminal record? What about patient confidentiality while she was at the pharmacy? Could she give them some details of her background? (Irish), her friends (none to speak of), and any hobbies (ditto). Could she get references from current and previous employers (no problem)?

Doctor Alison Grendon was slim, dark and very precise. For the first 20 minutes, she shot question after question at Rowena. Then, quite suddenly, she stopped, relaxed and asked if she would like a coffee.

While waiting, she apologised for the strict interrogation and told Rowena to ask her any questions in return, but cautioned that there were many things she could not tell her at this interview.

"Why all the security?" asked Rowena. "Is this MI5?"

Doctor Grendon smiled for the first time.

"You might well think so. I wanted to see how you reacted under pressure. We already know you are a competent pharmacologist and administrator and we have already taken references. I work in a special team looking at some of the wider aspects of the human genome. This work is highly confidential, and we need someone in the team who understands the basic science and whom we can train to be a geneticist, and most of all who is discreet. I would like you to meet the head of the unit, Professor Cozens, here at the Novotel next Monday at 6.15pm. We will advise you of the outcome within a few days of that meeting. We will tell you whatever the result, as we don't want applicants kept in the dark.

If we offer you the position and you accept, we will ask you to sign a declaration of confidentiality. You will be given a three-month trial. We can release you at any time without notice during the trial period, and if you don't think the job is right for you, you can also leave at any time subject to a thorough debriefing. This could last up to three days depending on how much of the trial period has passed. This is outlined in the confidentiality declaration.

The unit is in Central London and, if you are successful, we will show you around as soon as you have signed the declaration. We will ask the pharmacy to waive your period of notice and will compensate them for the inconvenience. We don't want people waiting and wondering — it can lead to unfounded rumours. Assuming the three-month trial period is successful, you will sign a more comprehensive declaration of confidentiality. The salary is £42,000 a year and you will have five weeks holiday. There is private health cover and a generous defined contribution pension scheme, details of which I will give you if we offer you the position.

You have to tell us where you are going if you leave the UK and must remain within phone contact. This is for your own security. We retain your passport until the day you go, and you must return it the day you come back to work."

Rowena was astonished. She had never felt so important in her life. Although she was disappointed that she wouldn't see the lab unless she got the job, she knew this position was for her. The intensity of her prospective new employers and the language of science all seemed right. And the money? Well she could move out of that ghastly flat for a start and distance herself from the "lascivious Len."

CHAPTER 35

(Blackmail?)

Conor did not receive many hand-written letters. He got plenty of bills, as well as the usual junk mail, emails from the archdeacon or telephone calls from parishioners, but very few letters.

He picked up the plain, white envelope. The writing was unknown to him and the postmark unclear. On the letter itself, the correspondent had given no address and no date. Conor judged it was composed by an uneducated hand, especially as the letter began without any greeting.

"I hope you enjoyed your morning in Westminster. You really have not set a good example to your flock. Your bishop is not pleased. I don't think you would want him to know any more about your misdemeanours. I can prevent him knowing if you are prepared to give me some information. You and I should meet, but if you attempt to tell the police or the church authorities, your fraud will be revealed to them."

The mystery voice continued. "I will leave a contact point in the hymn book in the third row in front of the pulpit, five spaces in from the central aisle. You will collect it after the 8.30am mass on Sunday. You will take the 11am as usual. Do not attempt to switch the mass with Father Ngeni. Do not attend the earlier mass or try to identify the people sitting in the third row by asking any parishioner who was sitting there. The message will be in hymn number 647, 'O Star of the Sea'." The letter ended abruptly without further instruction.

The word 'revealed' sent shivers down Conor's spine; he believed it was a deliberate reference to the unfortunate horse. The letter was not a bluff. The writer clearly knew all about the church roof fund and the equine investment.

Conor was certain the letter was sent by the woman who had seen him at Kempton, but he could not think of any reason for her to blackmail him. If she knew so much about him, then she must also know he had no money. In truth, she hadn't asked for money, and he thought the demand for information was a cover. He had lost his personal savings as well as the church roof fund when Revealed broke its neck, and he had no information which could be of any possible use to anybody.

He agonised about going to the police or to the bishop; he was well aware he had committed a criminal offence. The church might try and hush it up, but they would certainly deprive him of his parish and send him to some third world hell-hole. If he went to the police, he could be arrested.

Conor sat in front of a bottle of malt whisky, or more precisely, a half-empty bottle. He was convinced he would be sent to Banjul, the capital of Gambia. He had read in *The Catholic Herald* that there was a real shortage of priests there as the number of Catholics was expanding rapidly, and that several of the Gambian priests needed some experience in Europe before they could return to their own parishes. Apparently, they were looking at older priests in Britain who were looking for a new challenge (or had a new challenge imposed on them in his case). Banjul sounded a most unattractive alternative to St Augustine's. Poor food, no booze, lots of really poor people, three masses a day, six at weekends, hot churches full of flies, malaria, TB, AIDS. No, he really couldn't face it.

He reached for the malt again, knocked the bottle on the floor, and, uncharacteristically, blasphemed as the precious liquid spilled onto the carpet.

CHAPTER 36

(Donald's Suspicions)

Café Nero on Euston Station was a shade too public for me, but Bridget had insisted that Donald was suspicious of her every movement out of the lab. I noticed she was carrying a cappuccino with her sandwiches even though she was already drinking one as I arrived.

"Have you become a caffeine junkie?" I enquired, as I greeted her with a brotherly peck on each cheek.

"Hmm, nice aftershave, and smart suit. Are things looking up at Fife?"

As she had ignored the coffee question, I persisted.

"Latte to go with it?"

"I have to have a reason to leave the lab, or I get an interrogation from Donald. I really got angry with him yesterday."

"Surely I can get my own sodding lunch?" she said.

"Last week, I had gone out for a coffee with my old friend, Pam, from medical school. You may remember her.

I was only out for about 20 minutes. "Where have you been?" he screamed when I got back.

"I can tell when you've just had a coffee because you always leave some of that revolting foam round your mouth. "Well, I went ballistic. I threw one of those rubber pears at him — you know the ones that employment agencies send you with their Christmas card. It has a little nipple on top so men can fiddle with it. Apparently, it calms them down and takes their mind off the crisis at work."

"Really! I must be using the wrong agency."

Then I remembered, my agency had, after all, sent me Hurriyet, who was the real thing as far as distractions are concerned.

"But you can't work with an idiot like that."

"Tell me about it. But there is something funny going on. Donald can be a bastard, a real shit at times, and, sure, he shuts himself away and won't talk to anyone when he's in one of his moods, but he always comes around and is truly sorry, and is really sweet to me and promises it will never happen again. Then I forgive him and well, you know, he takes me out to dinner, and we finish up in bed — until now."

"So, you *are* an item?"

"*Were* an item would be more accurate. This has been just too much, but he's my boss and this is the project to which I have devoted the last four years of my professional life. I believe in it completely and absolutely, Sean, and it will help the world. I can't quit now. I've got to see it through, but little brother (I could never resist looking down at the curvature of my stomach whenever she called me that), whatever you get up to, never have a relationship with someone at work."

"Oh, absolutely not. Never," I said, thinking of Hurriyet, my lovely Turkish delight.

"B, I really must carry out the tests on the live cases soon. If I am going to save Fife, I am going to have to know the death dates of all 14,000 who still have no covering gilts. I am due to meet Jewell at the end of next week."

"I know, I know, and frankly Donald can go and stuff it. I have no idea why he is holding out on me and I am going to go ahead anyway, even if it breaks every fucking confidentiality agreement l have ever signed…and even if it means the end of my relationship with him… it's probably over anyway."

"Wow B, that's a bit rash. Can Donald fire you? Isn't he the unit director?"

"Yes, in theory, but he would have to get permission from the governing council — and he wouldn't do that."

"Because…?"

"Because he would have to give a very good reason, and he would have to explain all about the fourth dimension, which he is terrified of doing."

I was very confused by this and was about to ask why.

"Don't go there," said Bridget. "One day I will explain it all to you. "Look, I can't download that much data. How about 3,000, that's my absolute limit. Sean, I can understand why you need all this information, but surely Phil Jewell will want to know how you can be so sure, and what science you are relying on?"

"I will show Phil the results of the Death Date Gene tests applying to the 270 annuitants who have all died on their due dates, but I will amend the results so they appear to have died within 18 months, say 40% before their time and 60% afterwards. Not even Phil would fall for a DDG-type prediction at this stage. 18 months is about as far as I can stretch it. If I deviate further, then I am at the mercy of interest rate movements and the gilt market. I can attribute this to the new actuarial methods which are being used in the US. It's called the Mesalinoa Prediction."

"What!"

Bridget looked horrified.

"You mean you are replicating DDG with an algorithm? Who is this Mesalinoa? I've never heard of him."

"Oh, yes, you have. In fact, you're having coffee with him right now, a brilliant Irish cum Italian mathematician, well, anagram expert actually, out of Dulwich, England, m'am…at your service!"

"Sean O'Liam, you arrogant bastard. They'll spot it straight away."

"No, it's only for Phil, and he absolutely hates anything actuarial, especially with an Italian name. Then I will explain how many of the living annuitants out of the 270 have responded, how many have given up smoking, how many already have emphysema and so on, and he'll believe me. He's desperate for a solution. His neck is on the line. He loved my audit preparation justification. He is putty in my hands," I said, getting slightly too excited.

Both cappuccinos were completely cold by now, so she bought another one and hugged me like a sister should. We agreed to meet the next morning on the 17 bus, which she boarded at Archway Station. She texted me as it passed through the former Holloway prison and I was to get on outside Pentonville. Yes, it really does pass close to both establishments. I always knew she had a warped sense of humour! If possible, I was to sit next to her, and she would get off at Kings Cross. Each day, I would pass her one hard disc, and collect the downloaded disc with the 3,000 names.

Next morning, I was waiting furtively outside my putative new home in Caledonian Road.

CHAPTER 37

(Meeting the Boss)

Alison Grendon was already waiting in the foyer at the Novotel in Euston Road even though Rowena had arrived 10 minutes before the agreed time. Beside her was a sombre-looking man of about 45. Rowena presumed this was Professor Cozens. He made no attempt to acknowledge Rowena's arrival.

"I have briefed Professor Cozens and, although he has one or two questions to ask you, he is happy with your CV and my report on our meeting."

Professor Cozens looked up and spoke very quietly in a broad Yorkshire accent, which Rowena found difficult to follow. The Novotel foyer was overheated and, in Rowena's eyes, a far too public a place to conduct an interview. Although Doctor Grendon had removed her own coat (grey, belted MaxMara, Rowena noted), the professor was still wearing a heavy trench coat, despite the heat. She was beginning to feel quite uncomfortable and decided she would take the initiative.

"Professor Cozens," she started cautiously, in case there had been some confusion and because she wanted to be certain this was the man she needed to impress, "may I take my coat off, and would you mind if I sat on your right?"

The Novotel was over-lit and under-carpeted as well as too hot, and Rowena did not want to have to ask him to repeat his Yorkshire vowels against the background of high heels on the wooden flooring.

"Yes, of course, I'm so sorry. It is very warm in here," though he made no attempt to remove his own coat. "And I think we can dispense with pseudonyms. My real name is Professor Donald Sheard and Alison is really Doctor Bridget Hughes-Renton. We have to be so careful in this field."

Bridget was astounded. She had never heard him introduce himself as Donald Sheard before; he always assumed any new staff would just find out, leaving them in the embarrassing position as to whether to call him Professor (which he liked), Doctor (which he detested) or Donald (which he ignored). He had made it a strict rule always to use what he called 'agency names' before any new recruit had signed the confidentiality agreement.

"Rowena, may I call you Rowena (he didn't wait for an answer)? I really only have one question." He addressed the top of her head, as though he was trying to talk to someone behind her. "This organisation stands at the very pinnacle of knowledge in this particular field of genetics. We cannot risk any breach of security. Over the next few weeks, we will progressively release the key factors as they become credible to the scientific community as a whole. We would like you to become part of our team and to have much of the responsibility for the release of the data."

Rowena almost looked round, half expecting a voice from behind her to answer this. She re-crossed her legs, for once feeling quite proud that her tights were not laddered, and smiling that his gaze had moved from the mystery person behind her to just above her knees and then back to the ceiling.

"I have been searching for something at the forefront of medicine for several years. I have turned down several offers in existing disciplines, knowing that I would just be a labsbody. From what Doctor Hughes-Renton has told me about the project, this is just what I am looking for. I really believe I am ideally qualified for this position."

She'd sold herself to Donald, though Bridget now began to have some misgivings. She could tell Rowena was lying, but Donald had already decided. She tried to convince herself that Rowena could be a little labsbody after all, but she doubted it.

CHAPTER 38

(Old Friends)

Once back home, Rowena decided a small celebration was in order. Of course, the job wasn't in the bag, but she felt it was hers, so she opened a bottle of Gordon's, the dust on which confirmed she had had no occasion to rejoice for several years. She added some very flat tonic and repeated the process three times.

Fuelled with alcoholic courage, she decided she needed someone with whom to celebrate, so she walked a couple of blocks to the City Fox. It used to be The Fox and Hounds, but it was clearly no longer PC to allude to hunting. It was, apparently, perfectly acceptable to commemorate the mangy dustbin-raiding sub-species rather than his cunning country cousin.

It was a long time since she had passed the pub, and more than just the name had changed. The fine brass railing around the bar had gone, and so too had the familiar London brews. They had been replaced by guest beers from Slovakia, Belgium and Mexico, and the heated cabinet of pies had yielded to sushi and lasagne.

She used to be a regular here a few years ago, but after all this time, she hardly expected to see any old drinking companions, but, to her surprise, tucked away in the corner, under an enormous mural of an urban fox chewing the remains of discarded fried chicken, sat Kelly and Knicks. These were friends who, like her, had not been afraid of behaving badly in the '90s. This could be a fun evening after all.

The three women had a lot of catching up to do. Kelly had recently dumped her long-term partner for conspicuously failing to apply for any job following his not so recent redundancy.

"He was a negative on my balance sheet," said Kelly, proudly recalling the limited knowledge she had gained as a temp at a local accountancy firm, and hoping Rowena wouldn't challenge her on any accounting technicalities. "All I found were betting slips and unpaid credit card statements. And then there's my girls; you try controlling fourteen-year-old kids going on nineteen. And they're lookers as well. Blokes outside the 'ouse like dogs when there's a bitch in heat. Spend, spend, spend, make-up, clothes. God knows what they get up to. Just as well I put them on the pill when they were 12."

Rowena looked a bit shocked at this, but said nothing as she had no children of her own, let alone two man-hungry teenagers.

"I think it's time I had a baby. I'm nearly 39," said Nicks, who had a reputation for changing her eponymous underwear as frequently as her boyfriends, and whose aversion to small children was legendary.

"I wouldn't start trying for another 15 years, if I were you, Nicks, just in case!"

"Well, maybe I could borrow your girls for a bit, and we could all go out clubbin' together."

"You're welcome," said Kelly, "But their blokes are a bit young, even for you…and personal hygiene's a bit low on their list."

"Yuck, how gross. Don't you know any 40-year-olds?"

"Do you think I'd let you have first sight of them? What about you, Row, you still on your own?"

The earlier gins were now having an effect on Rowena, assisted by a Bacardi Breezer which Kelly had bought her, and which the modest collection of crisps did nothing to take the edge off.

"Not really interested, they're all shits underneath."

"Oooh no, they're all shits on top. Underneath is the only worthwhile bit!"

They all collapsed in hysterics. This was Nicks at her best. Rowena was beginning to enjoy herself.

"Well, I've just been offered a job, well *nearly* offered, and my new boss, well, he is…he's…"

It was no good; she just couldn't finish the sentence. Donald remained undescribed.

"He's alright *underneath*, you mean," said Nicks. More screams of laughter and Rowena bought another round of Breezers.

"I haven't got that far. I've only just met him."

"Yes, but you're going to soon, just like I'm going to throw up… soon…no, now. Kelly, help me!"

Kelly did her best with a tablecloth and a few tissues but left a moaning, groaning Nicks in the loo to finish cleaning herself up.

"Wow, Row, but sleeping with the boss. I mean, don't you want the job, anyway?'

"God, yes. You bet I do, but it's all *sheecret*, so you mustn't tell anyone!"

She told Kelly rather more than she should have done. She confessed that her fascination for Donald was probably just a dream, that he was almost certainly married and that the other doctor, Bridget, was definitely waiting for her turn and maybe had already taken it.

After an hour or so, and with the help of a couple of quiches and a coffee, they were both beginning to sober up.

"I suppose we better go and see if Nicks is alright," said Kelly, "I'll go and check the Ladies."

"There was nobody in there a few minutes ago. She must have cleaned herself up and gone home."

"Well, you might have told me, Row. She's quite incapable of walking home on her own, even though it's only just around the corner."

"Sorry," said Rowena quietly, though she wasn't. She was livid with Nicks for exposing her obsession and didn't really care what happened to her.

Kelly was relieved to see the lights were on in Nicks's flat. She rang the bell, with its 'Twinkle Twinkle Little Star' tune (Nicks had insisted that it was installed with both verses to give her time to put her make up on and at least partially get dressed). To their amazement, she heard Nicks rushing down the stairs before the song had finished. She flung the door open and looked absolutely stunning in a long and very revealing red dress. Whoever she was expecting, it clearly wasn't Kelly and Rowena.

"What a transformation! Two hours ago, you were covered in vomit, your blouse and skirt were ruined, and you asked me to absolutely promise never ever to take you to the City Fox again. What happened?"

Nicks clearly wasn't going to ask them in, despite the extreme cold.

"Well, I stayed in the toilet for absolutely ages, and as I came out, I literally bumped into this lovely man who had also been ill and said he'd seen me go in and thought he'd wait until I came out to see if I needed any help getting home. Wasn't that kind?"

"And how did he know when you felt well enough to come out?"

"I dunno. Well, actually, I think someone once drilled a tiny, tiny little hole through the wall between the boys' and the girls' toilets and maybe he just happened, I mean by chance, to be in the one opposite where I was sitting, like at the other end of the tiny, tiny little hole."

Kelly noticed Nicks only put a 'h' on the word 'hole' when she was pissed.

"And how do you know about this hole?"

"You remember Aggie?"

"Aggie the Shaggie? From school?"

"Yes."

"What's she got to do with it?"

"Because…" said Nicks very carefully. She seemed distracted.

"Oh, sod it; he ain't comin', is he? I'm not gonna bovver wiv 'posh', but 'e was nice."

Kelly was getting impatient.

"Who is *he* and what's he got to with Aggie?"

"Dunno his name, but the one who walked me home, he was real posh, see. I said 'e could come back for a coffee and that when I'd cleaned myself up."

"What? Come back when you had had a bath, put on your deep ravine red rag and sprayed yourself with "Eau de Sedooce"? You must be mad. He could be a multi-killer rapist."

"I suppose."

Rowena was very confused and very, very cold.

"If he's not coming, can we come in?"

"Yeah, I suppose."

Once upstairs, Kelly saw the coffee pot and cups were already waiting for Mr. Posh to arrive and the kettle to boil.

"So, how do you know about the hole?"

"Aggie drilled it, see, and I was wiv her when she did it."

"What? 20 years ago, when we were at school? Never. The pub's had a complete makeover last year. They've built new toilets."

"Nah, this was at New Year, see. Aggie'd been flirting with this bloke, body builder type, all 'ceps and tats', you know?"

"Ceps and tats?" said Rowena.

"Yeah, biceps and tattoos. I mean he had tats everywhere and he says real loud, 'I'm going off for a piss' and Aggie wants to know if he really does have the tats *everywhere*. I mean *everywhere*. Anyway, she doesn't quite 'ave the nerve to go on her own and she asks me to come wiv 'er. So, we go into this stall and she gets out a screwdriver, and I 'fink she's tried it before 'cos it comes out you know where in the men's, see. But, of course, he'd long gone. Anyway, I always use that stall just for fun."

"Even when you are violently ill, and you think you are dying? And you still have time to pick that stall?"

"Yeah, well old 'abits die 'ard."

Rowena poured them all a coffee. "I'm sorry, but I really don't think Mr. Posh is coming and if he does, I think we should be here too."

"Yeah, you're right. Thanks for thinkin' of me. I'll make up a bed for you. Don't mind sharing, do you?" "Nah, coke and that. Offered me some. Says she can get it cheaper than the Cowbridge Estate gang. Lives dangerously, that girl."

By the time Kelly and Nicks had caught up on Aggie's last 20 years, Rowena was fast asleep.

***

Rowena went home the next morning to find a smartly-typed envelope containing a letter offering her the position of 'Unit Administrator' and inviting her to be at the lab on Monday 8th March. It was signed by Donald Sheard, who had asked her to confirm her acceptance by calling his mobile. Wow!

CHAPTER 39

(Family Connections?)

Claire was at home reading *The Sunday Times* in front of a warm log fire. 'Not warm enough,' she thought, 'but much warmer than that freezing flat in Edinburgh.' She had exhausted *Style* and the *Magazine*, dispensed with *Sport* (having just checked if there was any news on the pectorally-advantaged Ghanaian runner she rather fancied (there wasn't), and was wondering whether she should read the main section and the *News Review*.

The other part, which lay crisply unread, was the *Money* section, which was normally used to light the fire at this time of year, but had somehow escaped incineration.

As she stacked it next to the kindling, Claire's eye was drawn to a small photograph of a good-looking man whom she thought she recognised but could not place.

Preoccupied with where she had seen this man, she almost forgot to read the article which was attributed to him.

FIFE LIFE 'BONUS' UNDER SUSPICION – BY JON HEELY, OUR SPECIAL CORRESPONDENT.

> *The 123-year-old Scottish mutual life company, Fife Life, came under fire from a number of its annuitants last week for offering free medical checks and a bonus for attending, provided they went to special medical centres arranged by the company.*
>
> *A number of annuitants have written to the company protesting that it was extremely inconvenient having to travel to a medical centre when they could have been seen by their own GP in their own town. A few had even suggested that this request could be linked to a cut in Fife's annuity rates. Rumours had been circulating in the City that several Mutuals are in trouble because of the continuing low level of interest rates, which have severely reduced their investment income.*
>
> *An annuitant for over 20 years, Hugo McLaren, 73, from Dunfermline, Fife, said he had declined the bonus offer because "mutual companies just don't*

do that sort of thing. I think it's a bribe ahead of some bad news, like a cut in the regular annuity payment in the future."

Sean O'Liam, Fife's Chief Actuary, denied there was a problem and confirmed this was simply a pre-audit procedure, which had been approved by the company's auditors.

***

Claire shouted to her mother in the kitchen.

"Mum, you've got to read this. The paper's got an article on Fife Life and uncle Sean is quoted…and Tom's father. Apparently, he's an annuitant. Isn't that just weird? And the guy who wrote it; I know I've seen him somewhere recently. What is a special correspondant, anyway?

Bridget almost snatched the paper from Claire and read it over and over again.

"Well, does that mean uncle Sean's in trouble, and is that just a coincidence that Tom's dad wrote the letter?"

Bridget looked shaken.

"I don't know. It could just be a coincidence. I mean, Hugo could easily be an annuitant, but it's asking too much to believe the journalist picked him out of thousands, maybe out of tens of thousands. I'll call Sean to make sure he's read it."

"Mum, I've just remembered how I know the name Jon Heely. He was on the train when I was going to see Tom's parents.

He was at the next table working on his laptop. His laptop case had his name, Jon Heely, kind of embossed on it."

"Oh, come on, there are lots of Jon Heelys."

"I'll tell you why I remember the name. He was quite fit, you know, good-looking, in a casual sort of way, and I found myself thinking, "That's the first time I've looked at a guy in that way since Tom died," and I was weighing up whether I was being disloyal to Tom, or whether it was healthy that I was experiencing normal emotions again. Anyway, I think it's really spooky that I saw him on the train, and the next thing I know he's writing in a Sunday newspaper connecting my boyfriend's father with my own uncle who may never have met each other. It's an omen, not just a coincidence. Maybe I should call Hugo and tell him I've read the article and that Sean O'Liam's my uncle."

"The guy's just a freelance journalist trying to make a story and get himself a name with *The Sunday Times*. He looks quite young. I guess he must be if you fancied him! So, he needs to make his name. Mark you, I can't see how you can be so sure he's the man on the Edinburgh train from that tiny photo. And no, I don't think you should bother Hugo. He might be quite embarrassed talking about his personal financial arrangements with you. I know that Tom's parents are very fond of you and they would be mortified that they might have offended you by giving the interview."

"Mother, you're so negative. You said yourself that it can't really be a coincidence picking Hugo out of all those thousands of annuitants, and uncle Sean is not personally implicated. He's only Fife's spokesman giving a holding statement. Go on, you call Sean and I'll call Hugo. Don't be a wimp."

***

Bridget realised she couldn't call with Claire in the room, as the conversation was almost bound to reveal the collaboration, something she had sworn to keep confidential. She dialled a random mobile number, which fortunately defaulted to a recorded message. "It's me," she said, "have you seen *The Sunday Times*? Call me tomorrow."

CHAPTER 40

(Longevity, Mice and Men, the Fourth Dimension)

The laboratory was not at all what Rowena had expected. She thought the team would be much bigger. Apart from Donald and Bridget, the only other members were Ruth and Craigie, middle-aged women who talked incessantly to each other, but barely said a word to anyone else. They clearly disliked Bridget, treated Donald with great reverence, and having been introduced formerly to Rowena, did not offer a single word of welcome. Rowena knew their type. They had established their boundaries early on, both in terms of friendships and job limits. No amount of sweet-talking was going to help her integrate with them.

Donald and Bridget each had their own rooms, both of which were linked to a much larger office, in which Ruth and Craigie sat, each with their own computer. Rowena shared this office, which was on the top floor of a 1930s stone office block in Bloomsbury. It was light and airy with a glass ceiling. The old-fashioned heating system was fighting a losing battle against the February cold. There was little decoration in the room. Bridget had bought a few pastoral views, which could have been anywhere in England, as well as a large whiteboard, which occupied the shorter wall, with telephone numbers of the unit's contacts. These were confined to Ghana and Sweden where the DDG tests were taking place. Rowena had expected a real laboratory rather than a typical office. She was already feeling disappointed. Ruth and Craigie were not likely to dispel that gloom either.

The only bright spot for Rowena was seeing Donald every day. He seemed particularly attentive to her, to the extent that her fantasies developed like a teenage girl. She even caught herself practising a Rowena Sheard signature. Every month, as instructed, she changed her password. Each time, it was an abbreviated variation of their two names, followed by the number of months she had worked in the unit. It was only when Craigie had spotted her trying anagrams of the first four letters of each of their names, and interrogated her rather too intensively about her password, that she became conscious of her obsession.

Rowena had still been given no real idea of what the Institute intended her to achieve, but she had soon realised that the tasks she had been given were distraction activities. Whether this was a deliberate ploy by Bridget to make her appear superfluous to the Institute's requirements, or simply the result of Donald not having any plans for her, Rowena was not sure. She sensed that Bridget still distrusted her, but was this because of Donald's unaccustomed familiarity at the interview or a desire to restrict the Institute's secrets to the privileged few?

She was reaching the conclusion that the administrative work she had been given by Bridget was designed to test her patience and tempt her to resign. Why employ a qualified pharmacist on £42,000 a year to order stationery? Rowena had no intention of resigning. She had set her mind on Donald and nothing was going to stop her.

It was difficult for her to define the relationship between Donald and Bridget. Ruth and Craigie made occasional remarks at Bridget's expense, which implied there was still, or at least, had been, a relationship between the two scientists; something which was rather more than professional.

The two women were speculating about Donald's recent conference in Zurich, which Bridget had not attended.

"I wonder why she didn't go this time? I reckon it's all over," Ruth giggled.

"Not before time – miserable cow."

"Well, you know my feelings about it."

They had been interrupted by Bridget flinging the door open and staring fiercely at the two women. Rowena was certain she must have heard every word.

The following week, Bridget had taken the day off to take Claire to the hospital for a post-trauma check-up. Was it just coincidence that Donald, who had been cocooned in his office for two weeks, unexpectedly emerged from his cave, all sweet and smiling? He bestowed his good humour on the two shrews, who returned obsequious greetings.

He gazed at Rowena benignly. Was she imagining that this unnatural behaviour was due to Bridget's absence or because he was now able to see her charms without the implied criticism from the loveless Doctor H-R?

"Could you give me your opinion on these, Rowena?"

"Yes, of course, erm…"

How she wanted to call him Donald, but "Ruthand Craigie" (she thought of them as one horrible 'she-monster') would have commented as soon as he left the room ("You've only been here four weeks. You really should show more respect" or "You're lucky Doctor Bridget didn't hear you being so familiar").

Donald pushed some spreadsheets across Rowena's desk and then retired to his room, rather sheepishly (or so she thought). She had seen the Ghanaian statistics before; they had been lying on Bridget's desk. Actually, those were a different set. Gloria had sensibly emailed a copy to Donald, who always printed in Trebuchet on yellow paper. Bridget always printed on plain white in Arial. This was clearly his own copy. He had printed the whole report himself even though he could have easily given Bridget's copy to Rowena. 'Interesting,' she thought.

She also wondered why Bridget had never discussed the report with her, even though she had left it in such a prominent position on her own desk, knowing Rowena would be bound to read it.

Donald was also apparently unwilling to explain the report (doubtless expecting super-brain Rowena to interpret it, she believed). Although she had seen the sheets on Bridget's desk, she had not had the opportunity to study the meaningless figures, but now she had been authorised to study them, there was clearly a pattern. Then it occurred to her that Donald also didn't know the key to the stats. They were clearly encrypted in such a way that only Bridget and Gloria, their Ghanaian representative, could decipher them. If only Rowena had the formula, she might make her first useful contribution since she has been employed at the institute.

CHAPTER 41

(Pure Odium)

The Secular Post is published monthly and has a small, but dedicated, readership. Opposed to every organised religion, it stands at the extreme end of non-belief. Even prominent atheists do not subscribe to it. In fact, they abhor its extreme illiberal approach, since the publication does not even concede the right to personal belief. It is not a Communist broadsheet. It holds quite the opposite position, promoting the accumulation of wealth, endorsing free love, and despising guilt. While *The Secular Post* accepts the law of the country (just), its stance is largely libertarian. Its editor, an obsessive American named Heldon Pontowsky, takes any opportunity to rubbish belief, or indeed commitment to any cause which is not self-serving. He reserves his greatest dislike for charities.

Exactly how Heldon had heard of the DDG is not clear, but he had collated various articles from the British and Swedish press. Heldon reckoned that if the DDG had any credibility, then the beliefs of organised religions could, finally, be disproved. Nothing would give him greater pleasure.

He was notoriously anti-Semitic, and lays the blame firmly on the priestly class in every faith, whom he sees as perpetuating their privileges throughout the centuries. No priest, no rabbi, no imam could be excused. According to

Heldon, they all practise their beliefs solely for the preservation of their caste.

He uses history to support his views, citing the acquisition of extreme wealth by the Christian Church, the rigid rules imposed on their followers by all religions (rules, which, according to Heldon, were never practised by the priestly class) and the suppression of women.

Heldon had some experience in this field, having been married five times, usually concurrent with a wifelet (married in tandem as he put it).

At last, with the help of the DDG, at a time when all the world's major religions were blighted by scandal or division, whether it be child abuse, extremism, views on homosexuality, or misogyny, he could see their nemesis coming. Atheism was on the up, religious scepticism on the rise, governments finally bowing to the power of reason, not historical belief. If the Death Date Gene really predicted the date of a man's death, then 'God's will' was out of the window. All that was needed was evidence that man, not God, could tell the date.

The problem for Heldon was how to convert this DDG information into a credible story which would be picked up by the national press. *The Secular Post* often publishes outrageous stories about clerics of all denominations, but they were so absurd (monk builds house on the moon for 14 virgins) that nobody bothered to sue. It was well known that *The Secular Post* had no money, but Heldon did have a close call when he accidentally used a real bishop's name in his year-long submarine orgy story. The real bishop, a Canadian in his seventies with a blameless career, was rather amused. The Vatican, previously oblivious to Heldon's publication, demanded a retraction and a public apology.

This came at a very difficult time for Heldon, as he was facing a charge of sexual assault on a short-term wifelet. He, therefore, published the retraction and the apology in the next edition. Coincidentally, it was the affair with the battered wifelet which gave Heldon his idea.

Tabby was the 19-year-old Kansas starlet whom Heldon had met and seduced while she was on a three-day trip to London. It was acknowledged that she was a willing party to the seduction (hence the assault charge had not been elevated to rape). He was prone to being a bit rough with his girls, and when Tabby had complained that Heldon had not introduced her to his friend, a theatrical agent who specialised in having full-bodied American girls in his shows, she became extremely angry. In a heated row in broad daylight in a London street, she pushed Heldon away and he retaliated in similar manner. He had the youthful American pinned against a wall when two police officers happened to pass. While this might have been passed off as a domestic quarrel, Heldon had 'previous' as far as violence towards women was concerned. He was happy to be bound over to keep the peace after Tabby had been persuaded, by another heinous Pontowsky lie, that he could get the poor girl invited to a garden party at Buckingham Palace.

Tabby really wanted to get back to the US, as her brother was seriously ill with cancer. Just after the Buckingham Palace incident, Tabby's mother called her from Kansas begging her to come home to see her brother, Street. His cancer was spreading, and she believed he was not expected to live for more than a few weeks. It was true that Street had cancer, but the medics had predicted it was not going to kill him for several months, even years.

Naturally, the thought of dying so young depressed him and he had turned to the bottle for comfort. He had worked as a mechanic and had a collection of rusty old Pontiacs, as well as his prize Chevy. He took to drinking heavily and then jumping into one of his old bangers and charging around a nearby dirt track. Soon, the bourbon spurred him onto riding the motorway. He hit the central reservation the first time he did. The second time he was not so lucky. Swigging a bottle with one hand and trying to light a Marlboro with the other, he sang one of his own compositions.

"I just heard my girl say to the farmhand I pay.

Why wait until June? He's gonna die soon,
I'm ready for you, so here's what we do,
I'll spin him a yarn, we'll meet in the barn,
We'll romp in the hay, make love all day.

If he should come by, I'll pretend to cry,
Say you tied me with rope, and I had no hope,
Say you took me by force.

Street, get down from your horse,
And give me your gun, so revenge is done,
Then I will turn round, once the trigger I've found,
Shoot Street in the head, and let him drop dead,
On the floor of his shed, not sick in his bed."

Street was seriously pleased with his song writing, but the combination of the bourbon and the blues was fatal. There was a gap in the central barrier this time and his Chevy was no match for the oncoming truck.

Tabby returned to the States for the funeral, but not before Heldon had added to her distress by forcing her to tell him the exact time of her brother's accident and bribing her to bring back his medical records and death certificate.

***

This still left Heldon with a problem. Even with a convenient outcome in the US, and some experienced counterfeiting which could justify his much-needed prediction, he needed access to someone in authority who was working on the DDG. Putting the two strands together, he was convinced he could get a platform to convince a prominent atheist to endorse his theory and obtain a much-needed boost to *The Secular Post's* circulation and his own finances. Little did he know, there about to be a dramatic change to his fortunes.

CHAPTER 42

(Kidnap)

The driver was waiting at Terminal 5 with a large placard saying "Gloria Okane." She was very relieved to see him, as Bridget had given her no details about her travel arrangements in London, other than that she would be met at Heathrow.

She shook hands with the driver, whom she thought might also be Ghanaian. She asked him if he was from Accra, but he only said he was not from West Africa. He clearly did not want to start a conversation. This was disappointing. The sheer size and speed of London amazed her, and she would have loved to have known about the buildings and places she was passing.

After the freedom of the M4, there was the customary traffic jam on Cromwell Road. She asked the driver what the hold up was, but he said, tersely, "Just normal Friday traffic." Clearly, however, he had a deadline. After a few minutes, he called an office (presumably the Institute, Gloria imagined). She reckoned it was a woman on the other end of the line (Bridget, maybe). The voice instructed him to call back if they had not reached what sounded like Escort Road in ten minutes. Gloria had bought a London street map, but could not find Escort Road. She really would like to know where she was.

"Are we far from the Institute? I could always walk if you could tell me the way?"

No reply.

She looked around her. She saw a repeating advertising sign with four different products, each allotted 10 seconds before the sign rolled down. She thought how clever this was, especially if cars were always caught in jams like this. Then she read; 'Starting March 19*th* Ideal Home Show, Earls Court Road'. That's what the voice must have said. She searched for and found Earls Court in the A to Z. A lorry moved forward a few yards, revealing a road sign: Central London 2 miles. No way could she walk that far, especially with her bags. She was beginning to feel increasingly uneasy about this driver. Surely, he would have been friendlier if he was an employee of the Institute.

He called again. He told the voice at the other end that Cromwell Road was blocked and that police were directing traffic down Earls Court Road. Gloria worried that she would have to pay the driver if they could not get any further.

Surely the Institute would arrange that. She had not withdrawn any pounds from the ATM at the airport, as Bridget had said she would be given money when she got here, and she did not want to risk a financial trail.

The car set off down, what she assumed was, Earls Court Road. Gloria thought it was a rather cheap and crowded street. She passed Earls Court Station, which at least confirmed her position. The car phone rang. The traffic stopped and started, which at least gave the driver time to write down the instructions. He reset his Sat Nav and set off slowly. After a few more blocks, he turned right into a slightly seedy crescent, where every other house was either a cheap hotel or brandished a large sign offering a room to let. Suddenly, he stopped outside a grubby, narrow, four-storey building which called itself the Harlington Hotel.

"This is where you will be met in about 10 minutes. You must wait in the hall."

He got out and extracted her bags from the boot and deposited them on the pavement. He glanced briefly in her direction as he got back in the car, but said nothing. As he moved off, Gloria noticed he was on the phone again. By now, she was genuinely scared. Bridget had told her only to call her on her mobile in an emergency. Surely this was an emergency; alone in a strange city with only Bridget as a contact? She pulled her mobile out of her bag and tried the number.

Nothing.

***

Then, she thought her Ghanaian phone might not be enabled for the UK. She saw a glass shelter across the street, which she hoped might be a phone box. 'I can call her from here,' she thought. She carefully read the instructions and put her credit card in the slot. It rang briefly, followed by a few clicks and a message which stated clearly "This number does not take incoming calls. Please check and try again."

She hardly had time to find out the number to call the police when a leather glove covered her mouth, a hood was pulled over her head and two strong arms hustled her into a waiting car.

CHAPTER 43

(A Test for Len)

His tobacco-stained teeth looked more grotesque than ever. The gaps between them seemed to have widened, or maybe some had just fallen out through neglect. Irresistibly, her eye was drawn to the dark bacteria-filled cavern that lay behind.

Rowena was seriously beginning to wonder if this exercise was worth it. She knew this one sample test could not disprove the DDG, but she had thought it would be fun, and lecherous Len was the perfect choice. A year ago, their lives easily overlapped, but Len had visibly deteriorated while Rowena had acquired a whole new professional image. Working at the Institute had given her confidence as well as money. Donald had provided something to aim for. While privately understanding he was an impossible target, the thrill of the chase had galvanised her into an amiability which had taken over her lifelong scepticism.

She had started to forgive the male species as a whole, and was even considering signing up for an internet dating site…but not before she had enjoyed a little revenge.

Len had been lusting after his tenant for several years, though Rowena had always dismissed his advances. Eventually, Len had given up all thoughts of conquest and had retired to his beer-stained existence. He had noted the new Rowena on a few occasions and decided she was out of his league.

Returning one night in his customary state from The Urban Fox, he found a message on his answerphone inviting him to join her for a drink in that very hostel. In his Guinness-filled dreams, Len assumed Rowena must have spotted him on the one recent occasion he had been properly dressed…at his aunt's funeral…and finally fallen in lust with him.

No such chance!

***

Rowena was waiting in her preferred quiet corner in The Fox, looking elegant in a Karen Millen dress with enough flesh above the knee to give Len some hope, but not so much that, after a couple of pints, it might have pushed him too far. For this occasion, she noticed he was wearing a clean(ish) white shirt.

Len, still sober at this stage, smiled toothlessly and aimed his lips at Rowena. She was comfortably able to deflect the approach to a minor graze of her left cheek.

She got to her feet and said, "Still drinking Young's?"

"No, Row, I'm into that Czech lager nowadays. You know, that Staropramen."

"That sounds a bit light for you, Len. I thought you old beer drinkers disapproved of that foreign stuff?"

"Oh no, that Velvet they produce is real nectar."

Rowena duly returned with a pint of Velvet and a gin and tonic. She had carefully considered how to approach the matter of giving her notice as a tenant now that she could afford an apartment in that smart new block, Orpington Court. While it would have been easy just to drop a note through Len's letterbox, she would then have had no chance of persuading him to join her for a drink and to listen to her other proposal.

"Good news or bad news first, Len?"

"Aw, I'll just have the good news, Row; there might not be any need for the bad news after that."

"Well, you can stop calling me Row for a start. There'll be no good news for you if I hear another 'Row' out of you."

"All part of the new image then, is it, Row-ee-na?"

"Careful, Len, don't overdo it. But it is more suitable for a scientist with a serious job. The point is that part of my role is research. I can't go into all the detail because it is confidential information, but the section I am working on is how people react to certain situations. The good news is that the sample cases we select get paid, and well paid."

"How much? And what do I have to do?"

"You get paid £30 an hour, and I guess the case I have in mind for you will last about two weeks."

"Twenty-four hours a day, that's over £10,000 quid! Yes, please, when can I start?"

"No Len, you don't get paid while you're asleep or while you're eating. I set you certain tasks and you keep a timesheet. I will meet you every evening and we will discuss how you got on and I will expect you to write a report, which I will check, and maybe revise a little, and then pass on to the project director. The tasks will vary, but you could expect to do six to eight hours a day."

She was making this up as she went along, hoping to remember all she had promised, but at the same time feeling quite proud of her ability to think on her feet.

"Still sounds all right," said Len, mentally calculating the profit. "And I'm ready for the bad news now?"

"Len, I want to leave the flat at the end of next month. I can get a mortgage on what I earn now, and I've put a deposit down on one of those new flats in Orpington Court."

"Can't say I blame you. It's pretty damp in that flat and I can use the money from this thing I'm doing for you to do it up properly and get better rent. Quid's in! What is this project you work for, anyway?"

"It's called the UK Advancement of Knowledge of the Human Genome."

Rowena reckoned Len would never remember that and, as it could never be traced under that name, it didn't really matter that he knew.

***

Rowena produced a sheet of questions which the 'Project Director' had prepared, and for which she had instructed Rowena to find a suitable candidate who fitted the right demographic criteria. The keywords were: poor education, prematurely ageing, limited resources and no strong religious beliefs. Len perfectly fitted the first two, but technically, he owned a house, admittedly in a poor district of London and in a terrible state of disrepair, but a house, any house, in London, must be worth at least £450,000, **even** No. 43 Solent Street. This didn't exactly make him poor, but Len thought like a poor man, so Rowena reckoned he qualified. As for religious beliefs, Len had never displayed any moral values of any sort, so she felt quite safe on that count. Besides, she had made up the criteria herself, so she could always change them.

The questions included: 'What would you do if you won 10 million euros on the Euro Lottery?' A number of options were then listed, such as giving it to charity, and if 'yes' which charity or charities and why, and if not, why not? The questionnaire also required a visit to certain charities after he had given his answer, to see if that affected his decision. The same applied to his family (did Len actually have any relations?

Rowena wondered). The process was quite lengthy and would easily take Len several hours a day. It then asked the participant to consider why he or she had chosen various luxuries such as a new house or a flat in Mayfair, a fast car, a trip round the world, even a new, beautiful, sexy boyfriend or girlfriend, but he/she would have to answer how they would deal with any existing relationship.

The question selected for Len, ostensibly by the mythical project director, but in practice by Rowena, was, 'What would you choose to do if you were told you were going to die in exactly one month, assuming that you would remain in perfect health during that time?'.

Len was not exactly in perfect health now, but he was sufficiently fit to do almost anything he wanted. As in the Euro Lottery questionnaire, a number of options were suggested to the respondent, who was then obliged to consider these in more detail.

Len studied the paper, looked at some of the options, and said he was ready to complete, reckoning he would finish it in three days.

"If I finish it early, do I still get paid the full whack?"

"We will meet every few days and there will be plenty for you to do, Len. It will take up the whole of the allotted time."

***

It had been a good evening with Rowena, and Len was feeling more than a little hungover. Still, from what he could remember, it would be easy money, with the added benefit of meeting Rowena every few days.

He was rather apprehensive about completing the family history, which Rowena said was essential, before he could start the case study. He knew he had not exactly lived a healthy life, but he had never seriously considered the prospect of an early death. He was only 56 after all, and men in the UK were meant to live until they were 80, weren't they? Still, she hadn't mentioned a medical, and that was a relief. The last time Len had seen a doctor was when he thought he had broken his arm falling over on his way home from the pub. The arm was only badly bruised, but the doctor had given him a right ticking-off for his drinking and smoking habits, saying he wouldn't see 55 if he carried on like that.

Well, that was seven years ago, and he had passed 55, so they are not always right, he believed. He reckoned he was good for 70, especially as he had recently taken up vaping. He certainly did not want another medical.

The question about his family also worried him. Sure, he knew his mum died when she was 67. He was 40 at the time, and doing a short (and, to be fair, his only) stretch at Her Majesty's pleasure in Winson Green, for an unwise career diversification into selling cars with false mileages and unmatching chassis parts.

He had been allowed out for the funeral, but he had never forgotten that he had not been able to say goodbye to her.

He still had the death certificate, so he could still check her age for certain. As for his mum's parents, he could only just remember them from when he was a child. He would have to call his sister, silly bitch, but he wasn't sure she would speak to him after all this time. Still, needs must.

His dad was a different problem. He couldn't ask his sister about him, because it was generally agreed they did not share the same father, even though his mum had remained married to the same man for 30 years. Actually, that was the cause of the unsettled argument with his sister.

During a furious row about Len having borrowed money from their mother, which he allegedly had never repaid (it was a long-term loan, recalled Len), his sister had accused him of having 'rogue genes' and being 'not a real child of their father'. Certainly, Len and Brenda bore little resemblance to each other, and her father was, without a doubt, her mother's husband. Len always thought of him as his dad, and he had been a clean-living, teetotal electrician; a bit too clean-living actually.

So, he felt deeply insulted by his sister's suggestion of his bastard status and had not spoken to her since, while privately nursing the possibility that his lovely, lively mum might have been a bit too lively on a few occasions.

The insult stuck, but the real issue of his paternity only bothered him on his dark hangover days. It did occur to him that Rowena could arrange a DNA test through the UKAGP *or* whatever her institute was called, but the only outcome would be to prove Brenda was right or that it all remained uncertain. So, what was the point? He also thought about getting a copy of his birth certificate, but his mum was hardly likely to have told the truth.

CHAPTER 44

(Mystery Scientists)

Bridget opened the letter with some trepidation. It was signed by a Professor Quessington-Adams and on behalf of two other apparently eminent scientists. She did not recognise any of their names. They claimed that they represented an organisation called the Humanist and Scientist League (HASL). She would make a point of checking them out in a scientific directory.

Dear Doctor Hughes-Renton,

The diligent research by your team on the human genome has been brought to our attention, and in particular, the analysis which has been applied to the DDG. We would like to publish your conclusions in our periodical, The Humanist and Atheist Scientific Letter (HASL).

We would welcome the opportunity to discuss your research prior to publication. If you feel that such a meeting is premature and may compromise further analysis, we do, however, reserve the right to publish without attribution to the UKAGP.

Any publication in HASL would follow the strict scientific guidelines set down at the time of its foundation, and will not pass any legal, ethical or moral judgments on the implications on the DDG or any variant thereof.

We are especially keen to publish the facts at this stage for two reasons. Firstly, we are aware that a speculative and uncorroborated article may shortly appear in a publication called The Secular Post, which has no scientific authority, and will almost certainly focus on outrageous ethical and social claims.

Secondly, we believe that the government is suppressing the information about the DDG, partly because it is quite unprepared for the possible consequences in terms of public disorder, and partly because of the influence of the Christian churches in the UK. We believe that the Roman Catholic Church in particular has impressed the ethical implications on the Prime Minister. We strongly believe that the government should no longer withhold the information from the British public.

> *Yours sincerely*
> *Gordon Quessington-Adams (Chairman, HASL)*
> *Petr Volontsoch (Chief Scientist, Scientists and Humanists of the Czech Republic and Slovakia (SHOCS))*
> *Bertrand-Urban de Gregoire (Academie de Sans-Dieu)*

Bridget was shocked to the core. Did the geneticists really know the outcome of the DDG tests? If so, how had they acquired this information? Should she arrange to meet them to forestall publication? Should she tell Donald, who had been unwilling to talk about the project for the last few weeks? Indeed, why had they written to her and not to Donald? Were they aware of his current state of mind?

What is *The Secular Post*? Is it a serious publication? Does the government really know anything? Has the pressure the Catholic Church is allegedly putting on the Prime Minister got anything to do with Conor?

'God almighty, where am I going to start?' she wondered.

***

"What the hell is wrong with Donald?" Bridget verbalised her thoughts. "He has refused to see me for three weeks. It's not my job to do the PR." But privately, she knew Donald would never do it. It had to be her; there was no-one else. She decided to email Quessington-Adams.

CHAPTER 45

(Voices on Hampstead Heath)

Conor had been careful to remove all the hymn books from the third row in front of the pulpit, after the 8.30 Mass, in case there was any confusion. If they didn't know the words to 'O Star of the Sea' by now, it was about time they went to confession!

Actually, he reflected quickly, it was about time *he* went to confession himself to admit using the church roof funds for purposes it was not intended for.

***

Conor couldn't actually think of a priest to whom he could confess. He imagined the scenario: "Bless me, father, for I have sinned. I have spent my church's roof fund on the purchase of a share in a horse, which has subsequently died, uninsured."

"And which church roof might that be?"

Not much chance of anonymity there.

However, Conor took the 11am as agreed and retired to his room after Mass, taking a strong cup of coffee with him, to read the message in Hymn 647:

Tomorrow at 10am, but not before, you will go to Hampstead Heath. There is a bench 50 metres left of the Kenwood House entrance to the heath. You will recognise it because there is a green bin immediately on the right of the bench. Wait there until you receive further instructions.

***

Conor was still clutching the hymn book, flagged with a betting slip and the directions to what he hoped was the particular bench identified. He hoped that this would not take long, as the icy wind was penetrating his black clerical coat only too easily.

He had been irresistibly distracted by the discarded remains of yesterday's *Racing Post* in the adjacent bin, when a voice appeared to rise from the depths of that same receptacle.

"Hello, Conor. How are you? Well, I hope."

Conor was terrified. Was this some type of modern-day miracle? He was not great on technology, but this seemed to be a pre-recorded message from the litter bin (normal rubbish, he was relieved to see, not the dog-poo variety). Just a recording machine, he supposed, operating remotely. He looked round to see if there was anyone in the bushes behind.

"No, I'm not there, Conor, but I can see you."

He looked in vain for a CCTV camera in the trees.

"Nor there," the voice laughed.

Was it male or female? It sounded like one of those electronic voices from an Indian call centre. They sound electronic, only they are real people, trained to speak like Leekons.

"Now, listen," the voice continued, "it's a shame we can't meet in person, but that's the nature of the business we are going to do together."

"What business?" squeaked Conor. "I don't know who you are or what you want."

"Hopefully, you will never know who I am, but I am about to tell you about the deal. You already know that I have all the knowledge I need about your crimes, the ones you have already committed under your own roof (the bin paused, chuckled and cleared its throat), and the ones you may not have committed, but which I could easily persuade that idiot bishop to believe."

Conor tried to interrupt, but the voice in the bin anticipated him. There followed what sounded like a clicking of tapes.

"You will reply when I tell you," it said. "The people I represent have a proposition. We are looking for some information."

This time, Conor stayed silent.

"We know your sister works at the UKAGP. More than works there, in fact; she is really running the programme for the DDG, otherwise known as the Death Date Gene."

"I don't know anything about this," protested Conor.

"Possibly not," said the voice, "but you could find out."

"Look, I don't get on very well with my sister. I don't subscribe to her humanist views, and the last time we met, we had a blazing row; I haven't spoken to her since."

"That's not very Christian of you, Father Conor. Don't you think it's time you made it up with her? We think you should…unless you were looking forward to Banjul."

'Banjul,' he thought to himself. 'They know all about Banjul. It must be the church, but it can't be. The church doesn't do blackmail. But whoever it is wants me to spy on Bridget, my own sister?' Conor thought about it again. He could, he would, and he *had* to justify it. Of course, anything to do with the DDG was unethical, immoral, and sinful. Bridget would realise the error of her ways. He would bring her back to the bosom of the church.

"Damnation to him or her who tries to obstruct the Maker's plans." He couldn't pinpoint where this was written *in The Bible*, but he was sure he had read it. He quietly regretted not being a more diligent student. Weren't the church's laws quite clear on euthanasia? Surely DDG was the same, probably worse? No justification whatsoever.

He had a duty to stop it, all the more so as the brother of one of the main proponents. It was very dodgy, doctrinally, and in his heart he knew it, but he made up his mind. He had no choice.

"It's time you asked Bridget to lunch," trilled the voice from its place of refuse.

"We want you to say to her that you have been approached by an anonymous organisation seeking information about her and the DDG. You must say you are very concerned for her. She is very vulnerable right now; she is under a lot of pressure. Say you have had this conversation but that you have no idea who is behind it. On no account should you mention the church, the roof, or the possibility of your being transferred to Banjul. Arrange the meeting by the end of next week. We will speak again, the following Sunday."

There was a sort of flushing sound from the bin, followed by complete silence.

CHAPTER 46

(Mystery Abduction)

Gloria figured she must have been asleep for nearly a day. It was shortly after midday when she had been snatched, and, despite her terror, she had detected a growing sense of hunger, especially as the last meal she had had was breakfast at 5.30am.

By now, she was starving and thirsty, though she did notice that some of the water in the glass by her bed had been drunk, either willingly or forcibly, to accompany some sleeping pills.

It was beginning to get dark again, and the few streetlights suggested it was around 4.30pm. As she had been blindfolded at the time of her abduction, Gloria had no visible evidence that she was in the same run-down Victorian building, but she was convinced she was on the top floor of the Harlington Hotel.

The room was very sparsely furnished, with a bedside table and reading lamp, but no cupboard and no chest of drawers. Her suitcase and her briefcase lay by the door. She had no recollection of bringing them up, though she remembered being carried up several flights of stairs. Clearly there was no lift.

The suitcase seemed undisturbed, but was unlocked. As she had been wearing the same jacket, cream blouse and trousers since she left Accra, she was anxious to find some clean clothes. She had been woken by the chill of a London afternoon in early March. It occurred to her that someone must have put her to bed and removed her jacket. She shuddered at the thought of the invasion of her privacy, but she was relieved that there was no sign of her being molested.

But where was the jacket?

She was desperate for a shower, and anxious to distance herself from her abductor's memory. She considered throwing all of yesterday's clothes from the top floor window to attract attention, but it was locked and sealed. The shower cubicle was at a strange angle, having been squeezed in under the eaves, and only just usable, even for a woman of Gloria's slight stature.

From the shower, she could see a tiny shelf and what appeared to be some wet fabric lying on it. This could be her jacket. The shelf was at the apex of the room, where the eaves met. There was no way she could reach it. Dripping wet (there were no towels either), she went back into the bedroom to search her suitcase for a piece of clothing so she could dry herself off, and perhaps a couple of clothes hangers to twist together to reach the jacket.

She tried the bedroom door, but, unsurprisingly, it was locked.

She was so preoccupied with escaping that it was only then that she noticed a full tray of breakfast on the bed. It must have been placed there while she was in the shower. Or, worse still, while she was standing stark naked, trying to reach the jacket.

Then she noticed that there was a second switch beside the light in the shower room.

There was a small orange light on this switch, which, she was certain, had not lit up before. The switch itself did not appear to control any light in either room, but was untidily tacked to the shower room wall. It led to a hole recently drilled through the skirting board to the landing outside.

Clearly, someone was watching her, whether for a cheap sexual thrill or to monitor her sleeping patterns; it was not clear.

She poured herself a cup of real coffee from the cafetière, and swiftly consumed the boiled egg, toast and apple. Now she felt strong enough to open the letter which had come with the breakfast.

"Welcome to London, Gloria. I am sorry if the reception was somewhat abrupt. We can make your stay a much happier one from now on. I am afraid we have had to 'borrow' some of your statistics. Don't worry, we shall return them to you, and we can provide you with a cast iron alibi for being 24 hours late for your meeting with Doctor Hughes-Renton.

"I also apologise for the state of your jacket. It is essential that our identity is not disclosed, and, obviously, your jacket would be covered in the DNA of my colleagues. Clever stuff, DNA, and, as far as I know, there is only one method that can destroy the identity of the owner. There is a powerful chemical, which, when the fabric on which the DNA is found, is absorbed in water for 20 hours, leaves no trace. Sometimes, the best plans go wrong for the simplest of reasons. My colleagues had the chemical, but not the water. We had to soak your jacket in the shower, but had to keep it out of your reach for at least 20 hours. I am sorry you had to have such a long sleep. This letter and its envelope have also had the chemical treatment.

"Gloria, in the bedside table you will find a phone linked to a bespoke number. There are no other numbers. It cannot be detected by the police or any other agency. If you co-operate, you will come to no harm. You will signal your willingness to co-operate by lifting the phone and saying, 'I agree.' My colleagues will collect you within one hour and take you to a more comfortable location, where we have an attractive proposition to make to you, which will make you one of the richest women in Ghana. Do not attempt to revoke the arrangement during that hour, either by attempting to smash the window (it is triple glazed) or flooding the building (we have turned off the water supply, and do not attempt to flush the toilet). Do not try to wave from the window (if you go near, a steel curtain will fall at such force that it will break your arm).

"We have had to 'borrow' your two mobile phones, your watch and your cosmetics; we did not have time to check these for electronic gadgetry, but they will all be returned to you if you co-operate. If you try anything of this nature, the telephone is primed to self-immolate within one hour, and, as you will know by now, this building has some of the safest fire protection in London, and will prevent any conflagration spreading to adjacent houses. Everyone will be totally unharmed, unless, of course, you are unlucky enough to be on the wrong side of the door and window."

Terrified, Gloria gingerly opened the drawer under the bedside table, expecting a sleek mobile phone. But, inside, there was an old-fashioned 1940s-style instrument, nailed to the wall. She lifted it and to her surprise, it started playing *The British Grenadiers*. On reaching 'and such great names as these,' it said, with a strong American accent, 'Please speak now.'

Gloria did as she was told.

CHAPTER 47

(Advice from his Sister)

Len had last sat in Brenda's front room on the day of their mother's funeral.

"I am *quite* pleased to see you again, Len; you have been on my mind a lot recently. I mean, neither of us is getting younger, and with mother gone, I suppose we are the only family left."

Len grunted. It was his best sort of grunt; the sort of grunt Len gave the landlord when he presented him with an empty pint glass but asked for a half and the landlord filled it beyond half way!

Len's emotional capacity was severely limited, but he felt he should do something. He couldn't bring himself to kiss his sister on the cheek, but he stood up, walked over to her chair, and shook her hand vigorously.

"Well, I suppose that's the best I could expect," said Brenda.

"Thing is Bren, I've had a bit of luck. I've been asked to do a sort of survey. It's easy money, enough to spend a bit on the flat, do it up, and get better rent."

"What about that grumpy tart that lives there; the one you had the hots for?"

"Ah, well. She's gone and got all smart. She's got a proper job, and she's a real professional woman now. She's moving out, see, but she's the one what wants me to do the survey, see."

"Really?"

"Thing is, Bren, the first question is what would I do if I won 10 million euros on the Euro Lottery, but was told I was going to have exactly one healthy month left to live? Would I give some of the money to charity?"

"Well, would you, Len?"

"Don't know much about charities, Bren. I mean Ken at The Urban Fox, has that tin for the Dogs' Trust chained to a beer pump. Dunno why, there's nuffing in it. I was a bit pushed to buy another pint a few months back. Rattled the tin, seven bloody p. It's all chained up and that, but Ken don't realise anyone can unscrew the bottom. So, no bloody pint!

"Woman from Dogs' Trust came round the other day. Nine pence in it.

'Only 9p,' she said. 'You don't like dogs much round here. Don't you know they're man's best friend?'"

"Man's best friend? My arse! Got attacked by that bloody great chihuahua what lives at the end of the street last week. Size of a small horse, it is. No wonder the bloke has it chained up. Bloody great teeth, 'uge mouff. Went straight thru' my jeans, big scars on my knee —."

"I don't think that was a chihuahua, Len. Sounds more like a rottweiler."

"Yeah, whatever. I'm not giving nuffing to dogs."

"What about Oxfam, or Save the Children, or Lifeboats?"

"Look Bren, I don't have no kids, as far as I know, I hate the sea, and Oxfam's all abroad in' it? Abroad can look after itself, can't it?"

"There are lots of hungry people in England, Len."

"I never seen any; anyway, they got the food bank."

"Well, give something to the food bank."

"Give to the food bank? They're meant to be giving to people like me, when we've had a heavy night in The Fox, and can't afford a burger!"

"But you'll have a million euros, Len. You won't run out."

"Yeah, but them banks are giving all them euros away, aren't they? To the Greeks and that. So, no, I'd keep them euros in case I was going to Sandown for the odd flutter... and, of course, I'd lend you a few bob for a month or so, if you were short."

"Lend me!" Bren screamed.

"You want it back within a month. What, so your mates can have a monumental piss-up in The Fox when you go? Not bloody likely. As it happens, unless you've made a will, it would come to me as your nearest of kin. I'd arrange the cheapest funeral possible, with a cardboard coffin; I'd make out you were one of those green people and you'd told me you didn't want to burn good trees. I'd invite nobody from The Fox, and split the money with the girls."

"That's not very nice. Your only brother, and you'd treat me like that. Anyway, your daughters don't need no money. They all live with smart blokes. Look, I'm not going to die. This is only some silly exercise that Rowena and her team at the Institute spend our money on. Course Bren, if I was gonna die, I would leave some to you. Then you could give it to

Gwen, Hen, and Jen."

Brenda began to feel she had gone a bit too far. It was, after all, only a silly exercise, and it was certainly not in her interest to make sure Len died without a will.

"Well, you like horses, Len. Why not give some to a charity for sick horses or injured jockeys? If you said you were thinking of leaving a big sum in your will, and you were not expected to live very long, they'd probably invite you to a day at the races and a visit to the sick horses themselves!"

"Then I could finish the bit in the survey on what I thought of the charity. Brilliant Bren, I'll ask for your help on the next part...which is all about our family."

Len left abruptly, filled with rare enthusiasm to locate an equine charity. Bren was left to fret about the forthcoming discussion about the family.

***

Len thought about all the luxuries he could have in his remaining weeks. He didn't drive, and there wasn't time to learn in a month. He did still like women, though that wasn't usually reciprocated, but with one million euros, and a proper clean up — haircut, waxing (whatever that was), and real grooming by that lovely Vietnamese masseuse down the road. In fact, he could treat her to a proper dinner after the massage, and then, well, you never know what might happen!

What about a horse? He had to be a winning owner before he died.

In fact, he was so immersed in his thoughts that he let five taxis go by while waiting at the bus stop, completely forgetting that money was no object, at least as far as a taxi was concerned.

CHAPTER 48

(Stubble Man)

"Hi, this is Gloria."

There was a long pause… so long that she thought she had not followed the instructions correctly. Then, finally, there was a voice at the other end. It spoke with an American accent.

"We are sorry you have had an uncomfortable time. Unfortunately, we have to take extreme precautions in the interest of security. So, you will have to be blindfolded again. We will take you a few miles to a more comfortable location.

We would prefer you to apply the blindfold yourself. When you press 47#, on the phone, a blindfold will descend from the ceiling. It is easy to detach it from the wire. The time is now 4pm. By 5pm, you should have collected all your things and be ready to leave. Put on the blindfold. Two members of our staff will then knock on the door; one will take your case. The other will handcuff himself to you and help you down the stairs to the car. Do not attempt to remove the mask while you are in the car. We have fitted childproof locks so any attempt to get out will be pointless. The journey will take about 40 minutes. When you arrive, you will be taken to your room. You will find the accommodation very comfortable. A meal will be sent up to you at six-thirty. We look forward to meeting you."

More clicks followed and then silence. Gloria knew she had no choice. She had done all she had been told to do; she had tried on the blindfold. It was comfortable enough, but Gloria did not fancy wearing it in the car. The two men arrived on the stroke of five.

She deliberately left covering her eyes until the last possible moment, enabling her to catch sight of the first man. As he saw her fix her lava-lamp, he caught her glance almost as though he expected her to sneak a look at the expressionless face with fashionable stubble staring back at her. His cheap aftershave invaded the room and was enough to convince Gloria that he was the same man who had delivered her to her hotel prison.

As Gloria had expected, travelling in the back of the car while blindfolded, even with handcuffs off, severely disorientated her. In a further attempt to confuse her, stubble man circumnavigated several roundabouts, which made her feel nauseous. After an especially tight turn, taken at some speed, she threw up over the driver.

He swore at Gloria in an indecipherable language, and then, in plain English, threatened to put her in the boot for the rest of the journey. Gloria was terrified, but stubble man's colleague, to whom she had been shackled, calmed him down. Not long after this event, they arrived at their destination.

Stubble man completely disappeared but the shackle man took the risk of pointing her towards the Ladies, so, he said, she would be vomit-free when she met the director of this mysterious organisation.

Gloria cleaned herself up and was taken to meet the No.1.

"My name is Heldon Pontowski," the director said. "Gloria, welcome to our home. I am sorry you have had an uncomfortable ride. You will be well treated here. We hope you will be able to answer a few questions for us. And I promise you will not be late for your meeting with Dr Bridget."

CHAPTER 49

(A Week with Hurriyet)

Jon Heeley stepped off the Ryanair flight from Alicante. He had never been so relieved to be back in Britain. A week with Hurriyet was exhausting…in every way. She was truly high maintenance. She complained about the hotel, she sent the food back at every meal, she insisted on the best wine, and she bought every trinket at every market stall. On the sixth day, she finally gave him some useful information. It was only a telephone number, but it was Claire Hughes-Renton's number and address and it was the address he desperately needed.

"Why you want it, Jon? The Claire girl is okay now, right. So, no point you seeing her. Anyway, I much more attractive, sexier. I only met her once, but she was thin, very thin, probably even thinner now after accident. No fun at all. Jon, you much better with me."

"Hurriy, of course you are much more fun."

It was probably the most blatant lie he had ever told and when he found out she had had the number and the address all the time, he despaired. He had promised her a whole two weeks in the sun, only there wasn't much sun in Benidorm that March. Now another week beckoned, and there was nothing more to be gained.

"You said it would be sunny but is cold and it rains all the time."

"Hurriy, it's only early March and it has to rain in Spain sometime. I can't control the weather."

"Warmer in Ankara," she replied.

Jon knew this was untrue as he had seen a newsflash showing Turkey had had its worst snowfall for years, but it wasn't worth picking a fight with Hurriy.

They had retired to their bedroom, where Hurriy, despite her anger, was beginning to look demanding, and had even turned down the sheets.

"No clean sheets again. Jon you must call reception."

But Jon was spared another battle with the hotel staff by the telephone ringing. During a brief respite from Hurriy that afternoon, Jon had called another freelance journalist friend with instructions to call him back pretending to be *The Sunday Times* and wanting him to chase up some vital new information on another story he was following.

"Okay, thanks Dan, I'll try and change the flights to tomorrow. Hurriy won't be happy, but I'll try and find another week with her later in the year."

"I'm really sorry, Hurriy, I've got to go back to London for *The Sunday Times*. We can go to Nice next time."

Hurriy, worn down by the weather, conceded surprisingly quietly.

"I promise," he said, quietly priding himself on his fast-developing fibbing ability.

***

Jon had not counted on the sheer weight of Hurriy's recent purchases. Heavy pieces of junk jewellery, three pairs of trousers and even a coat, in addition to what she had brought with her, greatly exceeded both their 20 kilo allowances. Ryanair was not prepared to make any concessions on hand baggage either.

Twenty-five euros each, but worse was to come. During the week away, Hurriyet had been fiddling with her new EU passport. She objected to the absence of the two dots above the letter u in her name. She insisted that adding the dots determines the correct pronunciation. She filled these in quite boldly with a ballpoint pen. She had also changed the luscious looking brunette in her passport photograph for the one of her as a blonde, which she always carried with her, and which reminded her of her early days in London.

The Spanish authorities were not amused. Although the document clearly showed her as a British citizen, the mutilated passport, the unrecognisable photograph, together with Ankara as her place of birth, and, when challenged, her strong "Middle Eastern" accent, all convinced the passport authorities to detain her beyond the flight's departure time.

Eventually, Jon (with the help of a call to *The Sunday Times* travel department, who kindly created a record of an Anglo-Turkish female employee) persuaded Spanish Border Control to let her pass. The cost to

Jon for an amended ticket for a passenger with a corrected name and two tickets for the next flight plus the excess baggage was 450 euros.

"It's either that or you leave the lady here," said Ryanair's passport and immigration chief, admiring Hurriy's distinctive physique. Jon was sorely tempted.

***

Once home, Jon had second thoughts about phoning Claire. Bridget could answer the phone and that would really blow his cover. He was not sure if Claire had resumed her studies in Edinburgh.

As a journalist, Jon was accustomed to making quick decisions, but this one took him some time. What would her reaction be? Had she read his article in *The Sunday Times*? Should be bring his laptop with his name clearly visible, as a reminder?

He was confident that she would remember him, because he had spotted her looking in his direction and scrutinising his laptop case on more than a few occasions on the long train journey to Edinburgh. Had he not had a few Turkish things on his mind, as well as solving the Fife Life connection, he might well have chatted her up.

In the end, he decided to take the tube to Highgate, and within a few minutes, he was on the doorstep and ringing the bell of the imposing Hughes-Renton residence. If Bridget answered, he could easily respond with the number of the house next door, and slink away quietly with an apology. If it was Claire, then he would quickly flash the laptop, lettering side up.

It seemed like an age, but actually it was only 30 seconds, before he could see the outline of a younger woman opening the inner glass door.

"Claire?"

There was a very long pause.

"God, it's you."

CHAPTER 50

(Fourth Experiment)

The data which Bridget had let me use seemed pretty convincing, but I appreciated there was an element of luck. At first, I was completely bowled over by the accuracy of the statistics, especially as the figures came from such diverse sources. It just couldn't be coincidence that the predictions were nearly 100% accurate from the UK, Sweden and Ghana. Okay, someone could have been given a few backhanders to 'reconstruct' the figures in Ghana, but in the UK and Sweden? Surely someone would have spotted it? The more I thought about it, the more improbable it was.

How *could* there be a gene which predicted *exactly* the day you died? Yes, of course, smoking, bad diet, pollution, stress, they all take years off a life…but actuaries have been factoring in those issues for years. They could take 1,000 lives with 200 who had never smoked, 200 who gave up a 10-a-day habit when they were 40, 300 who stopped after 25 a day when they reached 50, and 300 who puffed until the day they died. But there were always variations; some smokers lived to 90, some had unrelated accidents or suffered violent deaths. Women seemed to die in their 80s, men in their 70s. Why? These statistics covered a wide enough sample (32,000), but they seemed too accurate. 95% is just not credible, even from three countries with very different demographics.

Still, my job as the chief actuary of a life company was to rely on the evidence. This I had done. This was clearly evidence from a seemingly respected and reliable source. True, no other life company would be using it. True, there remained a question mark as to whether it would ever be published, and, most pertinent of all, the data had been given to me by my own sister.

The situation at Fife was still critical. I had to take a chance. All the evidence pointed to our annuitants living longer lives. This is late 2009. The worst banking crisis for 80 years has been going on for a year. No UK investor will consider investing in a bank, nor in any fixed interest investment, except for UK government stocks (gilts). Lehmann Brothers collapsed only a few weeks ago. The equity markets were dire.

Fife can't meet its liabilities as its annuitants are all living longer than the government stocks, in which Fife has invested. But there are still opportunities to buy longer dated gilts, which won't be redeemed for 20 or even 25 years. The rates will be lower than the stocks which are coming up for redemption very soon, but I can make up the difference by buying corporate bonds. Nobody is prepared to buy those yet, because of the risk of default, but they offer 2% or even 3% more than the ultra-safe gilts.

Over the next few weeks, I switched the 'shorts' to the 'longs' and made up the difference in income by buying longer-dated corporate bonds to match Bridget's projected death dates for Fife's annuitants. Then I produced a very pretty spreadsheet and emailed it to Phil Jewell. Phil never understood the gilt market, and I had deliberately made my figures even more incomprehensible by putting in columns for days' accrued interest, gross redemption yields, EPIC codes, ISIN codes (completely meaningless for a layman, but essential for an investment manager) and a day count (even I don't know what that is).

"I leave all the investment side to you," said Phil, "so it better be right. But I am interested in the revised death dates for our annuitants."

"I'm afraid they're worse, Phil," I said. I pointed to the spreadsheet showing by how many years and months the original dates had been exceeded.

"Sure, I get that," he growled in a very Caledonian way, "But where did you get the new data from?"

I had prepared myself for this question. Phil was no fool. He wanted evidence, even if he might not understand it.

I knew he would not believe that all our 270 annuitants had died on their due dates (I had doubts myself) so I varied the data, making 40% die up to six months before their time was due, and 60% after their due date. The six-month timescale was within an acceptable range for me not to be too affected by interest rate movements. He swallowed this and the use of the UK Genome Association and a passing reference to the Mesalinoa Prediction, championed by a fictitious American actuarial group, based in Phoenix, Arizona, miraculously translated to Dulwich, England.

Phil was delighted, and unexpectedly offered me a place on Fife's board.

I guessed this was to have someone to answer the technical points if things went wrong, but as I was already in it right up to my not inconsiderable waist, I accepted. together with a useful increase in my remuneration.

CHAPTER 51

(Doctor Knows Best)

Rowena insisted that Len should have a full medical if he was going to qualify for the trial. This would be a lot more convincing than just receiving the results of a gene test from the Institute, which even Len would suspect. She was still good friends with Caroline, a local (but not too local) GP, with whom she had regular dealings when she managed the pharmacy.

Len had protested strongly at the prospect of a medical, but when Rowena had shown him a photograph of a particularly pretty nurse from an advertising campaign to recruit new staff, he had quickly agreed.

Rowena had persuaded Caroline to do the medical, rather than risk one of her nurses asking questions. Caroline was an attractive and extremely professional doctor, who could be quite severe with patients. Rowena could only imagine how the medical would unfold.

Meanwhile, Len was working hard on his bucket list, featuring wine, women and horses. Of course, it was all a figment of his imagination. Little did he know that two letters would shortly drop onto his doormat and create an ugly reality.

The letter from the surgery arrived on the day that Len was about to catch the train to Newmarket. He was due to discuss a possible substantial donation to the Injured Jockeys Fund in exchange for (he hoped) a share in a horse. He hoped the horse would produce a few wins in the last few weeks of the season. Doctor Caroline had listed a number of unpronounceable medical conditions, which Len had apparently endured for some years.

There were references to courses of treatment and instructions to report to the surgery as a matter of urgency. Len dismissed these requests, reasoning that if he really only had a few weeks to live, he might as well enjoy himself without drugs disturbing his fun. He had apparently lived with these conditions for several years, so what was the point? This was exactly the response that Rowena had expected and indeed hoped for. Now, with the symptoms which she had identified in the second letter (from the Institute) clearly stating 29th April as his predicted date of death, Len began to panic.

CHAPTER 52

(Despair)

Donald Sheard put his head in his hands; grunts of despair emanated between his fingers. Privately, he had been harbouring doubts for some time. The DDG was really a product of his arrogance and his extreme reluctance to admit his failure. Only Bridget really believed in its authenticity.

He loved Bridget, or he thought he did… certainly he did when they slept together, which was an increasingly rare event these days. He certainly admired her, if only for her tenacity. But, really, despite all the stats from Ghana, Sweden and the UK, there was something that didn't add up. He knew he was widely acclaimed in the world of genetics, but the failure of this project would destroy all his genuine achievements.

For years to come, he would be known as the DDG man, the famous genetic fraudster, the scientist who fabricated death dates. He could see a future for himself appearing on chat shows as Doctor Death!

And then along comes Rowena with her 'proof', her analysis of the spreadsheets and her experiment with 'lecherous Len'. She had been so keen to join the team, and now it appears that her intention was to sabotage its work.

And then there's me. I know Donald just regards me as the errant Irishman, and contrasts me with my dedicated, metropolitan, sister. Donald had, at first, steadfastly refused to allow me to use some of the figures on a cohort of Fife Life annuitants, as he was going through a bout of DDG-inspired depression, conscious of its shortcomings, and convinced of its imminent exposure as the press closed in. He felt like a mass murderer on the run, with suicide being the only escape.

But that mood passed. He allowed Bridget to apply some of the figures to Fife's clients in a final desperate bid to prove his doubts were misplaced. Another period of self-reflection followed, and a further era of denial, during which he refused to talk to Bridget.

Donald's mood didn't rise and fall like a barometer, predicting blue skies followed by thunderstorms. His mood was even more irregular than that. He wanted to expose the duplicity of his own creation. He even penned a letter, admitting as much, to a national newspaper, in response to an article exposing the concept of the DDG, signed by seven prominent scientists and gerontologists.

But he couldn't bring himself to post this testimony of guilt; certainly not in the letter column of a national newspaper. He was unsure whether the avalanche of correspondence that would follow would be more sympathetic in *The Times*, *The Guardian* or *The Daily Telegraph*, so he posted it to himself. He pretended to receive it as though he was an uninformed scientist, whose reaction he could measure afresh.

It was no good. He destroyed the letter and was on the point of swallowing a bottle of Paracetamol when Bridget finally caught him on a day when he had forgotten to lock himself into his office; she snatched the pills and called his doctor.

CHAPTER 53

(Harriet Wants Reconciliation with Sean)

Harriet hadn't heard from Jon since they arrived back in London. The truth was that one week in Benidorm had been more than enough. Jon did not return her calls, and he stayed with his mother in Guildford until he considered it safe to return to London, hoping that the area around his flat in Clapham was now a Harriet-free zone.

Harriet had to resort to waiting for an agency to provide her with temporary employment. Because her English had not improved, she was quickly consigned to a receptionist role, for which her impatience and discourtesy to visitors ensured that most of her assignments were extremely short-term. If she was fortunate enough to be hired by a straight male in the HR department, then she could use her most noteworthy assets to maximum effect, and the employment might last to the Wednesday of the first week. More normally, a professional woman would not tolerate Harriet's shortcomings beyond lunch on the first day.

And so, it was unsurprising that the need for a more lavish lifestyle brought her back to the donor of last resorts, none other than yours truly. Her timing was most fortuitous. The phone in my office was ringing as I returned from a most excellent lunch to celebrate my promotion to the board of Fife Life, and, more relevantly, the accompanying increment to my salary. Fortified with at least one bottle of my preferred establishment's best Chablis, I was in the mood to accommodate anyone, certainly an attractive young woman, the worst memories of whom seemed to have miraculously disappeared under my alcoholic haze.

"Seanie, I know I got you into big trouble and I really sorry. I have really boring job and they don't like me. Can we meet up, so I can say sorry properly? Maybe you know someone who can give me more interesting job! Also, I have new British passport with the right spelling!"

"Hurriy, it's really nice to hear from you, but I am on the board of Fife Life so I must be more careful about creating false identities even if you do have a new passport."

"So, you are a richmanfatcatdirector (she rolled it all into one word) so you can look after me and I am really, really good girl now!"

"Well, Hurriy, I will buy you lunch tomorrow, but I am not promising you I can find you a job either at Fife or anywhere else."

"Okay," she went very coy. "We meet tomorrow – 1pm at Martha's bar and I wear long skirt and closed shirt and jacket, so all very smart and 'spectable, right?"

Nothing much could disguise Hurriyet's contours – even a 'closed' shirt, and the way she was already organising me, spelled disaster.

CHAPTER 54

(An Equine Purchase)

Len was at Tom Pullen's yard, looking at a beautiful horse, and was suitably dressed for the occasion. His attire consisted of a check sports jacket (complete with elbow patches), yellow wasted cords, and a trilby. Finally, as an afterthought, he had bought a pair of very smart brogues, which he had admired many times before on racecourses, but which he felt did not really fit his image.

Now, at last, he felt he was a real owner, and he was rather pleased he had gone to the trouble of dressing up, especially as all the purchases were being financed by Rowena's Institute.

Tom was explaining to Len how important his contribution was to the Injured Jockeys Fund and the Retired Racehorses Fund. Tom assured him that his yard would never destroy a horse whose racing days were over, as long as it was healthy.

"I can't speak for all the yards," said Tom.

Len nodded sagely. Even he was pleased to know that 'his' money was being used to care for an injured jockey or a retired racehorse. He recalled one of Rowena's questions about how he felt when giving something to charity; this was a concept which, to date, had passed him by. To his surprise, he felt really good about it.

"And what about a name?" asked Tom. "Melanie's Eyes, a lovely filly, is about to foal, and with modern technology we can tell if she is going to have a colt. The names we have chosen provisionally are Railroad, after his American sire, and Eyesight after his dam. I'm sure you know we are obliged to maintain the same theme to assist other breeders."

"Oh, I wasn't thinking of waiting two years for a foal to reach racing age," said Len knowledgably.

"I really am so excited about becoming an owner, because I may…"

Len just about stopped himself from saying, "…as I may not be alive."

"Have you any horses which are racing already, but where the name is, well… unsuitable?"

"Well, we have been racing 'Last Few Days' in the yard's colours, because no prospective owners like the name. The problem is that we are getting no contribution towards her keep or training. She's a fine-looking horse, very reliable, with two seconds and a third last season, even with very limited time on the gallops. Come and meet her; she's in the last stall on the left. The trouble is we can't change her name now she is four years old, but if you don't mind…"

"The name's perfect," said Len, a little too enthusiastically.

Len's eyes glazed over as the prospect of winning a classic filled his head.

This was the only time that Len had fallen hopelessly in love, but the object of his affection was chestnut brown, had four legs, a very swishy tail and stood 16 hands high!

"Of course, Mr. Shefford —"

"Call me Len, please."

"Of course, Len. We would not expect the full price. I think 8,000 guineas would be enough, plus the cost of her keep and training for the rest of the flat season, which finishes, as I am sure you know, on 31st of October."

Len really loved being treated like someone who knew all about racing, even though most of his knowledge was limited to brief instructions to on-course bookies. He grimaced at the price, but then he realised he would only have to pay a month's keep and training if Rowena's prediction was correct, and if it wasn't, he would still be alive, and he would disappear as soon as possible with the Institute's cash, leaving Rowena to pick up the bill.

"As you know, Mr. Pullen —"

"Call me Tom, please."

"As you know, Tom, I have never owned a racehorse. Last Few Days is somewhat under-raced. I am happy to give you 1,000 guineas now, but could I leave the remaining £7,000 until after his first race, which I think you suggested will be at Folkestone on 25th of May."

"Absolutely, no problem, Len."

Len shook hands with Tom and signed a form confirming his intention to pay the outstanding £7,000 on the 4th May, assuming the result at Folkestone met the agreed criteria. He confidently completed the formalities, using Rowena's new address, which he had memorised carefully, so as to avoid any suspicion. There was no way he could risk using her name, but he would be well out of the UK by the time Tom Pullen started chasing him for the money.

***

Len walked up and down the street past Long Nu's massage parlour several times. So, if all went to plan, he would still have £7,000 from Rowena's float for his own future plans, but he realised he would need a lot more than that to live in Brazil or Peru, or wherever train-gang member Ronnie had held out for twenty years.

Finally, he decided to approach Long Nu with a proposition.

"Have you had massage with us before?" she asked, with a smile that left Len speechless.

"I have had a massage before, but not here. Your parlour looks so much better, and now I have inherited some money, I thought I would treat myself to something special."

"Well, we do special rate massage for regular customer," said Long Nu.

Len was already distracted by Long Nu's charms, and reckoned several visits would be required before he achieved his desires. He had assumed that she was Chinese, but neatly folded on a table in the corner of the salon was a copy of *The Saigon Daily News (SDN)*. Len was just about informed enough to know the difference between Saigon and Shanghai.

"Ah, you are Vietnamese."

"Yes, but my English very bad, and I want to join family in Brazil. Can you help me? I have money for ticket, but I need visa and form for new girl who is taking over shop next week! I show you her if you are here Monday and you can help her."

Len clearly misheard Long Nu. The possibility of a naked treatment, if he ever got back to London, persuaded him that two weeks in Brazil with Long Nu, followed by an eternity with the new girl was something he couldn't refuse. When she heard him trying to speak Vietnamese for what she thought was her sake, she gave him her special smile and he promptly went down the street to Beach Travel, and bought two tickets to Rio.

CHAPTER 55

(One More Chance)

This time, Conor did not have to listen to the Mekon voice on Hampstead Heath.

These days, apart from his three regulars, whom Conor thought were all well past the age of serious sin, the confessional box was rarely used. Conor thought this was a shame, because, apart from the spiritual benefit of confession, it was also profoundly entertaining.

A blue curtain covered the top half of the box, maintaining the penitent's anonymity, so Conor was surprised to see this was already drawn so soon after the evening Mass. He was tempted to look inside to see if it was a youthful prank. Then he remembered the threat from the mystery voice in the bin.

He went into the box, donned his surplice and waited. To his horror, the first words came from the Mekon.

"I said I would return to complete our business," said the voice.

"I did raise the issue with my sister," Conor replied.

"She said it would be very difficult to get any information from her boss."

"Donald Sheard is having a breakdown," said the voice on the other side of the grill. "Right now, he won't listen to anyone. I'll give you one more chance. I want the information by next Sunday. I will come down on you in a way you won't be expecting, just like your Holy Spirit, only in a much more malevolent form. Do not leave this horrible little box for five minutes; I do not take kindly to being stalked."

The penitent's door clicked open, the blue curtain rustled, and Conor sat perfectly still, covering his face in prayer for a full 10 minutes.

CHAPTER 56

"Death Date Prediction is a Scam"

Jon Heely did not reveal his source. His article was unfinished, leaving *The Sunday Times* reader thirsting for next week's edition.

It was two months since he had met Claire, and had managed to persuade her to give him the background on Sean O'Liam of Fife Life and his relationship to Bridget Hughes-Renton. Claire was still sore about Tom's fatal accident and what she considered to be the gross misuse of the Death Date Gene.

Her relationship with Bridget had not improved. She was torn between accusing her mother of perpetuating what was either an outrageous scam at the Institute, or an unforgivable betrayal of letting her beloved Tom die and herself be seriously injured. If there was any truth to the DDG, surely Bridget could have used her knowledge to warn her own daughter to avoid the traffic in Princes Street that fateful night.

Paradoxically, Claire still maintained some loyalty to her mother, being painfully aware of how dedicated Bridget was to the work of the Institute.

So, Jon started his approach sympathetically. It was a risk asking Claire out to dinner. There was a slight chance that she could report him to the Press Association for stalking her, but he was confident that journalistic charm would win the day. It was a long shot that she would remember him from the Edinburgh train, but the interval between the trip to Scotland and the unplanned visit to Highgate was not too long.

"I was really sorry to hear about the terrible accident in Edinburgh. I guess losing your boyfriend and having your own serious injuries and trauma to heal will take a long time."

The candlelight in the Hampstead restaurant was very dim, and Jon could hardly read Claire's expression. He had noticed, however, that she had clearly gone to some trouble to apply a serious amount of make-up.

"Thank you," she said, smiling.

"Are you going to sue the rider? *The Sunday Times* would willingly help you get some compensation, especially as I believe he was Turkish and it might be difficult with Turkey being outside the EU?"

"Yes, I thought his name was Hurriy Ham-ish. Did he survive?"

"Hurriy Ham-ish? Turkish? No, he was, and regrettably, still is, Hamish McFenn, very definitely Scottish. He lost a leg, but if I hadn't been on life support, he would have lost a lot more body parts than that. Fucking bastard."

Jon didn't know why he was surprised at Claire's bitterness. Was it just Tom's death and her injuries?

"The insurance people are sorting it out. His parents will get a big lump sum, but what's the point? Tom was all they lived for. Their lives are ruined. I'll get about £10,000 for my injuries, assuming there is no lasting damage, but nothing for losing a boyfriend. The court's view is that I'm young enough to meet someone else and resume my studies and my chances of pursuing a good career are unimpaired."

"I'm really sorry to hear that," said Jon, gently.

"I suppose Tom will fade slowly from my memory, although I hate to think he will, but the issue that will always be there is my mother. You know she works for the gene institute, UKAGP?"

Jon nodded, careful not to acknowledge that he was aware of this information. He didn't know how much Bridget had told Claire.

"She's the key figure at the institute, both technically and on a personal basis."

"Personal basis?"

"The head of the institute is a guy called Donald Sheard. He's a nutter, actually he's having a breakdown right now, and doesn't want to publish anything about the project because he doesn't believe in it any more. My mother is still convinced of the whole death date thing and claims she has all the figures to prove it from the UK, from Sweden and from Ghana, though I've never seen them. Mother and Sheard have been an item, at least until he started locking himself in his office, but the only thing he is sleeping with now is the leather armchair! But she still believes in the DDG, and I don't get why she didn't warn me in advance about the accident and to stay well clear of Edinburgh that night. Surely my safety and my boyfriend's life shouldn't be sacrificed for the sake of a sodding dodgy project? The whole thing is crap to me so that makes it even harder to take."

"So, what are you going to do about it?"

"Well, for starters, I'm not keeping quiet about it any longer."

CHAPTER 57

(A Full-Bloodied Row)

Clare was getting very irate with Bridget.

"You are completely unsympathetic to my loss," she screamed. "If your bloody DDG means anything, you could have told me what was going to happen to Tom, and if I mean anything to you, you *should have told me.*"

"It's not like that," shouted Bridget. "The DDG predicts, but we can only be sure it was right after the event…"

"Event! Tom didn't have an event, he died. He was killed. He was fucking killed. He wasn't 'evented'. Anyway, what's the point of it if you can't predict it?

I suppose it's just to enable uncle Sean to make millions, or at least to stop losing millions, because people are dying at the wrong time."

"How do you know about that, Claire?"

"I just do," she said, suddenly impressed with her own composure, and unexpectedly aware of Jon Heely's persistent interest.

"And while we are at it, what about animals? If Wag was run over, could you have predicted his demise? Is the date of his death in one of the secret files?" Wag, the family Jack Russell, hated their arguments. The quarrels between them usually meant he wouldn't get a walk (Claire) or, worse, he wouldn't get his supper (Bridget), and almost certainly, he would be ignored and pushed away if he tried to cuddle up and create a happier atmosphere.

Despite the ongoing fight between mother and daughter, Wag, while dozing in his bed in the kitchen, was also keeping one ear open in case Claire thought a walk with him would be a calming influence, or, hopefully, the possibility of Bridget opening a tin might have the same effect.

He didn't know what 'run over' meant. It didn't sound very nice, but the very fact that he was a topic of conversation encouraged him to jump up in anticipation.

"I'm going to see uncle Conor to see what he thinks about your DDG," Claire said.

"You'll do no such thing; if Conor finds out about it, the project's ruined; he'll tell his bishop, and the church will tell the government. Actually, it's quite dangerous. Priests will be accused of conspiracy and attacked, churches will be burnt and..."

Claire wasn't really listening to Bridget's rant. She had taken Wag's lead off its hook, and Wag, already on his back legs and yapping with delight was pulling on his lead in the direction of Highgate Cemetery.

Claire set off across Hampstead Heath, and Wag, excited by the wide, open space and the range of scents, was beside himself. As she walked across the heath, Claire wondered if she should call Conor first. What do priests do on a Monday? Visit the sick? Teach RE at the local primary? Obviously, she wouldn't call on a Sunday. That would be a no-no, but a Monday? Claire and Wag walked on towards St Augustine's. Wag seemed to know the way. By this time, there was no point in calling Conor, as they were almost there. Claire was almost pulled off the pavement by Wag in his excitement. But why? Then she remembered. She had taken Wag to see uncle Conor at his church a few times before, but not for some time. Conor had made a bit of a fuss of him, given him a few biscuits and tickled his tummy. Actually, Wag was more interested in Conor's musty old clerical suit at the time.

"Claire, how lovely to see you. What a surprise," he beamed, opening the presbytery door.

"Sorry, uncle, I should have called you, but you can blame it on Wag. He pulled me all the way. He seems desperate to see you."

"Well, of course. He's a good Catholic dog! Probably wants to make his confession! All those pies he took at the church picnic last year! Actually, I think it's my old suit, lots of lovely smells. Wait a minute, see how he's sniffing around the sacristy door, and, of course, it's Monday. All the dogs I know love the smell of incense, but only the day after Mass. The scent's too strong for them on a Sunday. Only God knows why. Better let him out though. I don't want him lifting his leg on the pews!"

"Actually, uncle, it is Wag I wanted to talk to you about. You know this project that Mum is involved with, the Death Date Gene? Well, could it possibly apply to...?"

Conor closed his book and listened carefully.

CHAPTER 58

(Bridget Finally Meets Gloria)

Gloria was not impressed by the anonymous grey building which housed the gene institute. She pressed the buzzer marked 'Pregnacare' as directed by Bridget. As Gloria was very definitely not pregnant, she was somewhat embarrassed by this instruction. The door opened automatically and then closed behind her. The building seemed empty, and the wooden floorboards echoed with every step she took. She felt very afraid. Was she about to be abducted again? Whose side was Bridget on? She turned back towards the front door, but it was clearly locked.

Then, ever so quietly, another door opened. Gloria had thought this was just an oak panel. There was still no sound of human movement, though the scuttling of what sounded like a mouse, or, worse still, Gloria's greatest fear, a rat, brought even more terror. Behind the oak-panelled door, and further into the room, she could hear a drawer being closed and locked. Then a clicking noise — it sounded like a weapon.

Finally, a timid voice, hardly audible, broke the silence.

"Gloria?"

"Bridget?"

"Yes."

To her horror, Gloria realised that Bridget was pointing a revolver directly at her head.

"I'm sorry about all these precautions," she said, putting the gun on the table. "Heldon Pontowski will do anything to get the information. That's why you were abducted. I'm so sorry you had to go through all that. I had no way of contacting you."

Bridget appeared to show no remorse for all that Gloria had suffered. She was beginning to regret ever being involved, either in Ghana or in London. However, there seemed to be no alternative. She was under Bridget's control. She had no money and nowhere to live.

Gloria went through the information meticulously, but, having pressured her to 'give her every detail', Bridget seemed to lose interest and appeared more curious about her abduction.

"You were roughed up and drugged by Heldon Pontowski's boys, but could they have taken the stats, copied them and returned them while you were asleep?

"As you say, your clothes were disturbed, and you were asleep for a whole day."

"But I kept the information close to my body the whole time, and I was not assaulted."

Bridget's mood had darkened.

"Let me read the statistics. I think this is a plot."

Gloria pulled out the spreadsheets from her cleavage. Bridget studied them briefly.

"These mean nothing!" she screamed at Gloria. "These are just freak statistics about your Ewe tribe. No-one will believe them. Heldon swapped them with the real ones while you were asleep. Don't kid yourself. His men took the real figures from your so-called 'private hiding place'. Now I get it. You're on his payroll. No wonder you survived. You probably offered his henchman a fondle of those big black breasts while he was there. No wonder you were out of contact for a whole day. He knew you were coming to see me. The only thing he doesn't know is the new address of the institute. But you know, because I ordered the taxi to pick you up. And Heldon doesn't know if the spreadsheets he's pinched is the real thing. So, he can't take a chance and publish it yet. But he must be tracking you. He had your mobile. He'll follow you on GPS.

"Take off all your clothes. I want to make sure you can't be followed. Just wear this jumpsuit."

Bridget ordered another special taxi. She knew the driver well. She ordered him to take Gloria to Epping Forest. She didn't expect to see her again.

CHAPTER 59

(A Surprise Encounter)

Bridget left the Institute by the side door. She was still concerned that Heldon had the Ghanaian stats, but whether they were genuine or not, she couldn't tell. She was convinced, however, that she was being followed, and decided it would be unsafe to go home or stay in the office.

Rowena had long since dismissed the Swedish and Ghanaian data as worthless, and was certain that Bridget was close to a breakdown. Still, Bridget's secret escape from the Institute had not gone unnoticed by Rowena, and this was an opportunity to study Bridget's data again and to establish whether Gloria had brought any new stats from Ghana.

Alas, Bridget had not forgotten to lock her office.

Rowena kicked the door in frustration. Unexpectedly, she heard the lock turning from the inside. 'Oh my God,' she thought. Surely Bridget couldn't have gone around the building and come back, could she? Rowena did not want to face her in her present state on home ground. But the turn of the key was emanating from the adjacent door, *from Donald's office.* She had completely forgotten about Donald, assuming he was living in permanent seclusion in his office, and much though she would like to, there was no way of ascertaining *his* state of mind.

"Who's that?"

Donald's soft Yorkshire tones permeated the connecting door to Bridget's office.

"Donald, it's Rowena."

He said nothing, but slowly unlocked the connecting door.

Expecting to see a depressed, unkempt, scientist slumped over his desk, Rowena was astonished to find a pin-striped suited Donald, apparently dressed for a high-powered meeting.

'Wow,' she thought, 'now I know why I wanted to come and work here in the first place!'

Donald started the conversation before Rowena could think of anything to say.

"Actually, I was hoping you were in; I need to talk to you."

She cursed herself for not having worn anything smarter, but there seemed little point in these last few weeks, with nothing to do in the office except to wait for Bridget to provide more meaningless statistics.

Donald got straight to the point.

"I was due to hold a press conference tonight, but now you are here, I will postpone it till tomorrow.

"I think you and I would work well together; we have the same views. My intention is to come clean on DDG and start a new project, and I want you to be my partner in this exercise. There is no point in talking to Bridget, as she has very different opinions. We can discuss it over dinner tonight; just the two of us."

"But I only have my lab coat and my working clothes."

"You look great just as you are, but if you want to go home first, I would be even more impressed. I will book a table at Hervey's in Covent Garden. Do you know it? Is seven o'clock okay?"

Rowena was bowled over. Just when she was going to have to destroy her own career prospects by 'going public on DDG', the object of her desire appears, transformed and available. In her excitement, she forgot Donald was still married to Marion.

Hervey's turned out to be a discreet, but small, restaurant in a quiet corner, close to the Royal Opera House. It was full and classy and with lots of couples. Were they all having affairs or cryptic business deals? In her case, she hoped it was a bit of both.

CHAPTER 60

(A Fishy Revelation)

"I know that you have long realised that the DDG is a fake. Bridget has manipulated the figures, and even poor Gloria, about whom I am very worried, has been bullied to create a genealogical matrix, and has expressed her doubts. There is no possibility of predicting an EXACT date of death."

Donald had ordered turbot, and Rowena, a fish lover, thought she shouldn't follow sheepishly on what she hoped would be the first of many classy dinners, and so opted for halibut. As she scanned the room, she made a mental note to see if her dress sense was up to scratch. The men all looked casually smart, wearing open necked shirts from Jermyn Street, with really severe jeans. Only Donald had maintained a three-piece suit and tie, for the press conference, she supposed. The women were all remarkably tall. Many seemed to be lawyers, but she was pleased that her business suit had not gone unnoticed by the other female diners.

All this activity had distracted her, with her mind wandering to tomorrow's press conference. She must listen carefully to Donald, in case she was challenged as to why she had accepted a job at the unit, and whether she had ever believed the statistics.

"You can a have pretty good stab at it..." Did he mean the fish or the stats? "But life expectancy will only give Sean a 'best-guess' solution. He wants something much more accurate."

Oh God, Sean. She didn't know anything about actuaries. What happens if someone questions her tomorrow? In that moment, she reached the most succulent part of the fish.

"You won't need to answer any of the journos because they know the basics from the press release."

All thoughts of challenging questions were quickly dismissed by the prospect of working with Donald on a new project.

CHAPTER 61

(Criminal Minds)

"Twelve months," said the judge.

I nearly fainted.

"You'll be out in six," my counsel said. "That's the norm for ghosting. I'll try and get you into Ford, but I can't promise. Ford is usually the preferred destination for white collar crimes. Nice countryside. Not too far from London. I was at school right next door. I know it well," he said cheerfully.

"You can more or less come and go as you please. But they have tightened up following the riot in 2009. You really DO need to be on your best behaviour when you go before the assessment panel. You absolutely DON'T WANT to go to Wandsworth or Brixton or The Scrubs. Decent crowd in Ford. Still got a few clients there. I'll pop in when I next come and see old Mitch Coslove, though he, of course, is not white collar, or blue collar. No collar at all, actually. Strangled his bird's lover. Why did he go to Ford? Well, I found some *very* extenuating circumstances. Still got eight years, out in five. Will be out next year, actually."

I couldn't believe it. After four months on bail I was expecting six months at the most; suspended, I'd hoped. And now my first year will be with a strangler and then there's still the GBH boys. Starsteiner, my very eminent counsel, seemed to know them all.

No mention of drug gangs, thank God; at least not yet.

Starsteiner continued, "Still, there's a chance of a job when you get out; you'll find some very useful contacts. Callington-Royal (not his real name, of course) built up a lovely business. It's a franchise, of course, covers most of the UK's 'hotels' but strictly 'honest' blue collar lags are on the payroll; no pervs or murderers. Can't tell you more, but next time you take some money out of a cash machine - oh, God, sorry, I guess you won't be seeing one of those for a while, every cash machine that is pre-2008 is rather different..."

I was really shocked. Starsteiner was meant to be helping me reduce my sentence; instead, he was leading me straight back into a life of crime! No, I mustn't use that word. I'm just an actuary, an officer of a life assurance company doing my best to restore the fortunes of the company, which my predecessors had done their best to destroy. I never got to actually use the DDG. They were just sample exercises.

True, stealing (I prefer substituting) that Lancashire woman's identity was a bit chancey, but she wasn't going to be needing it again, and poor Hurriyet would have had to go all the way back to Turkey. Fancy the judge saying, "The law takes a very serious view of identity theft, whoever the recipient is."

He wouldn't have thought that if he'd seen her. I should have had her called as a witness. Poor Hurriyet. I wonder if she'll come and see me down in Ford.

Starsteiner woke me from a very nice dream.

"Be on time and well dressed for the panel. Ten o'clock on the 16th, 3 Longmire Court, off Chancery Lane."

CHAPTER 62

(Home Again?)

Len continued to behave as disgracefully as he had throughout his life, but he was pleased he had persuaded Long Nu to come with him to Brazil. She was sweet and accommodating and amazingly tolerant of his prolonged drinking bouts. Her English was poor and her Portuguese non-existent, so she felt increasingly lonely. Len would take her along to the bars along the Copacabana as a trophy. She was pretty and always smiling and it occurred to him he might be able to sell her on. She kept their flat meticulously clean and Len was proud to show how well maintained it was.

He was well aware that the other customers in the bar lived in squalor, with women whose principal purpose was very definitely not housework! Long Nu should therefore be a prized possession… if only she could say more than a few words in English.

Len was not intentionally unkind to Long Nu, but he never spent more than the basic necessities on food, and his western burger-orientated diet did not suit her. She also needed new clothes and essentials like cosmetics and washing powder, areas of domestic life which were unknown to Len.

He was, however, rapidly running out of money. Two simply could not eat as cheaply as one, even if the one only had the appetite of a sparrow, and especially if the other's principal diet was liquid. Rowena's unintended gift would just about pay for two flights back to London. Tempted though he was to leave Long Nu to the mercy of a Brazilian bartender, for once in his life, he couldn't bring himself to abandon a woman to her likely fate.

Would Long Nu get her old job back in the massage parlour? How long would he have to look after her before she got paid? Could she claim benefits?

In his usual manner, Len had tried to get much cheaper flights than the direct transatlantic ones to London. The unscrupulous travel agent had persuaded him he could save $1000 per head if he took a local flight from Rio to Marechal Rondon airport, deep in Amazonia. Len was not aware that this remote airport did not have a good safety record, with four incidents over several years causing over 50 fatalities. TAM, the Brazilian operator, used only small planes to cover this vast country, but despite Long Nu's concern, Len booked two seats on the earliest possible flight.

It wasn't long before Long Nu started to feel quite unwell. And even Len felt pretty queasy. The plane rocked from side to side, and the single stewardess gave them oxygen masks which made Len feel even worse. He looked out of the window and all he could see was hundreds of miles of jungle.

Len asked for a prayer book, but it was only in Portuguese. Long Nu twisted her hands into knots which Len assumed was her version of prayer.

The plane lurched violently and started to fall sharply. Worst of all, two unkempt-looking men came out of the cockpit and started threatening passengers to hand over their parachutes. The plane was clearly flying without any human assistance. It was 27th May.

CHAPTER 63

(Life Behind Bars)

I had been behind bars for only three weeks. So far, the other Ford residents had been most courteous, apart from asking for the occasional cigarette. As I have spent a large part of my life estimating how long people who smoke are going to live, it will not come as a surprise that this is a vice which I have studiously avoided.

My two cellmates are clearly white-collar and we spend our time swapping anecdotes about football, rugby and cricket, and exchanging books. We never discuss our 'crimes' and we never use that expression. I only discovered the correct description when there was a bit of a disturbance (never 'riot' or 'trouble') in D Block, and John (we only use first names) pointed out the very sick-looking culprit in the exercise yard the next day.

"Avoid that man at all costs. He fully deserves his detention and he gives this place a bad name."

I nodded and thought no more of it. A few months later, a young man of about 22 approached me in the yard. He was very polite and asked me how long I was likely to be 'staying'. The use of expressions which would be more commonplace in a hotel is quite usual. Indeed, there is a whole language to be learnt before you can really engage properly in a prison conversation. However, this was one sentence with which I was familiar. I also knew the correct answer.

"I'm told they will be tidying my room in three weeks." This is cell-speak for my expected date of release.

John told me later that I should never have said anything, but I was aware that there were a lot of 'trading places' if releases were imminent.

"Good luck," said the young man, and I thought no more of it.

A few days before my release, the lad approached me again. I thought he was going to ask me to carry out some type of drug switch and I was quite prepared to give him an emphatic NO.

"My cellmate is very ill," he said. "They won't let him have any medication. The screws say there is no point. He is going to die very soon, anyway. They just let him have the minimum of morphine. I'm told you have access to a drug, DDG, I believe it is called, which can predict the exact date of an individual's death."

This should have been a warning to me. Apart from providing custody for white-collar criminals, Ford also incarcerates a few dangerous men coming to the end of their term. Clearly, this man was in the latter category.

I was shocked. Who is this man? What use could DDG be to him? Why should I incriminate myself by dealing with the criminal underworld? But I had to admit I was curious. With no further information forthcoming from Bridget and Donald, apparently having abandoned the project, I needed something, anything, to restore my reputation. But surely, even though I didn't have access to the DDG (Bridget had never let me keep any of the notorious pharmaceuticals), I could take an inspired guess at the death date of this terminally sick man, give him a 'carotene special' and attribute the predicted date to *our* drug. No-one would ever know. I have no idea why I suddenly felt any proprietorial affection for DDG after all the trouble it had caused me, but I did.

So, toss a coin. May or June? June, okay, 1st to 15th or 16th to 30th? Okay, 1st to 15th? What do I do now? Go on tossing? Let's be more scientific. Date of my release? No, someone might make a connection. I know. My birthday! It's the 2nd June. Bingo. Solved! Medicine by numbers!

"I really don't think I can help you," I said to the sick man's messenger.

"Please," he begged. "I don't think he will live another couple of days."

"Just two days?"

"Well, that's what the MO says."

I was tempted. While he was alive, I could backdate the projection to maybe a year ago. He would need to be strong enough to sign his name and fill in the actual date he signed and his predicted date of death.

So, I agreed, and later that afternoon, armed with two mugs of 'carotene special' (chopped up carrots and virgin olive oil, heated until the carrots dissolved), I called the messenger (Jason was his name, I discovered) and delivered it to a far corner of the prison.

"What's his name, Jason?"

"Heldon... Heldon Pontowsky."

I froze. I had never met Heldon but I had heard about him from

Bridget. He was the nasty piece of work who was the promoter of all things selfish, the serial rapist, the hater of all charities and religions. No wonder he was ill. Every woman must have wished him dead and every faith on Earth must have prayed for his demise. Nevertheless, it was a shock to see him. Apart from his lack of respect for mankind in general, he had clearly not taken much care of his own body.

Every space on his grossly obese flesh was covered in tattoos. Some of these had clearly gone septic. I could hardly bear to look at the rainbow of colours across his inflated stomach, down his arms and around his neck. Obscenities preceded the name of every judge or politician who had crossed him, every woman who had rejected him, every cleric who had condemned him and members of his own family, particularly his own mother, for whom he had reserved particular words of hatred on every limb.

He distrusted doctors and had instructed the faithful Jason to scrawl down his back with a needle, which had clearly never been sterilised: "I'm going to live longer than all of you. Just wait and see." Well the odds were clearly against that now.

Heldon signed, but he was beginning to smell like a corpse already. I gave Jason the two mugs, saw him administer them and left as quickly as possible before Heldon turned orange all over.

***

Only two days to go before I am a free man. Curiously, I had heard nothing about Heldon's demise, but I was approached several times in the yard with enquires about the 'life' drugs. Tea-stained aspirin was not the most obvious placebo, and I struggled with creating the exact replica each time.

My guess was that these younger men were all Heldon's acolytes. These guys also appeared to be heading for an early grave, judging by the look of them. They were trying to work out who was the next to die after Pentowsky, but they couldn't manage it. There was a lot of competition to live the longest, but I was in no mood to supply DDG even though I knew the medicine on which I had based it was completely fake. I could only imagine it would all finish in a huge fight between a group of very sick young men.

In that case, the DDG was doing a great service to humanity. I was the happiest man alive when they finally let me out.

CHAPTER 64

(Rowena's Doubts)

Rowena didn't have to check her notes. She knew that the 27th May was exactly the forecast date for Len to die. Curiously, his letter, confirming he had completed all the tasks she had set him, together with the completed schedule, had arrived three days before. So, had Len been convinced that the death date gene was genuine, and there was nothing he could do about it? Or was it sheer bravado to travel with a dodgy airline from the least safe airport in the country on his proscribed date of death?

Had he told Long Nu?

Was he playing roulette with her life as well?

The really weird thing was that Rowena didn't actually remember telling Len the date. The purpose of the exercise was to demonstrate to herself that the DDG predictions were a myth. Now Len had shortened the odds by taking all these additional risks. Was Len being funded by some other source? She knew Len had bought a horse and only paid the first £1,000. Len had also agreed to let her have Last Few Days, or the £7,000 balance, if, by chance, 'something happened to him,' Tom Pullen had a copy of these notes. As it was her money anyway, she was not too upset. Len had not been allowed to touch the 'fetlock fund' until after 27th May.

Tom called her later to ask if she had heard about the crash, and whether there were any survivors. As far as she knew, there were none, she told him. Unaware of their relationship, Tom expressed his condolences. It was as much as Rowena could do to stop laughing, until she remembered that poor Long Nu must have perished as well as Len.

She genuinely hoped that the end was not too unpleasant for either of them.

CHAPTER 65

(Dogs Know When Their Days Are Over)

"Well, Claire, when your mother and I were children, we had another Jack Russell — Wag's grandfather, actually. Like Wag, he was a very intelligent dog. He had incredible hearing and he could detect the engine noise of our father's car from about 400 metres, so he was ready to welcome him home with a ball or a slipper when he came through the front door.

"Father named him Dig, because despite our efforts to restrict his territory with elaborate fencing all round our garden, which was sunk over a metre below the soil, he was always able to escape!

"Now, we had another dog, an Irish terrier (what else!), called Kelly. Dig and Kelly were devoted to each other, but as Kelly got older, he became quite sick. Actually, he had a tumour, which was very sad. He must have been in some pain, and Dad should have taken the vet's advice to have him put down. So, Kelly had to go to the vet quite often, and Dig would always be waiting for him. Eventually, Kelly seemed to get better, and we were all very happy.

"Then, Kelly's tumour got worse and we made the awful decision to have him put down. We took him to the vet, and we left Dig in the house with all the doors and windows shut. When we came home, there was no sign of Dig. Somehow, he had got out and we found him in the garden, digging a huge hole (Irish terriers are one and a half times the size of a Jack Russell) exactly where we had planned to bury Kelly.

"Dad tried to stop him digging, but Dig wouldn't let him; he even snapped at Dad, which he had never done before. Eventually, he escaped from the garden. Two days later, we found him; he had been run over on the North Circular."

Claire was in tears, and even Conor's eyes misted over. Unbelievably, Wag jumped up onto Conor's lap, and let out a single bark.

"So, dogs can read the future through their sense of smell, which is 50 times stronger than our own, but, no, Claire, only God knows our date of death."

CHAPTER 66

(Happy to Be Home)

Hurriyet was happy to be back in London. I had found her a very small flat in a rather poor area. To her credit, she had found herself a job. Her English had improved, but only marginally. However, the thousands of migrants, against whom she was competing for employment, had even poorer English language skills than her, so she got the job.

The Parks Department of the London Borough of Camden might not be the start of an especially promising career, but physical though it was, sweeping leaves was cathartic. She had no idea what that meant, but she hoped that they would allow her to drive the council sweeper. The sweeper was a much more efficient method and allowed time for short breaks in the warm autumn sunshine.

But Hurriyet soon reached her boredom threshold. Park-keeping was no substitute for a job paying hard cash, even though I charged her minimal rent for accommodation. And one day, her burgeoning career in the Parks Department came to an abrupt end. She was keen to show off the performance of her powerful mower/leaf sweeper, but faced competition from a young Lebanese man, who was more interested in collecting Hurriyet than leaves. He took a corner too sharply, catching the front of Hurriy's Stiga Park 340, and caused enough damage to cost a month's wages for each driver. End of two careers.

Hurriy was quick to bounce back from her dismissal. Somehow, she had found her way to Ford, having, even more surprisingly, discovered the date of my release. My wife, Clodagh, had served papers for divorce by special messenger while I was in prison, and had obtained an injunction for me not to return to the family home, barring an agreed date sometime in the future. I had nowhere to go except for the tiny flat I was renting to Hurriyet.

I was therefore more than pleased to see her.

We took a taxi to Barnham Junction (conveniently close to Ford), where we waited patiently for the London train. I hadn't really noticed that winter had arrived while I had been inside. Clothes for 'leavers' were provided by the prison, but they were of such poor quality that I must have looked like a criminal to all the other waiting passengers.

Hurriy was unexpectedly sympathetic, asking me about the conditions in the prison, and how I got on with my cellmates. As she had asked me similar questions in the taxi, and was not normally inquisitive, I began to smell a rat. Note: Sean hates all rats and mice.

"Seanie," she said, "I have something to tell you. I am having baby. How you say in English? I am up duff. I have been gone six months. You will be Daddy again soon! Is very exciting for us, yes? Anyway, who is 'duff'?"

I thought this was just one of Hurriyet's games. After all, I had been in prison for three months and I hadn't seen her for seven months before that. It was impossible, but looking at her, she did look as though she had at least put on some weight. This was clearly a con, but I had learnt to be very careful before jumping in and accusing her of sleeping with some stranger.

"So, when is the baby due? You don't look six months pregnant. You would be huge by now. And it couldn't be mine."

"I not sure when. I need to see Turkish doctor! So, English baby takes nine months? Yes? But in Turkey, baby take 15 months, especially as he is a boy."

"Fifteen months! Don't be ridiculous! You must be having a foal, not a baby," I quipped. "Besides, you shouldn't have been racing mowing machines, if you are that pregnant."

"So baby is yours, because you care if he gets hurt!" she retorted. "Also, our baby is not fo-oal. He will be very clever. You accountant, me Turkish. Perfect mix."

This was not going very well.

"How do you know it's a boy?" I asked tentatively.

"When I went to shop, I take the test and the bottle turns blue, so I know. Blue for a boy, okay. Maybe you not so clever accountant after all!"

"The blue could mean you're pregnant, though it's not a very reliable indicator, and it certainly won't tell you the sex of your baby. Otherwise every baby would be a boy. Anyway, I can't be the father."

"You are telling me I have slept with other man. Never. I never sleep with other man since you. Somehow, maybe I am having Turkish 15-month baby, so I am not big yet, but he will be very big Turkish man one day…"

At this point, much to the disappointment of the listening passengers, she collapsed in tears on my lap. I felt like doing the same.

We got to East Croydon before she said anything else. This time, she whispered, "Who is duff?"

I had had a little time to think about it by now, though I wasn't sure I was right. "Duff is not a man, but a pudding. It's a flour pudding boiled or steamed in a cloth bag. It could be the shape of a woman's belly when pregnant. It could also be like a dumpling. Sometimes, a pregnant woman is known as being in the pudding club."

She whispered again, "I'm not pudding or dumpling, am I, Seanie? I'm not having baby. I just live quietly with you, okay?"

"Okay." This time it was my turn to whisper.

CHAPTER 67

(Side Effects)

I had only enjoyed my freedom for a few days when there was a knock on the door of the flat. How criminals track you down, I just don't know, but there he was...*Jason.*

"Heldon wants to see you."

"Heldon? I'm surprised the old bastard is still alive!"

"Oh, he's alive alright, but he looks very different. He wants more carotene cocktail, but he's worried about the side effects."

"Side effects? What side effects?"

"He wants to meet you."

"Oh, no. Not bloody likely."

"I thought you'd say no, so I took a photo of him. As you can see, the carotene cocktail has created a uniform brown colour. No bright orange any more, but a huge growth of hair all over his left cheek right up to just under his left eye and across to his ears and back down under his chin. Just half a beard, as you can see. The rest has no hair at all, just smooth brown skin. He wants a full beard of course, but he just can't get it. He's taken several litres of carotene cocktail, but all to no avail."

"Several litres? That stuff costs a fortune. How did he get hold of so much?"

"I don't know, but he dips his half-beard in it, and rubs it on his right side, but it's still completely smooth. He thinks you've conned him!"

"I'm not getting involved with the criminal underworld any more, and if I were you, Jason, I'd finish with Heldon immediately."

"As it happens, I am due for release tomorrow. I am straight off to Spain, where I come from. By the way, I have never touched a drop of that cocktail. It smells disgusting!"

"Jason, one favour, please. I would like a phial of the undiluted Beta Carotene, just for laboratory purposes."

"Sure thing, Sean, I'll drop it in tomorrow."

'At last,' I thought, 'I can get some real pharmaceutical evidence about the Death Date Gene. I wonder if that bright new chemist, Rowena, is still working with either Donald or Bridget. She must know if it's for real or not.'

CHAPTER 68

(Jon Heeley's Lucky Break)

Jon Heeley knew the DDG story would break sooner or later. Press rumours had quietened down, and neither the government nor the Catholic Church felt it was necessary to make any further announcements.

A freelance journalist does not earn a lot of money, and since the new press regulations had been introduced, speculative stories were hard to come by. Jon was waiting his turn at his regular hairdressers, Salvi's, and found himself thumbing through a recent copy of *The Secular Post*. His eye drifted across to the Canadian bishop story. Surely it couldn't be true?

"Hey, Salvi, where did you get this rubbish from?"

"Some guy came in for a cut this morning. Said his boss had taken some funny potion and one side of his face had hair like a forest and the other completely smooth. He said his boss desperately wanted to have hair all over his face, and he wanted me to rub it in. He had tried but it had no effect. I said, "Send him to me, I can sort that out." "No, no!" he shouted. He has a disease and he smells like a rotting corpse. You must not go near him. He was clearly very distressed. He threw the mag on the pile and rushed out without paying, but with only one half of his head shaved to a number one."

Jon was fascinated.

"Salvi, can I take this mag home?"

"Sure you can, Jon. Funny thing, I was tidying the pile of mags and I noticed a 'Property of Ford Prison' label on the back. That's miles away, in Sussex, isn't it?"

"It sure is, which makes it all the more interesting, Salvi. Let me pay you for the half bald man's cut as well as mine. I'll keep in touch, but if he comes back for the other half of his head, tell him I'll pay him good money for any information about the potion."

"Some chance of that, guv, but thanks anyway."

CHAPTER 69

(Going Viral)

Donald had always let Bridget do the talking when it came to telling things to the press. She had always been very good at fending off difficult questions. He kept a low profile at these events; so much so that journalists often did not recognise him as the CEO of the UKAGP. On several occasions, he would surreptitiously leave the building before the journalists could identify him.

This time was different. Smartly dressed and with a chic-looking Rowena by his side, he positively boomed into his microphone: "The DDG is dead. There is no evidence that this drug, or its liquid alternative can enable the user or, if you prefer, the consumer, or, indeed, his or her physician, to predict the exact date of death of the individual taking it."

CHAPTER 70

(Journalists Everywhere)

There was complete silence from the 20 or so assembled journalists. Eventually, Lindsay Zells, the Health and Beauty Editor from *The Daily Mail* spoke up.

"Is that it? No explanation? No apology to those thousands of people who took DDG271 and who were under the illusion that they had five years or three months to live and who planned the rest of their lives accordingly? It's outrageous. You should be in prison for fraud, for misrepresentation, for everything."

She was apoplectic. How many *Daily Mail* readers had taken this drug? This must be the scandal of the decade, and *The Mail* will champion the poor innocents who have taken the pill in good faith. If only that idiot, Bonner Caldy (Editor of Social Affairs) would pick up his phone, she could get the okay for the first edition and she, Lindsay Zells, would get all the plaudits, while those other journos, still hanging around in the basement of the George the Third, trying to get signal, would be left miles behind.

'Journalist of the Year'; she could see it now. She would step over Callum from *The Express*, Jeremy from *The Times*, Gavyn (with a y) that pompous prick from *The Telegraph* and even Lister ("How do you spell that pill, dear?") from *The Sun*. Oh, yes, here I am, star of the show at the Press Association awards. I'll wear that really tight green sparkly dress and there'll be 'oohs' and 'aahs' all over the hall.

Unfortunately, Lindsay hadn't waited for the next question from the man at *The Financial Times*.

"How much has it cost the taxpayer to fund the gene institute to develop the DDG?" and "How many pills have you had manufactured, and how many drugs have you actually sold?"

"We have only manufactured 10 prototypes. No member of the public has swallowed a single pill or drunk any of the liquid equivalent."

Perversely, Donald was becoming increasingly proud of this classic non-achievement.

Finally, he said, "We have not earned a single penny from this exercise."

Meanwhile, Lindsay was desperately trying to hail a taxi to Notting Hill Gate. None seemed to want to stop, and it was beginning to rain. She was looking for her Uber priority number when a rather attractive young man, who had followed her out of the George the Third, got their first. It was Jon Heeley.

"Share it?" said Jon.

"Do you mean the taxi or the story? No way am I going to share either."

"Then your editor is going to be sadly disappointed."

Jon played back the recording of Donald's admission.

"You will see there is no scandal. No-one has lost money; no-one has taken any dangerous drugs; and the UKAGP is in the clear."

"Play it again. How do you know who I am and where I'm going?"

"Come on, Lindsay. You're not exactly unknown in the tabloid world. I don't have the connection with *The Mail* that you have."

"I recognise you. You're Jon..Jon Heeley. You wrote that expose about the fake healer of the blind in Turkey. Brilliant story; I loved it."

"Thanks. Now listen. There is a story, but it's not this one. I am prepared to trust you, because only *The Mail* would be prepared to run with it. The villain is not Donald; it's Bridget Hughes-Renton, his partner. She's still a believer in the DDG, and she won't give up, just because Donald Sheard has gone viral."

"How do you know all this?"

"Because Claire Hughes-Renton, her daughter, is my girlfriend. Claire was engaged to a guy called Tom. They were both at Edinburgh University when he was killed in a road accident and Claire was badly injured. Her mother convinced her that she was spared because she had not reached her death date, but Tom had reached his. Claire was so badly hurt, and her grief so deep, that she accepted that explanation."

Lindsay was distracted. 'Pity about the girlfriend,' she thought. 'I could happily work with Jon.'

"Olay, so what do you want me to do?"

"Just wait. Obviously, there is a story about Donald's disclosure, but it will be over in a few days as nobody got sick or lost money. Like you and most journalists at the George the Third, I believed Sheard was going to make some incredible claims for the DDG. Lindsay, you were absolutely right with your indignation at his bland statement, but only he would have known they had never really got started. The FT guy got straight to the point.

I have to say, I've saved you a lot of embarrassment, but I am giving you an opportunity to share in this story because I think you are a great journalist with a history of punchy stories. *The Mail* would never accept them from me."

"I must tell Claire that Donald has informed the world that the DDG is a fake. I don't know what her reaction will be, but I thought the sharp reporters would go looking for Bridget whatever he said, as she wasn't at the press conference. I thought it would be safer if Claire wasn't there when they went sniffing around her mother's house, so she's safely installed in my flat. It'll take me a few days to get Claire's reaction and to see what Bridget is going to do. I suggest we meet next week, say Thursday. Do you know The Fair Brother pub in Highgate? How would two o'clock suit you?"

"If I've got to go all the way up there, you better be waiting. I find men are *so* unreliable, especially journos. Always some excuse, and it's usually they've just spent too long over lunch. Here's my number, and if there's any change in the arrangements, let me know — at once."

Jon had never met a woman reporter quite as tough as Lindsay, and he didn't know quite how to handle her.

"Yes, of course," he said sheepishly.

CHAPTER 71

(Second Confession)

Conor recognised him at once. These days, he didn't hear many confessions, let alone from a professional-looking man who was confessing for a second time in three months. This was going to be difficult. Conor vividly remembered the first time, but each sin demanded separate repentance and required individual absolution. In the case of adultery, it was acceptable to say 'many times', although he was never too sure whether he could give one absolution if the penitent could say 'with many women' or 'with many men'. Was it incumbent of him to ask 'how many?', and should that affect the severity of the penance?

This case was unique. Conor remembered how the penitent described how he had developed a drug which could predict the exact day on which an individual would die, and the impact that would have on society. He recalled the license this would give a gullible person to sin, whether that would be by murder, hate, dishonesty, deception, calumny, fornication and every conceivable commandment in *The Bible* and many more besides, yet be able to confess the day before death and go to one's Maker with a completely clean slate.

Of course, Conor didn't believe it, so there was no reason to give him absolution. But it did remind him of the speculation in the newspapers and the rather scurrilous articles this provoked. It also prompted him to undertake the meeting he had with Bridget, and, more recently, the chat he enjoyed with Claire, and the stories about Wag the dog and his parents.

So, he wondered whether there was a connection with Bridget. It seemed too much of a coincidence. Was he coming back to tell him that someone had been prescribed the drug, and had then actually taken it? Perhaps he had been given the date and had decided to seek revenge while he was still alive, then had actually committed a murder and died himself, incriminating the penitent as an accessory. It all seemed too far-fetched.

"Father, do you remember my asking your forgiveness for developing a drug which foretold the date of an individual's death? I think I left some identity, my initials, DS, in case I should return for further advice in the secrecy of the confessional, and because someone we both know might well try to extract details of our discussion."

"I do, indeed, and I still record the initials you left with me, but I should tell you that it is only God who can forgive your sins, assuming you have committed any, which based on our earlier conversation, you had not, at that time. However, even if you are now telling me that the drug has been issued, I can no longer help you. Through other channels, I can see that you have been working on the same project as my sister, Bridget. I have implored her to desist from the development and distribution of the Death Date Gene, and I can only make the same plea to you. Remember, I am only God's carrier pigeon, and sometimes the holy wind takes me into areas in which I have no business."

"You are Bridget's brother? I had no idea. Then you *must* help me. Father, you must hear me out. I have today held a press conference at which I have declared the DDG to be fake. I confirmed the UKAKHG have only produced prototypes, and never sold or even manufactured this drug for consumption.

"Bridget is in serious trouble. Not only is she still convinced that the DDG is genuine, but she is being pursued by a criminal called Heldon Pontowski, who wants to demonstrate that all religions are rubbish, that mankind is intrinsically selfish, and that any evil should be encouraged. Bridget is scared of Pontowski, and might be prepared to consent to using the DDG to protect herself. You have probably never heard of it, Father, but his ideas are published regularly in a trash magazine called *The Secular Post*."

"*The Secular Post*? Oh, yes, I know it, although I've never read it. The church follows it with great interest. Some of it is obvious rubbish, of course, but some of it is vicious and dangerous."

Conor was shocked. It was cold and silent in the church, but the cleaners were due in with their hoovers shortly. The church flower lady would also be in soon.

"And you? Are you in danger too? This is surely a matter for the police. I don't think I am bound by the confidentiality of the confessional in your case, so I think I can pass this information to them. We must move quickly.

Although Bridget and I don't agree on many moral issues, she is my sister after all, and I must protect her from this evil man. I think we should retire to the presbytery, and you can stay with me for a few days until your revelations about the DDG settle down. And, by the way, what is your name?"

"No Father, I don't want you to put yourself at risk by knowing my name or going to the police. Just call me DS, but yes, I will accept your offer to stay in the presbytery for a few days until I hear from Bridget, and no, she won't know I am staying with you."

"It's the last place she'd think of looking," said Conor.

CHAPTER 72

(Fife and Wife)

After a few weeks, I was just beginning to get my life back, when the phone rang. "Who on earth rings at this hour?" It was quarter past seven. A sense of foreboding came over me. It was Phil Jewell, Fife's erstwhile company secretary and now main board director.

As I had been disqualified from holding the office of director or company secretary (I had taken on Phil's role just in time for prison), I had really lost interest in what was happening in financial markets. Phil had made no attempt to visit me while I was doing time for Her Majesty and I was planning a new career.

"It's good to talk to you again, Sean. How are you? I suppose I shouldn't say 'How was Ford?' Listen, I've got some good news for you. Those gilts you bought in a brave but vain attempt to match our smokers' lives didn't suit us, but are just right for Shetlork Life. Apparently, the locals live much longer in the Northern Isles. Shetlork really need those maturities and, of course, the Bank of England aren't issuing any more. There aren't that many in institutional hands, and once old Callum checked the register and saw Fife Life still held £20 million, bingo, he was on the phone like a salmon in spring. Of course, he knows our problems, so I had to settle on a sliding scale of 1% per annum discount for every year to redemption."

"So, it's a Win-Win. Good for the annuitants, good for Shetlork… and… erm, good for you."

"Yes, and you, Sean."

"Come off it, Phil, have you forgotten what part of Sussex I've been sleeping in for the last eight months? A prison record disqualifies me from holding any financial office for 10 years. So, I don't benefit from being an officer at Fife Life."

"Yes, but you didn't go inside for any financial offence, just for stealing the identity of the deceased lady from Lancashire! I mean, I say 'just', it certainly wasn't a good career move."

"Oh my god, Phil, I am even more stupid than I thought. Mark you," I said, looking across the room at the lovely Hurriyet cuddled up with the pillows. "She was worth it."

"So, what is the smokers' lottery going to pay me?"

"Can't be sure yet, but I think about £1.5 million!"

"I think it would make a nice Christening present. This time, baby is real, and you ARE the Daddy and I think we have wedding too. So, I am really Fife Wife." The voice came from deep beneath the pillows.

"Oh, yes, and we call the baby Angus. That's next to Fife. See, I know Scotland better than Turkey soon."

CHAPTER 73

(The Legacy)

Rowena was not pleased. She had read every national newspaper over and over again. They all said similar things:

Top Geneticist Apologises. It's A Fake.
We Invented Death Date Claim, Says Pill Man.
Nobody Took The Pill; You Really Can't Tell Death Date After All.

'But where is he hiding out? He's not at home with his family; he's not in his flat in Pimlico; and the Institute is all closed up,' she thought. Obviously, this new drug which he had promised her they would work together on was also a sham. He had cheated on his wife, he had gone public on the DDG without consulting Bridget, and he had lied about the new drug. 'This man is not to be trusted,' she thought.

She was on her way home, having collected a bundle of notes and calculations from the Institute. She hadn't expected to find him or Bridget there, but fortunately, she still had her key and password. There were a few reporters outside, but as she had dressed like a cleaner, that is exactly what the press assumed she was. The man from *The Sun* asked her if she knew where the scientists were, and she replied in a strong cockney accent that she had just cleaned and that the building had been empty for months.

She found a used Tesco bag, roughed it up a bit, put her paperwork inside and covered it with some brushes, rags and dusters. The ruse worked and the bored young men outside didn't enquire.

When Rowena got home, she sorted her own notes from the calculations which she had copied from Bridget, just in case she decided to write a book about what Lindsay, *The Daily Mail* reporter, had called 'The Scam of the Decade'.

Thinking about it more deeply, where was *The Daily Mail*? This was right up Lindsay's street, but she had scanned every edition since Donald's revelation, and there was no mention of it. Rowena wondered if Lindsay might be interested in the twist in the story with Lecherous Len, dying on the due date in an Amazon plane crash.

She had reached the bottom of the bag, where she found a crumpled note which she realised was from Donald.

"I have not deserted you, Rowena, but I have had to lie low for a bit. If I get through this, and Pentowski and his boys don't get me, I want you to take this forward. As a qualified pharmacist, you will know about Alzanifil, which I developed, and which is now being tested by the FDA in the States. Hopefully, I will survive, and we can work on Alzanifil together, but, if not, take these papers to Professor Kamaratchan at Princeton and you will have a dazzling career, and many horrible diseases will be prevented. This is the drug we discussed over dinner. Keep the information away from *all* prying eyes. After 22nd June I will be safe. Until then, my darling, I shall think of you each day, and look forward to our future projects together."

Rowena was not convinced. It was 'my darling' which made her want to puke. She knew she could never trust him. She shredded the note into infinitesimally small pieces. 'As far as I'm concerned,' she thought, 'you can lie low, very low, forever.'

CHAPTER 74

(Bridget by Bike)

Bridget was alone in her house in Highgate. She had turned off all the lights and drawn the blinds. She could hear the press camped in the road outside, chatting to each other. Cigarette smoke still managed to seep through the windows. In the morning she knew she would have to run the gauntlet of the reporters and photographers, but she was already thinking ahead to the meeting with Donald. For once, she felt quite comforted by the thought of Conor acting as referee.

He had suggested the ponds on Hampstead Heath. She couldn't imagine Conor swimming. Surely, he wouldn't strip down; he was far too modest.

What would be the safest method of travel?

Bus? But that would require two changes. However, Pentowsky's men would not be expecting it. She felt safe on a bus. Getting away quickly, if necessary, could be difficult, but there are plenty of buses going to Hampstead Station. She could always jump one going in the wrong direction.

Walk? No, she didn't fancy looking behind every tree in case they were hiding, and it would take 30 minutes.

Taxi? Bridget thought they were very expensive, although she had signed up with Uber last year but had never used it.

In the end, she decided to use her bike. The bathing ponds were at the bottom of the heath, and it would be downhill most of the way. The return journey? Who knows how she would be feeling after meeting Conor and Donald.

Bridget was still very angry with Donald. His very name gave her palpitations. The phone call she had with Conor had not reassured her. While she was happy for Conor to arbitrate, she was not convinced that he was going to provide protection from Pentowski's thugs. And what sort of protection would that be? Not very effective, from a 67-year-old priest who hadn't done any exercise since he was in his seminary.

The prospect of a Superman-style prelate (would he be wearing his black clerical suit with a huge red and yellow S across his chest?) made Bridget lose concentration, and she swerved violently, narrowly avoiding some school children. Their teacher swore loudly, and the children clapped, more because they had added several new words to their vocabulary than out of loyalty to their schoolmaster. Still, she had read recently that the S was not S for Superman, but a symbol of hope. She took this to heart.

So, it must be divine protection that Conor was intending to provide. Doubtless, Conor was at this very moment arranging for a guardian angel to sweep down across the Heath and carry off a Pentowsky bruiser.

CHAPTER 75

(Rigor Mortis)

Bridget was nearly there, having careered down Parliament Hill at a breathless speed towards the ponds, without having great confidence in her brakes. A few bathers were huddled by their respective pools. It was a sunny, spring day but there was a stiff breeze from the north-east to deter any swimmers from staying in the water for too long.

There was no sign of Conor and Donald. It was quite possible that Conor's Austin Cambridge (b. 1961) had not managed the short journey across North London. In the distance, she could hear the throaty roar of a marginally more modern sports car. She could see Jon Heeley hunched over the wheel, with Claire in the front passenger seat and a woman she had never seen before squashed in the back, looking very angry. But Jon stopped the car in East Heath Road. He opened the door for the unknown woman who started walking towards the ponds.

Jon and Claire appeared to be having a heated conversation. All Bridget could hear was Claire saying, "I'm staying here."

Bridget also noticed a woman pushing a bike towards the ponds from the other direction.

"My God, it's Rowena. What the hell is she doing here?" Of course, Bridget knew nothing about Donald's attempt to develop another gene-testing technique with Rowena, only that he had gone viral, disavowing the efficacy of the DDG. She had hidden in her house in Highgate, isolating herself from the world, and refusing to listen to the journalists who demanded that she acknowledge the DDG was a fake.

She knew Rowena was sceptical about the DDG, yet she had not attempted to reject it totally. In fact, she was aware that Rowena had experimented with tests of her own, because, on one or two occasions, she had called on Bridget for advice. She also knew that Rowena was still 'sweet' on Donald, a condition which she herself had endured, but from which she now recoiled with horror. She noticed that Rowena did not approach her, but rather lingered by the women's changing hut.

After a short interval, Jon Heeley introduced Lindsay Zell to Rowena. It soon became clear to Rowena that Lindsay was a journalist, and that she and John were co-writing the story of the DDG. Rowena was clearly asking a good price for her part.

All three turned around quickly when Conor's Austin Cambridge rumbled into the car park. A rather scared Donald sat in the back and declined to leave the car. Whether his terror was a result of Conor's driving, or because they had apparently been followed by two of Pentowsky's henchman on extremely powerful motorbikes, was not clear.

Conor walked briskly over to Bridget and gave her a big hug.

"Let's go back to the café by the station."

"What, with those thugs standing outside?"

"They're just pussy cats."

He waved them away and they retreated to the road. At that point, Donald scrambled nervously out of the car and made a run for the café.

Once seated, Bridget started the attack straight away.

"Donald, you always were the perfect wimp. Useless at making decisions, hopeless in bed, and now you've stuffed my prospects with your grand announcement to the press that the DDG is a fake without even consulting me. And, now look at you, running away from our helmeted friends."

"I'm telling you the DDG has still got legs. Do you know what they are talking about over there by the pond? Rowena is telling them the whole story, including Ghana, and including the bloke and his Vietnamese girlfriend who died in a plane crash in the Amazon jungle on exactly the day she predicted. I tell you, Rowena is the only one who is going to make any money out of this. We could both go down for misrepresentation."

"And you will go down for murder, Bridget."

"Murder! Me? Don't be so crass!"

"Bridget, where do you think Gloria is living?"

"Back in Ghana, of course."

"Tragically, she never returned to Ghana and she is no longer alive! I can tell you the whole story if you want, but I would prefer you heard it from the two gentlemen in the helmets, who are members of the Homicide and Serious Crime Command of the Metropolitan Police."

"Oh, and by the way, Pontowsky finally died this morning."

The two policemen, aided by a WPC, applied the handcuffs and led Bridget away to a police van.

Donald was so delighted by this turn of events that he had not noticed how close he was to the men's pool. He felt a sharp prod with a stick. Before he could stop himself, he was falling headlong into the deep, cold water.

Donald was never a strong swimmer, and his sports jacket and brogues weighed him down further. The shock of the cold water made it difficult for him to breathe. He was disorientated, and he made the wrong decision by striking out for the causeway which divides the two big ponds. Then, he realised that the wire netting, which was designed to prevent people falling into the water, had the reverse effect on bathers struggling to get out.

There was no sign of any of the group. Bridget was in the first police van, while Conor had been being taken away in another van for questioning, following his unfortunate use of the church roof money. Jon and Rowena had squeezed into his sports car and were heading for the *Daily Mail* offices to complete the sale of the story for a lucrative sum. Lindsay, now clearly without transport, had grabbed a man with just a towel round his waist and told him to 'follow the red sports car.' She told him all expenses would be paid for any inconvenience, including clothing. He was delighted to accept.

Donald turned back towards the bank, which was very steep. It was also extremely muddy due to the recent rain. Two dogs ran along the bank, barking at him. Donald was afraid of dogs, and they could sense his fear. One, a large German Shepherd, was especially aggressive, but the smaller one, a Jack Russell, jumped in and swam right up to him, barring the way to the men's changing hut.

The steps to the hut were his only means of escape, and he knew it. His cries for help went unanswered. Finally, in the quiet of the late afternoon, a voice called,

"*You* and my mother could have saved my Tom and spared me the time in hospital. *You* broke up my parents' marriage. *You* have deceived hundreds of people into changing their lifestyles because they believed they only had a few weeks to live. *You* deserve to drown…slowly. The time of your death will be exactly 19.15pm tonight when the water level in the pool will be just above your head."

When there was no response, she called for Wag, and a very cold and wet Jack Russell knew he had done exactly what his mistress had asked him.

Printed in Poland
by Amazon Fulfillment
Poland Sp. z o.o., Wrocław

49794735R00132